Blood of a Boss 5

Lock Down Publications and Ca$h
Presents

Blood of a Boss 5

A Novel by *Askari: The King of Philly Street-Lit*

Blood of a Boss 5

Lock Down Publications
P.O. Box 944
Stockbridge, Ga 30281
www.lockdownpublications.com

Copyright 2019 Askari
Blood of a Boss 5

Lock Down Publications
Like our page on Facebook: Lock Down Publications @
www.facebook.com/lockdownpublications.ldp
Book interior design by: **Shawn Walker**
Editor: **Shawn Walker**

Stay Connected with Us!

Text **LOCKDOWN** to 22828 to stay up-to-date with new releases, sneak peaks, contests and more…

Thank you!

Submission Guideline.

Submit the first three chapters of your completed manuscript to ldpsubmissions@gmail.com, subject line: Your book's title. The manuscript must be in a .doc file and sent as an attachment. Document should be in Times New Roman, double spaced and in size 12 font. Also, provide your synopsis and full contact information. If sending multiple submissions, they must each be in a separate email.

Have a story but no way to send it electronically? You can still submit to LDP/Ca$h Presents. Send in the first three chapters, written or typed, of your completed manuscript to:

LDP: Submissions Dept
P.O. Box 944
Stockbridge, Ga 30281

DO NOT send original manuscript. Must be a duplicate.

Provide your synopsis and a cover letter containing your full contact information.

Thanks for considering LDP and Ca$h Presents.

Acknowledgements

First and foremost, I would like to give a very special shout out to my beautiful princess, my granddaughter, Angelisa. I love you, Tinky Butt. I can't help but smile whenever I see your beautiful face. I love you always, and your Abi's got you. Believe that!

To my first born, Dayshon: I love you, Spank, more than words could ever express. I know things aren't everything you would like for them to be right now, but continue moving forward. You're coming into your own as a man, and that's a traveled road far from being easy. Especially for a young black man; trust me, I know. But as long as you stay the course, work hard, be determined and disciplined, everything that's already yours will naturally come to you. But you have to be HUMBLE. You have to be WISE. You have to conduct yourself as a KING at all times, never breaking your stride. Your daughter is depending on you, so your every move should be a reflection of her development, wellbeing and safety. And remember what I told you: measure twice and cut once. And never...EVER...give anyone more credit than they deserve. That's dangerous. But to those who deserve it, those who are worthy, be sure to give them your love, loyalty, respect and dedication. I love you, bul. Stay focused.

To the best part of my being, my heart and my soul, my beautiful daughters, Keyonti and Diamond: I love y'all so much. Y'all just so amazing to me, it's crazy. I'm literally infatuated with y'all. So beautiful, so intelligent, and just a big ball of awesomeness. Continue with the great work and never lose sight of y'all's dreams. I'm extremely proud! I love y'all.

To my youngest, my baby boy, Quamar aka Mujahhid. As-salaamu alaikum, young soldier. Front and center! I love you to death, Muji. I know things are hard on you right now, but you gotta stay focused. More than that, it's imperative that you keep your faith in Allah and follow the example of His Messenger. There're many things in life that you won't understand, but that's okay. The best you can do is take charge over everything that's in your control and walk your post in a perfect manner. Don't stress over the things you can't change. In many ways you remind me so much of myself, which is somewhat scary. I need you take from my past what's good, and stay away from everything about me that was bad. You already know what I'm referring to, so I'll leave it at that. I'm here for you whenever you need me. I love you, Muji.

To my little brother, NF Mitch: I love you forever and beyond. You're doing everything right, so stay on that path. Them streets are a short stop. So, it thrills me to see you doing your thing without engaging in the game. Keep that drive and focus. It's only a matter of time before we accomplish our goals. Never Fold Entertainment, we in the building. Let's get it.

To my nephew, Kanye aka King Ye: I love you, Neph. Stay focused on your dreams, and never forget that heaven lies at the feet of the mother. So, make sure you honor and cherish your miz. I see great potential in you, Neph, especially with the music. Keep spitting that fire, and who knows, you could mess around and be next.

To my beautiful niece Sahala: I love you princess, and don't ever forget that. Continue working hard in school and keep your eyes on college. A true Queen can conquer and accomplish all.

To my nephew Noah aka Powerful: I love you, main! (In that Memphis drawl you use when we speak. LMAO!!!) Keep crushing them on that football field. Last season, I wanted two touchdowns a game, and you gave me that. But next season I want three. BEAST MODE. I love you, bul. Stay woke.

To the big homie, CA$H, Queen Coffee, and the LDP Family: I appreciate the perpetual love and support. CA$H done elevated the roster with so much extraordinary talent, that I don't even know most of y'all. But I've definitely been watching and the heat y'all are bringing is without a doubt LDP certified. I salute.

Shout outs to all the real ones who are currently on lock; especially the brothas and sistas who support me and order my books. I know it's easier said than done, but hold y'all heads.

And shout outs to Meek Mill. On behalf of the brotha and sistas locked behind bars in Pa., we appreciate your efforts to make a change for us, bro. We constantly see you on the news and hear about you on social media advocating for our freedom, and it's heartfelt. I sent you a letter, as well as my Boss series, while you were locked down in SCI Chester, but I never got a response. Get at me, bro, and let's get this thing on the big screen. So, everybody reading this, I need y'all to post and share these hashtags:

#MeekMillStarringInBloodOfABoss #BloodOfABoss #AskariKingOfPhillyStreetLit

Hopefully, we can get Meek on board!!!

I would like to give a very special and *much needed* shout out to all of my readers: I humbly thank y'all from the bottom of my heart for all the love and support, and most definitely those blazing book reviews. So, shout outs to LDP's #1 ridah, Realtalk Helene aka Helene Young, Amanda Ried (my home girl all the way in Northern Ireland), Tumika Cain from the Say What?? Book Club, Meesha Turner (Don't forget to send that heat my way. That sneak peek of *Renegade Boyz 2* was FIRE!!! I need that entire series ASAP!!!), Destiny Skai, Mia Rucker, Jane Penella, Kim Leblanc, Sharonda M. Hughes-Neal, Viv Drewa, Andrea Holt Wright, Michele Dawn, Nic Jones, Tammie Byrd, Viola King, Sharon ChocltCrzy Toliver, Sheila Flowers-Wade, Velvet Gordon, Simone Woodberry, Sandra Atueyi, Tanya Perry, Rosezenia TeezyOne Cummings, Jeanette Ransom Frazier, Starr Dennis, Cheri Williams, Monica Robinson, TwinCyndy, Nikki510, Antoinette Tyree, Cat, Mz. Gemini, Dani, Feefee, D. Creamer, Lady Jay, S. Starks, Cheryl Lenoir, Sharon Nonchalant, Shirelle, X-Calaba, Ian, Jean38no, Christa Shields, Ms. Hudson, Monica Tention, Mike Jacobs, Erica Renee, Buffy Johnson, Blessed Lady, Yunetta Parker, Kay Gant, Genova Brown Rhodes, Yvette Cross, Sandra Marshall, Toni Trina Franklin, Donna Lewis, Shantel Johnson, Marcus Mattox, Aja LaGrand, Tranay Adams, Tina Hendon-Evans, Mahogony Our Naynay, VL Rome, April Thomas, Michelle Sharp, Wendy White, Author MzGlobal, Keesh, and my big cuzzo, Glen Morgan Sr.

I also would like to give a very special shout out to *LaQueisha Malone*, for featuring me in an upcoming issue of her magazine, *Strawberry-Lit Magazine*, and for her interview questions at the end of this book. If I inadvertently failed to mention anyone by name, and I'm pretty sure I did, please, charge it to my head and not my heart. Thanks, again. I salute.

Last, but certainly not least, I need to give a squad love shout out to Billy Bear and E. I love ya'll niggas. Hold ya'll head. If I make it home first, ya'll know what it is. #DFE4EVA

Askari

Previously in Blood of a Boss

Bdddddddddddoom! Bdddddddddddoom!
   Boc! Boc! Boc! Boc!
   "Get the fuck out of my way!" Rahmello shouted, as he tossed Flo's body from the back of his shoulders. He fired off a few more rounds and then popped up running with his gun still smoking.
   It was all happening way too fast—from the phone call he received from Olivia, to the dark-skinned nigga with the shotty who'd just tried to give him a wiggie. And now, hovering above the yacht, stealth black and deadly, was the war machine commissioned by Juan Nunes. The helicopter's Gatling gun was ringing nonstop, chopping down Rahmello's family and friends, but he simply didn't give a fuck. His only ambition was to make it back home to Omelly and Olivia. Everyone else had to fend for themselves, Nahfisah and Heemy included.
   Bdddddddddddoom!
   "Move, bitch! Get'cha fat ass out the fuckin' way!" Rahmello wolfed at a thick, redbone chick who was down on one knee blocking the exit. A stream of blood was squirting from the left side of her neck and her bulging wide eyes were locked on his, silently begging for help. She reached out to grab him around the waist, but Rahmello wasn't having it. He cracked her upside the head with the butt of his gun, and then pushed her out of the way as he bum rushed the exit.
   The stampede of people running down the exit ramp were hot on his heels. So, to give himself a little more room, he back aimed his .45 and commenced to busting until the gun went *Click!*
   Sweaty and sticky and fresh out of bullets, he dashed through the parking lot moving like his ass was on fire. Sporadic flashes of gunfire lit up the night. A bullet whizzed past him, but he kept his stride, completely unaware that the muthafucka shooting at him was a few cars away steadily creeping up from behind.
   "*Damn, yo, where the fuck we parked at?*" Rahmello questioned under his breath, looking around the parking lot for the two Lamborghinis he and Heemy arrived in.

Slowing his wind sprint to a steady jog, his blue eyes scoured the pier. He twisted his face from left to right, but he couldn't find them. The heavy smoke from the Gatling gun had wafted out onto the pier, and with so many people running and screaming, dodging bullets and busting back, it was hard for him to get a clear view.

Finally, he spotted the two Lamborghinis. They were parked alongside one another in the next lane over. With no time to waste, he pulled out his car key and quickly ran toward them. He deactivated the locks and tugged on the door handle, but surprisingly the door wouldn't budge. He repeated the process, and still the door would not open.

"*What the fuck is wrong wit' this muthafuckin' door?*" He cursed under his breath and banged his fist against the window.

Had he not been so amped up and anxious, he would have realized he was standing beside the wrong car. The headlights on the second Lamborghini were flashing every time he hit the button, but he didn't peep it.

After pressing down on the button a few more times, he finally caught a glimpse of the headlights behind him. He ran around to the driver's side of the second Lamborghini and tugged on the door handle. The car door lifted with ease.

"Aye, yo, Fuckboy? Lemme holla at'chu right quick," a feminine voice called out from behind.

"Rahmello had one foot inside of his car when he heard it. He spun around with his finger on the trigger, oblivious that his gun was empty. He squeezed the trigger three times, but instead of a loud boom, the only thing he heard was a *Click! Click! Click!*

Kia, who was dressed in all-black and had her twin .45s aimed at his chest and torso, licked her lips and smiled at him.

"YBM, baby."

Boom! Boom! Boom!

The first bullet crashed into his vest and spun him around 180°. The next two tagged him in his left hand and elbow, twisting him around full circle.

"Umm, fuck!" Rahmello grimaced when the back of his head banged against the flipped-up door.

Boom!

Another bullet hit him below his neck and torpedoed him to the ground.

Too gangsta to stay down, yet too dizzy to pop back up, Rahmello staggered up on his knees. He attempted to stand up on his wobbly left leg, but he lurched forward and slammed into the pavement chin first.

Bitching and moaning and gasping for air, he rolled around in pain expecting Kia to run over and finish the job. But when he lifted his head and looked back behind, the mystery bitch in all-black was gone. The only thing he saw was a misty cloud of gun smoke. That and the quick glimpse of a jiggling phat ass running past the back of his whip.

"Agh, shit!" he grimaced when he gripped his left wrist with his right hand. The bullet wound to his elbow was tender and sore, but the damage inflicted upon his left hand was ten times worse. His bloody, fat palm was swollen and blue where his pinkie and ring fingers *used to be*, but they were now the severed stalks of his blown away knuckles, popping out of his flesh like the whites of a spare rib.

"Please? Not my baby, no!" Olivia's voice resonated in the back of his mind. The painful sound of her voice was all the motivation he needed.

Moving solely off of adrenaline, he staggered up on his feet and slinked down inside of his Lambo. He didn't even care that his gun was empty, or that his left hand was out of commission. He had to make it back to La Casa Moreno. The lives of his little boy and fiancé depended on it.

***

A Few Minutes Later

Nahfisah popped out of the water gasping for air. Heemy pushed her body up on the pier, then he gripped the ledge with both hands and pulled himself out of the cold Delaware.

Soaking wet, he looked down at Nahfisah. She was dripping wet, curled in a ball shivering and shaking. Her blue eyes were zoned out in a trance, and over and over like a broken record spinning on repeat, she was rambling the words, "No. No. Don't shoot. No. No. Don't shoot."

The pandemonium from the yacht had spilled out onto the pier, and all around Heemy heard the booming of loud gunfire. The helicopter was long gone, so the additional gunfire was somewhat confusing.

Who was shooting and why?

"Come on, Nah, we gotta go," Heemy said as he reached down and grabbed Nahfisah by the hand. He pulled her to her feet and reiterated they needed to leave, but Nahfisah just looked at him with a blank face.

"No. No. Don't shoot. No. No. Don't shoot."

"Goddmanit," Heemy grimaced, flinching when the zip of a stray bullet whizzed past his left ear. "Come on, Nah, stop bullshitting! We gotta go!"

"No. No. Don't shoot. No. No. Don't shoot."

"Man, fuck this shit!" Heemy lashed out, as he grabbed Nahfisah by the waist. He threw her over his shoulder and took off running, praying they didn't catch a stray bullet.

The parking lot was jam packed with people running and screaming. A chick that he knew from the neighborhood was gunned down right in front of him, but he ran right past her. The pinging of bullets penetrating every car he ran past made it seem as though someone was shooting at him. But as he looked around the parking lot, the only thing he saw was people running and screaming.

Finally, Heemy made it back to his Lamborghini.

"*I shoulda killed his ass when I had the chance,*" he snarled under his breath when he saw Rahmello's Lamborghini was gone. "*Ain't even stick around long enough to make sure his sister was safe. Bitch-ass nigga.*"

Glancing around the parking lot, Heemy pulled out his car key and deactivated the locks. After flipping up the passenger's side door, he pushed Nahfisah inside and then pulled it back down.

Making his way around the front of the car, the pinging of bullets tearing up the Escalade beside him made him crouch down low.

Who the fuck is out here chopping at me?

He looked around the parking lot, but it was nearly impossible to identify a specific shooter. He wanted to bust back, but at that point, his only concern was Nahfisah.

He popped open the driver's side door and hopped down inside of the Lambo. Pulling the door closed, he looked over at the woman who had without a doubt stolen his heart. She was curled in the fetal position, rocking back and forth and shaking her head *no*.

"No. No. Don't shoot." Nahfisah began to cry, as images of her best friend's brains bursting out the back of her dome made her rock even faster. "No. No. Don't shoot," she spoke more adamantly. "No. No. Don't shoot!"

"Damn, Nah, you gotta snap outta that shit." Heemy released a long sigh. Not knowing what else he should say or do to keep her from going catatonic, he pressed down on the push start and gripped the steering wheel with his left hand.

Tap! Tap! Tap!

The sound of someone tapping on his window made him peek over his left shoulder, guardedly.

Standing on the other side of the car door was Keeno. A menacing scowl was plastered across his face, and the barrel of his Glock .40 was pressed against the window.

"Yeah, nigga, what's up now?"

"Fuck!" Heemy shouted when he saw that Keeno had the drop on him. He didn't even get a chance to prepare himself for the impact of the blast. The Glock .40 was already flaming.

Boca!

Ping!

"Agh, shit!" Keeno screamed in pain. He stumbled into the Escalade behind him and reached for his right shoulder. The hot shit he tossed at Heemy ricocheted off the window and blazed through his hoody. The smoldering gunshot wound was pouring out blood. He touched the wound with his left hand, then quickly snatched it away when he felt the sting.

"What the fuck?" Keeno muttered in disbelief. Confused, he looked down at the front of his pistol where the barrel was still smoking. Baffled even more, he set his sights on the driver's side window. The only damage he saw was a dusty, black scratch. Behind the scratch, he locked eyes with Heemy. No words were needed. Keeno fucked up, and he knew it. He would have never imagined the Lamborghini was bulletproof.

Heemy, too, for that matter. Rahmello never told him when he gave him the car.

"Hey, yo, Heemy, man, I swear to God, I ain't know that was you," Keeno began bitching. He threw his hands up in a defenseless posture, hoping to make peace, but Heemy just ice-grilled him. "Real shit, Heem. That's my word, bro. I really didn't know that was you."

"Nah, nigga, don't bitch up now," Heemy mouthed the words through the window. "You did what'chu did, so it is what it is."

Heemy threw the transmission in *reverse* and backed out slow, not once taking his eyes off of Keeno. Shifting from neutral to first gear, he looked back behind Keeno and saw two shooters dressed in all-black. Both men were strapped with two pistols and had black ski masks covering the front of their faces.

The first shooter dropped to one knee, but the second shooter remained high. Simultaneously, they fired at the Lamborghini, eventually ducking for cover when the bullets came ricocheting back.

Ping! Ping! Ping! Ping! Ping! Ping!

Heemy scowled at the two dickheads, then he brought his gaze back to Keeno. Gripping the steering wheel with his right hand, he threw up the Fo' Hunnid with his left. He twisted the Fo' Hunnid into Big B's, and then fixed his fingers into the shape of a gun.

"*Pussy, that's on the set.*" Heemy mouthed the words, and then mashed out with his tires screeching.

WELCOME TO BLOOD OF A BOSS V: BLOOD IN MY EYES

Askari

Chapter One

"Hello? Mrs. Moreno? Is anyone home?" Savino called out from the doorway. He was standing on the front porch to Annie's house, looking at the bashed in front door. It was cracked down the middle and nearly knocked off of the hinges.

Her Mercedes-Benz S550 was parked in the driveway. The back-passenger's side door was pulled wide open, and halfway hanging out the car was a blood splattered car seat.

"*Something's extremely wrong here*," Savino mumbled under his breath, looking back and forth between the house and car. He pulled out his .38 Special and slowly pushed open the front door. Stepping inside of the living room, he saw the room had been ransacked. The black, suede furniture was slashed open and flipped over. The coffee tables and lamps were shattered to pieces, and the 60" flat screen that hung on the wall was slanted at an awkward angle. A penny-sized bullet hole was placed in the center.

"Mrs. Moreno?" Savino called out in a shaky voice. "Kids?"

There was no reply. The only sound he heard was the whimpering of a wounded animal. Clutching the .38 like his life depended on it, he slowly made his way toward the sound. It seemed to be coming from the kitchen.

As he moved through the dining room, he saw the condition of the room was similar to the ransacking of the living room. The crystal chandelier that once hung from the ceiling was laying on the floor, and right beside it was the dining room table. It was cracked down the middle and smeared with blood. The dining room chairs were scattered all around, and laying on the floor sprinkled with blood, was a baby doll and two stuffed animals.

"*This is bad*," Savino mumbled under his breath, thinking about Sonny's mother and children. "Kids?" he called out some more, barely above a whisper. "Mrs. Moreno? This is Mario Savino, Sontino's attorney. If you guys are in here, you can come out now. You're safe."

Again, there was no reply. The only sound he heard was the whimpering of the wounded animal. Swallowing the lump in his throat, he continued making his way toward the kitchen.

"Jesus Christ!" Savino yelped out loud when he turned on the kitchen lights. The entire kitchen was covered in blood. There was blood on the floor, blood on the walls, blood on the cabinets, and blood on the ceiling. Blood was everywhere. The refrigerator, the stove, the dishwasher and microwave were all splattered in blood. *Uuugggrrrrr!* The wounded animal began to growl.

Savino couldn't see him, but could tell from the sound that he was somewhere on the other side of the granite island in the center of the kitchen. He tightened his grasp on the rubber-grip handle and continued making his way toward the sound.

When he reached the other side of the island, he looked down and spotted Rocko. The oversized Rottweiler was looking up at Savino with bloodshot eyes. The bullet holes embedded in his face and shoulders were oozing out blood, and with his two front legs snapped in half, he was using his hind legs to push himself forward.

Still determined to defend his family to the bloody end, Rocko's razor-sharp canines were clamping up and down biting at the air, desperately trying to latch on to Savino's leg.

Uuugggrrrrr! Urf! Urf! Uuugggrrrrr! Urf!

Savino took a step back and aimed the barrel between the dog's red eyes. There was nothing left to do, except put the dog out of his misery. Taking a deep breath, he pulled back on the trigger.

Boc!

Rocko's brains went scattering across the floor, and Savino dropped to his knees crying like a baby. In a twisted, weird way he felt somewhat responsible for what he now realized happened to Sonny's mother and children. Had he only made it there sooner.

Shaking and trembling, he pulled out his cell phone and pressed down on the number that Sonny called him from.

Ring!

"Yo, Savino, holla at me," Sonny's voice boomed through the phone. "Are they safe? Did you get 'em?"

"Sontino, I—I—I really don't know how to tell you this," Savino sobbed.

"Tell me what?" Sonny's heart dropped into his stomach. "Did you get 'em or not?"

"Your mother? The kids? They're gone."

"*Gone*? Fuck you mean *they're gone*?"

"Sonny, they're gone. And there was nothing I could do about it."

"Nah, man, no. *Fuck no!*" Sonny lashed out in a fiery fit of rage. "What the fuck is you even telling me right now, Savino? You're saying like *dead gone*, or *gone* like they're not there?"

"Sonny, they're not here," Savino clarified, still sobbing and breathing hard. "They're just—They're just—gone."

"*Sonofabitch!*" Sonny cranked his volume up another level. He was pacing back and forth from one side of his jail cell to the other and gripping the phone so tightly, that if he squeezed any harder, he'd might fuck around and break one of his fingers.

"Muthafucka, I told ya stupid ass to go get 'em!" he spewed his anger at Savino.

"Wait. What? Sonny, I did. I swear."

"No, you didn't. 'Cause if you did, we wouldn't be having this conversation, now would we? *Would we?*"

"Come on, Sonny, just calm down."

"*Calm down*? Pussy, don't be telling me to calm down. This my muthafuckin' daughter we talking about. My muthafuckin' niece. *My goddamned mom, Savino!*"

"Sonny, I know. But just hear me out," Savino pleaded with him. "I got here as fast as I could, but someone else must'a beat me to it. Your mother and the kids were already gone, and the only one I found was the dog. He was shot up and bleeding and trying like hell to bite me.

"Oh my God, Sonny, there's so much blood inside of this house," Savino blurted as he glanced around the bloody-red kitchen. "There's fucking blood everywhere."

Steaming hot and pissed at himself for underestimating his enemy, Sonny walked over to the sink and splashed his face with two handfuls of cold water. He was thinking about his mother and niece, already knowing they were the two targets inside of the house. His stepson, Dayshon, was away at summer camp, and being as though Keyonti was Alvin's granddaughter, Sonny knew the chances he would harm his own flesh and blood were slim to none. So, naturally, because he knew there was nothing to warrant their safety, his main concern was Annie and Imani.

Intensely rubbing the water into the grooves of his face, he looked up at his wall full of family pictures. A group selfie of his mother, daughter and niece stood out from amongst the rest. Annie's beautiful brown face was wedged between Keyonti and Imani's, and both girls were kissing their grandmother on each one of her cheeks. The smile on Annie's face was like a dagger to Sonny's heart, and before he knew it, the fresh tears welling at the rims of his eyes began to spill over, transforming the faces of his three lovelies into one brown blur.

He didn't want to think about it, but he couldn't help it. He couldn't shake it. In the back of his mind, playing over and over, were the gruesome images of his mother and niece being violated in the same manner that he'd just done to AJ.

The gut-wrenching premonition was so clear, it was almost as though he were watching a movie. He could see the shit clear as day: Annie and Imani butt-naked and bleeding, trapped in the dark cold basement of a Southwest Philly row house. The Reaper and his goons were crowded around laughing, every last one of them muthafuckas taking pleasure in dishing out to Sonny's peeps what he'd dished out to AJ. The shit was bonkers. And because there was nothing Sonny could do to make it stop, he closed his eyes and cried even harder.

"*Fuuuuuuuck!*" Sonny screamed out in a frustrated fit. "Fuck! Fuck! Fuck! *Damnit, I fucked up!*"

He knew Alvin would eventually strike back, he just never imagined his revenge would be so swift and harsh. And now, solely because his young nigga, Smurf, jumped out of the jet and made a move on AJ without first giving him the opportunity to properly think things through, the lives of his mother and niece were dangerously hanging in the balance. He *had* to think of a way to get them back, he had to.

"Hey, ah, Sonny," Savino called his name in a low, hushed tone. He was looking across the kitchen at the back-patio door, where a bloody palm print was smeared over the door handle. Down below, trailing from the island to the door, were a bloody set of boot prints. They moved through the crack in the door and stopped at the sole of a blood-speckled Timberland. The boot's heel was laying on the patio deck, right side up.

"*Sonny?*" Savino raised his whisper just a tad bit louder. "Are you listening to me? I think I might'a found something."

"Found what?" Sonny's voice came out strained. He didn't want to speak it, but internally he was already suspecting the worst. "It's my mom and my niece, ain't it?"

"No, it's not anything like that," Savino quickly replied. "I'm looking at a motherfucker laying outside on the back patio."

"The back patio?" Sonny perked up, instantly visualizing the layout of his mother's house. He wiped the tears from his eyes, and then took another glance at the picture of his mom and the girls.

"So, what's up wit' the nigga? Is he still alive?"

"I really can't say," Savino replied. He nervously wiped the sweat from his brow with the back of the same hand he was using to hold his .38, then he stood up on his feet and crouched down low behind the granite island.

"Fuck you mean you can't tell? Either he's still alive, or he ain't."

"The only thing I see is the bottom of his boot," Savino stated. He was peeking around the side of the island looking at the boot through the door.

"A'ight, so, go over there and check it the fuck out."

"Check it out?" Savino parroted. He was thinking about his private investigator, Arnold Troutman, and how his dead body was discovered outside of Sonny's mansion with a bullet in the back of his head. It was then, Savino realized he'd dug himself in way too deep, more so than he had ever intended. The last thing he wanted to do was dig himself in any deeper.

"Ummmmm, I'm not so sure about that," Savino said as he turned around, looking back behind at his only escape route. "Maybe it'd be better if I call Rahmello or one of the other guys to come do it."

"Call Rahmello?" Sonny snapped at him. "Ain't nobody got time for none of dat. This might be my only chance to get my mom and the kids back, or at least find out where the fuck them niggas took 'em."

"I know, Sonny, but I'm really not…"

"Nigga, stop bitchin'."

"—cut out for shit like this," Savino finished his sentence. "I mean after all, I'm only an attorney. An officer of the court for crying out loud."

"That, and a muthafuckin' drug dealer," Sonny spoke with conviction. "One who went behind my back and was serving my brother when I specifically told you not to."

Savino was floored. He had no idea, whatsoever, that Sonny was aware of the business he'd been doing with Rahmello. He attempted to justify his actions with a weak excuse, but Sonny shut his ass down.

"Nigga, fuck that. My mah'fucka folks is missing. So, all that monkey shit you talking I ain't try'na hear that shit, dawg. Now, stop bitchin' and do what the fuck I told you."

After mumbling under his breath what he didn't have the heart to say out loud, Savino moved from behind the island and cautiously approached the glass door.

"Alright, Sonny, I'm here," Savino softly announced. He pressed his forehead against the door and looked down at the fat, black man who was stretched out on the other side. He studied the man from his boot up, noticing right away that his left leg, the one attached to the boot, was blown away at the knee and dangling from a twisted array of spaghetti-like ligaments.

"Fuckin' disgusting." Savino shuttered, doing everything he possibly could to not look away. Moving his eyes up the fat man's body, the graphics were so horrified that he damn near threw up his dinner. The flesh on the left side of his face was mauled off and

24

peeled back, exposing the cheek bones and jaw muscles underneath. And slightly under his chin, clamped around his Adam's apple, were the four fang wounds courtesy of Rocko's death lock.

At first glance, Savino thought he was dead. But when he pulled back the sliding glass door and reached down to check the man's pulse, a deep guttural gasp echoing from the depths of his lungs, sent Savino stumbling backwards. Arms flailing, he landed on his ass and then popped back up in one swift motion.

"Sonofabitch!" Savino fussed when he saw he dropped his cell phone. It was laying on the patio deck, about a swipe away from the fat man's hand. He nudged it away with the tip of his shoe, then he reached down and scooped it up. He wiped it against his shirt and then placed it against his ear.

"Yo, Savino? Talk to me, fam. You good?"

"Yeah, Sonny, I'm fine. Just a little rattled, is all."

"A'ight. So, what's up wit' this nigga? Is he still alive?"

"Barely. He's fucked up pretty bad, but he's still breathing. From the looks of it, it appears as though the dog must'a taken a few chunks out of him."

Sonny closed his eyes and inhaled deeply. He knew that his next move needed to be his best one. So, after calming himself down and collecting his thoughts, he continued talking in a calm, leveled voice.

No sooner than Sonny said it, the fat man began to mumble. His gurgling words were unintelligible at best.

"Sonny, hold on. I think he's try'na tell me something," Savino said. He held the phone in front of the man's face and encouraged him to speak. "Go 'head, buddy, just take your time."

"P—P—Please," the fat man gurgled and stammered. "Don't let—your dog—eat me. I was—only—here..."

"You were only here to do what?" Savino pried. "Come on, buddy, help me and I promise to help you. Mrs. Moreno and the kids? I need to know exactly where I can find them. So, who took them and why?"

"I was—only—here—to help," the fat man spoke in between breaths. His punctured windpipe was growing louder by the second. "Tell—Sonny—G—G—*Grip!*"

"Fuck that nigga just say?" Sonny menaced when he heard the mentioning of his grandfather. "I *know* that nigga ain't just say Grip?"

"Did'ja hear him?" Savino asked, as he placed the phone back against his ear.

"You muthafuckin' right, I heard him. That nigga said *Grip*. Ask him what the fuck he's talking about. Grip what?"

Looking down at the fat man's face, Savino knew if he asked him anything else it would only be a waste of time. The burgundy gruel that was spewing out the man's neck was now calm and still. His chubby, bald head was lollied to the side, and his bloodshot eyes were locked wide open peering off into the unknown. "Yo, what the fuck is you waiting for?" Sonny persisted. "Ask him what the fuck I told you to ask him. *Grip what?*"

"Sonny, I can't," Savino tersely replied. "It's too late. He's dead."

Sonny's intensifying rage had him trembling so hard that his teeth began to chatter. Saying nothing else, he disconnected the call and then tossed the phone up on his top bunk. Chest heaving and nostrils flaring, he moved toward the back of his cell where his ten inched shank was stashed in the wall beneath his desktop. After digging it out, he ripped a piece of his bed sheet and tied it on as a makeshift handle.

Tightly gripped in his left hand, the skinny icepick was shiny and long and more than capable of sending a muthafucka on a one-way trip to the city morgue.

The first nigga on his shit list was Smurf. Then after Smurf, he was determined to get his hands on Alvin. Not only him, but AJ, The Reaper and every muthafucka who was out there riding with them.

Fuck the YBM!

Then finally, before all was said and done, he promised himself he'd get even with his grandfather once and for all. If for nothing else, then solely on the strength of his baby mama, Riri, and the unborn seed she was carrying when two of Grip's henchmen ran her down in cold blood.

Nothing and no one were safe, not even his younger brother, Rahmello. Because brother or no brother, blood or no blood, any and every one that had ever crossed him, disrespected or violated was sure to feel the wrath of a vengeance that was similar to no other. The stage was set. It was time for Sonny to go out with a bang.

Askari

Chapter Two
At La Casa Moreno

"Miss Annie and the girls? Were you able to get 'em?" Alexis asked when Grip and Gangsta stepped through the front door. She was standing in the middle of the foyer, dressed in a black, one-piece jumper. Her arms were folded across her breast, and her thick shapely thighs were shifted to one side. The look on her face was all business.

Strolling up the hallway behind, were her two bodyguards, Pierre and Toiussant. Both men were strapped with a foot-long machete and wore blank, expressionless faces. Saying nothing at all, the two Haitians came to a stop, positioning themselves directly behind Alexis.

Every eye in the foyer was fixed on Grip.

"So, did you get 'em or not?" Alexis reiterated, placing her hands on her hips. Her questions were more so aimed at Grip, than they were Gangsta. However, instead of replying, the old man just stood there staring at her.

Grip's penetrating, transfixing stare shifted from Pierre to Toiussant, and then back to Alexis. The entire time, he was thinking about her mother, The Madam, Geraldine François, and the slick comment she made the day before.

"*Patterns, my old friend. Patterns.*" The Madam smiled at him, relishing over the fact she had him in checkmate two moves prior to their chess game being over. The reality that he'd been so predictable was something that Grip didn't take too well. It was then he decided to switch his pitch, to become more observant and play the game from a different angle; one his opposition would never see coming.

"Oh, so I guess I'm just standing here talking to myself?" Alexis sassed at him, irritated that Grip had yet to proffer an answer.

The plan was for her and her men to takeout Olivia, while Grip and his secured Annie and the kids. So now that Alexis had handled her business and Grip was reluctant to speak about his, she was beginning to grow suspicious.

"Well, just so you know, the Columbians are already waging war," Alexis continued in a snazzy voice. "They just made a strike at Nahfisah's party."

"Is that so?" Grip coolly replied. He slowly cracked his knuckles one at a time, and then gently caressed his goatee. "Enlighten me."

"Somebody tagged me in a video that was taken at Nahfisah's party, apparently it's all over Facebook. The video starts out with what appears to be a fight, but it's hard to really see who's fighting. The only clear shot is of Rahmello from the side. He's talking to Heemy, that's the young kid I was telling you about, the one who's down with Sontino. The two of them are going back and forth, and then all you see is a dark-skinned man with a shotgun creeping up behind Rahmello. Heemy must've seen him, because he whips out a gun and fires into the crowd. The crowd goes crazy. Everybody's pushing and screaming, and falling over one another trying to make it off of the yacht.

"Now, while all of this is going on, the video moves from the deck to the sky where an ashy black helicopter is hovering above the yacht. The helicopter's side door was pulled wide open, and a goddamned cannon was sticking out the side. Whoever was filming the video must have dropped their cell phone. Because the second the cannon goes off, the video goes black and all you hear is the gunfire. The only good thing is that before it did, I got a good look at the shooter's face. It was that fucking Chee-Chee. So, I *know* Juan was the one behind that shit."

The more Alexis spoke about the video, the angrier she became. Her breathing intensified, her brow began to furrow, and her tightly clenched fist became sweaty and hot. She was pissed off to the max.

Anxiously tapping her foot against the hard marble floor, she proceeded with her account of what she'd seen on the video.

"I replayed it to see if it showed Nahfisah, but it didn't, at least not from the footage that was uploaded to Facebook. I'm hoping she made it off safely, but there's really no telling. But what I *do know* is that Sontino's gonna fuckin' flip when he finds out. Obviously, that's the last thing we need right now. I tried calling him, but every time I did, he sent me straight to voice mail. So, I called my girl-friend back at the jail to see if she could get him on the phone. But this bitch wasn't even at the jail, she was out on a hospital run. Ac-cording to her, some crazy shit popped off between Sontino and the son of the of the YBM, whatever the fuck that's supposed to mean."

"The YBM?" Grip questioned the name of the organization he founded nearly three decades earlier. "And you're sure that's the name she said?"

"Umm-hmm." Alexis nodded her head. "That's exactly what she said, 'the son of the YBM', just like that. She said his name was AJ, and that Sonny and his boys had him hogtied in the mop closet, with a sock in his mouth, at least that's the way they found him. She said they damn near beat him to death and rammed a broomstick up his ass. It was so bad, they had to rush him to the hospital. Thank God, the boy's not a rat. She said the cops came to interview him, and even though he probably wanted to, he refused to implicate Sontino.

"Now, I don't know anything about the YBM and why the hell Sontino did what he did, but you seriously need to talk to him. His trial's less than two weeks away, and one slip could ruin everything that we've been working on."

"Don't worry about Sontino, he's gonna be just fine," Grip said as he casually removed his Bossalini. He sat the hat on the lion statue situated beside the door, and then slowly scoured the foyer.

"Where's the girl? You all didn't kill her yet, did you?"

Grip's cold, blue eyes were zeroed on Toiussant's machete when he said it. From the handle to the tip, Olivia's life fluid was dangling down, slowly descending like a glob of drool from a Pit-bulls' mouth. The syrupy, red goop slipped from the blade and dot-ted the marble floor beneath.

Grip's gaze came back to Alexis. Peering at her through his squinted lids, he said, "The girl? Tell me about the girl."

"No, we didn't kill the bitch." Alexis' ice-grill was just as deadly as his. "But we damn sure did a little slicing and dicing. Know what I'm talking 'bout? Just to let her ass know we're not playing any fucking games. So, if you want to see her, she's out back in the pool house."

"And my great grandson?" He looked at her with a cautionary raised brow. "You didn't bring him any harm, did you?"

"Absolutely not. He's upstairs, sound asleep in the nursery."

"And what about Shabazz and Aziz?"

Alexis shook her head *no*, indicating they were no longer among the living.

"Goddamnit." Grip flexed his jaw muscles. "That fucking Rahmello. Speaking of which, have you heard from him yet?"

"You could say that," Alexis spoke with a nod. "When we first made contact, that snitching-ass bitch was talking to him on the phone. And that's the reason I called Gangsta and told him to drive out to the house, in any event we needed more manpower. You know what I'm saying, just in case any of the guys he flew in made it off the yacht. Damnit, I hope he was able to save Nahfisah."

"Alright," Grip replied, casually checking the time on his diamond bezel David Yurman. "It's a quarter to midnight, and my PJ back to Cuba is scheduled for takeoff in a few more hours. So, how long ago would you say that was?"

"About a half an hour or so." Alexis shrugged her shoulders. "Give or take."

"That's good," Grip replied, smoothly extracting the hand-rolled Cuban that was sticking out of his shirt pocket. "That's really good. Because the longer I'm in the States, the more susceptible I am of being arrested." He gripped the stogie with his right thumb and index finger, and then dug down inside of his slacks and fished out his solid gold cigar-cutter. After clipping away both ends from the stogie, he placed it between his teeth and bit down gently.

"Gangsta," he spoke out the side of his mouth, glancing over his left shoulder, "gimmie a light."

The nerve of this nigga. Gangsta looked at him and gritted his teeth. When he first received the phone call from Alexis asking him to drive out to La Casa Moreno, he had no idea that Grip was back in the States. However, when he pulled up to the front gate and spotted Alejandro, Grip's newly appointed bodyguard from Havana, he knew his uncle was already there.

Alexis obviously knew the old man was back in the States, but she failed to inform him, which to Gangsta was somewhat confusing. The plan that was set in motion by Big Angolo was to keep Grip tucked away in Cuba, far away from the inter workings of The Family. But there he was, glancing over his shoulder telling Gangsta to give him a light.

Challenging the old man with his eyes, Gangsta reached inside of his hoody's pocket where his compact .9mm was snugged tightly. He palmed the handle and slipped his finger through the triggerguard.

Alexis, peeping Gangsta's demeanor, shot him a look that demanded he calm down. She then gestured for Toiussant to give her a light.

Grip shot her the look of death, well aware of the sneaky, inconspicuous look that she had given Gangsta. Pierre and Touissant, seeing the way Grip was looking at Alexis, took a step forward.

"I wish the fuck y'all would," Grip dared them to make a move. He spat the cigar from his mouth and then turned around to face Gangsta. He stepped into his nephew's chest, standing so close that the tips of their noses were damn near touching.

"You got something you wanna say to me, boy?"

Gangsta stared the old man dead in his eyes, contemplating on whether or not he should kill him right then and there. He settled on the latter. But just as he was about to whip out and jelly the old man's biscuit, another look from Alexis made him calm down and think more clearly.

Now was not the time, he thought.

So instead of moving off of impulse, he released his hand from the pistol and stepped back slowly.

"Not at all, muthafucka, you don't get off the hook that goddamned easy." Grip looked at him with a menacing glare.

"If you got something you wanna say to me, then say it goddamnit. We can straighten that bullshit right on out. You hear me, boy? I said speak!"

Boom!
Scurrrrrr!
Wham!

"Now, what the hell was that?" Grip bellowed, as he spun back around to face Alexis. "It sounded like a goddamned car wreck."

"How the hell would I know?" Alexis shot right back. "I'm standing here with you."

Grip's light-skinned face became red with anger. He removed the .10mm that was stuffed down in the small of his back, and then stepped outside on the stoop. Looking down at the far end of the driveway, he shook his head in disappointment.

"You two," he pointed back at Alexis and Toiussant, "go get the girl and the baby and bring them out front. Pierre," he looked up at the Haitian giant, "you come with me. And you," he squinted his eyes at Gangsta, "take your ass out back and bag up the brothers. And hurry the fuck up, I want this house cleared out within the next half an hour. Then after that, tie up whatever loose ends that need to be tightened, and have your ass back in Cuba by tomorrow night. I'm hosting a dinner party with a few of the bosses from the roundtable and as my head of security, I expect you there. Now, move."

Chapter Three
At SCI Graterford

"Look at the way these muthafuckas did my boy," Alvin said to his cellmate, Bruno. The two men were sitting in their cell paying attention to two different things. Alvin was watching the video of AJ being violated in the mop closet, and Bruno was smoking a cigarette and texting on his Samsung. The six-foot-five, two hundred- and eighty-pound Bruno was seated on the top bunk with his back propped against the wall. Alvin was seated at the desk in the rear of the cell. The two men had spent the majority of their bid at the infamous SCI Graterford state prison, and their thirty-year relationship was the same as it was when they were back out on the streets—Alvin was the boss and Bruno was his bodyguard. Both men were fucked up when Alvin first received the video of AJ being violated.

"I took this nigga in, Bruno. I gave him my daughter's hand in marriage and loved him like son. I even did my best to teach this nigga the game, all so his cocky ass wouldn't end up the same as me. And how does he repay me? He kills my baby girl and then does this shit to my son?"

"His ass gon' feel it, A, so don't even sweat that shit," Bruno told him while responding to his last text. "The stupid lil' nigga done fucked up and fucked wit' the wrong crew. So, now we gotta spank his ass. Niggas ain't letting this shit slide, A. What he did to AJ, he's gonna get done to him ten times worse, believe that. He's about to get his ass broke off sum'n proper."

"You muthafuckin' right he's about to get his ass broke off sum'n proper. We gon' hit his ass where it hurt, right in his muthafuckin' heart. Rip that muthafucka out and stomp on it."

Vrrrrrm! Vrrrrrm! Vrrrrrm!

"About fucking time," Alvin stated to himself when an incoming text message vibrated his cell phone. He was hoping the message was confirmation from either Gangsta or The Reaper, that Sonny's family had been successfully kidnapped. But when he looked at the messenger bubble and saw a picture of Pablo Escobar, he knew the message had been sent by Juan Nunes.

Shaking his head in frustration, Alvin opened the message.

12:02 am: Juan: *Just sending you a bird's eye view from the first itch Sontino's gonna have to scratch. Go on Facebook. I tagged you in the post.*

"What the fuck is this?" Alvin questioned, as he pressed down on the Facebook notification. A video appeared on the screen showing the mayhem from Nahfisah's yacht party. The video's angle was taken from a bird's eye, so he knew whoever filmed it, they must have done it from the helicopter's cockpit.

Bdddddddddddddddddoc! Bdddddddddddddddddoc!

The perpetual ringing of gunfire was coming through the phone so loudly that it forced Alvin to turn down the volume. And even then, given the fiery red flashes and the nonstop shell casings spewing out of the Gatling gun, it was hard to get a clear view of the yacht's lower deck.

"*What the fuck is this nigga doing?*" Alvin mumbled under his breath when he finally set his sights on The Reaper. Instead of locating and kidnapping Rahmello, he was walking down and firing his shotgun at a scrawny looking Mexican. To make matters worse, Alvin was able to zero in on Rahmello.

"Fuck is you doing? You're letting this nigga get away!" Alvin snapped when he saw Rahmello shooting his way off of the yacht.

"What? What's that?" Bruno leaned over the bunk and looked down to see what Alvin was looking at.

"It's a video that Juan just sent me," Alvin replied. "This stupid-ass Rayon, he let Rahmello get away."

After clicking out of Facebook, Alvin went to his call log and pressed down on The Reaper's number.

Ring! Ring! Ring! Ring!

"*This Double R. Leave it,*" The Reaper's voicemail sounded Alvin's eardrum.

"This stupid muthafucka," Alvin said as he disconnected the call. He looked up at Bruno and shook his head in disbelief. "This fucking Rayon let this nigga get away."

36

***

Rahmello's entire ride from Penn's Landing to Bala Cynwyd was one big blur, as he could not stop the tears from falling down his flush, red face. The gush of blood pumping out of his left hand had him woozy and weak, so lethargic that his only means of staying awake was the cool breeze blowing in through the cracked open Lamborghini windows

Slobbering at the mouth and looking back and forth between his hand and the road, he veered over into the next lane, violently sideswiping the back-left fender of a Pepsi-blue Chrysler.

Whacka!

Pop!

Blurrrrrrrrrrrrrrrrn!

"Come on, nigga, stay focused." Rahmello checked himself, as he whipped the steering wheel back to the left. The Chrysler's driver was blaring his car horn and screaming at him to pull over, but pulling over was fresh out the fucking question. Rahmello's only response was his glowing taillights as he zoomed right past. He banged a left on City Line Avenue and zipped up the hilly road that led to La Casa Moreno.

Cruising down the other side, he noticed the front gate was uncharacteristically left wide open. He also took notice of the black Mercedes Sprinter Van and the two black Chevy Suburban's that were parked out front. The Sprinter Van was parked in between the two Suburbans.

Standing on post beside the first Suburban, was a tall, light skinned man he'd never seen before. He was standing at attention—heels together, arms at his sides, with his chin up, looking straight ahead. A dark pair of sunglasses decorated his clean, shaved face. His shiny, black shoes and silk gray suit with a red bowtie had him looking like a Black Muslim.

F.O.I.? Rahmello questioned the man's appearance. *Grip?*

Seeing the Lamborghini cruising down the hill, Alejandro stepped away from his SUV and threw his hands in the air, signaling for the Lamborghini to stop at his checkpoint.

"This nigga got me fucked up," Rahmello growled as he pushed the Lamborghini to a whopping 180.

"No, Papi, wait! Slow down!" Alejandro shouted, waving his hands more feverishly. He attempted to make a dive at the very last second, but the Lamborghini was already on him. It clipped him above his right knee and flung him through the air like a Chinese frisbee.

Boom!

Scurrrrrrr!

"Oh, shit!" Rahmello shrieked when his Lamborghini fishtailed out of control. He gripped the steering wheel with his right hand and stomped down on the brakes, but it was of no use. The sudden change of velocity was simply too strong. The Lamborghini spun into the grass, hit a ditch and ascended into the air with the tires still spinning.

Wham!

It crashed into the ground with a devastating force, popped back up and then rolled over twice before ultimately sliding across the grass, bottom side up.

"Fuckin' bitch!" Rahmello grunted and gasped. He was laying on his stomach and stretched over the suede console that separated the two front seats. The top half of his body was wedged in between the passenger's seat and dash board. A stiff, numbing sensation permeated his neck and back, and the feeling of being concussed had him nauseous and sick. He blinked his eyes and shook away the cobwebs, momentarily unaware of where he was and how he'd gotten there.

Still shaking his head, he caught a whiff of the raw gas seeping inside of the car. The rancid odor was like a stick of ammonia, instantly snapping him back to his senses. He coughed a couple of times, and then sucked in a deep breath, all the while trembling from the wretched sound of Olivia's voice in the back of his mind begging the intruders not to harm Omelly.

"Not my baby, no! Leave him alone!"

"Just hold on, Oli, I'm coming," Rahmello slurred the words, still shaking away the dizziness.

He attempted to slither his way out of the car, but for some strange reason he couldn't feel his legs. In a frenetic panic, he looked over his shoulder at his two dead limbs and screamed like a banshee.

"Aaaaaaggggggggghhhh! My legs! My legs! I can't feel my fucking legs!"

He gritted his teeth and did his best to wiggle his toes, but his ten digits disregarded the message. The numbness in his neck and back became rigid and tender, and before he even realized what hit him, a blistering pain ravaged his body from the waist up.

"Uuuuuuggggggggggggrrrrrrrr!" He clamped his teeth together, desperately trying to fight through the pain. He banged his face against the ceiling and hammer-punched the door, but nothing seemed to work. Then subtly, almost instantly, the blistering pain began to wither away.

Exasperated and flirting with the brink of unconsciousness, he rested his face against the gas-soaked upholstery and sobbed like a helpless man. He was thinking about Olivia and Omelly, and cursing himself for not being able to save them. Not only them, but Nahfisah as well. As far as he knew, his sister was dead and gone, shot up and twisted on the yacht's lower deck.

He wanted to blame Sonny, but how? The only thing his brother ever did was show love and support him. He gave Rahmello the game and taught him how to live by the code, but Rahmello refused to listen. So now he had to live with the consequences.

"Don't hurt us! Please?" Olivia's voice rang clear in the back of his mind.

"Nah, nigga, fuck that." Rahmello popped his head up with a new sense of urgency. "I ain't going out like a bitch."

He knew it was only a matter of time before the people inside of the house would come outside to kill him, so to even the playing field, he dug down inside of his pocket and pulled out his solid gold lighter. He flipped the lid back and gently placed his thumb on the sparker. One flick and he was sending muthafuckas to East Jablip!

"Fuck is you niggas waiting for?" he shouted like a madman, praying the home invaders would hear him and eventually come outside to investigate. "You hear me, bitch? I'm right muthafuckin' here! You pussy-ass niggas want a war? *Bring it!*"

The warm, oily accelerant was pouring in thicker and faster, so heavy that it puddled into a small pool quickly accumulating on the ceiling beneath him. It drenched the back of his head and trickled down the sides of his face.

"Tfft! Tfft! Tfft!" He spat out the few drops that slipped inside of his mouth. It was then he heard the sound of a voice that was all too familiar.

"Hurry up and get his ass out the car," Grip stated in his deep, raspy voice. "The goddamned gas is leaking. I can smell it from here."

Chapter Four
On Interstate 95

Beeeeeeeeep! Beeeeeeeeep! Beeeeeeeeep!

"Damn, lil' homie, I know you hear me beeping this mutha-fuckin' horn," Snot Box stated as he exhaled a thick cloud of Kush smoke. He was seated behind the steering wheel of his Escalade speeding down 95. The Valentine homie, D-Day from The Bronx, was leaned back in the passenger's seat, and hunched forward in the back was the little homie, Gizzle, from Pittsburgh.

After blasting their way off of the yacht, they made it back to the pier just as Heemy was mashing out of the parking lot. That was fifteen minutes ago, and since then they'd been trailing behind doing everything possible to get him to pull over. Unfortunately, though, Heemy wasn't having it. Because instead of pulling over, he hopped on 95 and tore up the highway like a young Dale Earnhardt.

Beeeeeeeeep! Beeeeeeeeep! Beeeeeeeeep!

After blaring his car horn a few more times, Snot Box flashed his high beams and then handed the blunt he was smoking to D-Day. He gripped the steering wheel with both hands and pressed down on the gas pedal, cranking the engine north of 120. But even then, it was no match for the Lambo.

Heemy shifted into fourth and the Lamborghini sprang forward. The faster he went, the more distance he created and the more distance he created, the more his taillights became two little red dots floating down the highway.

"Damn, Blawd, why the fuck this nigga ain't pulling over?" D-Day asked Snot Box. "I know he don't think niggas try'na murk him. If that's the case, niggas could'a been did that."

"Nah, bro, the lil' homie just being cautious," Snot Box defended him. He removed his right hand from the steering wheel and reached back to grab the Backwood full of Diesel that Gizzle was passing him. He hit the wood super hard and inhaled deeply, gagging a couple of times before blowing the smoke from his nose and taking another pull. "That was some brazy ass shit that just popped off, you feel me? So, it's only right for the lil' homie to be on tilt. Shit, I'd be the same muthafuckin' way, try'na figure out who's who and what's what."

Snot Box sucked in another pull, then he passed the Wood to D-Day, who was still smoking the Kush-filled blunt. D-Day accepted the wood with his right hand, then he reached into the back seat with his left hand and handed Gizzle the leaf with the Kush in it.

Settling back in his seat, D-Day adjusted the AK-47 that was laying across his lap. He cracked his window to let out some of the smoke, and then leaned back in his seat and puffed on the wood, while looking up ahead at the two red dots he knew were Heemy's taillights.

"This nigga, Rahmello, ain't playing fair, Blawd. This nigga ain't playin' fair at all," D-Day stated through a thick cloud of smoke.

"Rahmello?" Gizzle looked at him like he was crazy. "Nephs, Ike, that nigga ain't capable of bringing that type of drama, not no muthafuckin' Gatling gun sticking out the side of a helicopter. That was some Pablo Escobar, Griselda Blanco type of shit. And even if he did have that type of power, why the fuck would he put himself in the line of fire? He could'a easily caught somma that hot shit, the same as everybody else. Ain't no way in the world this nigga's that stupid, Ike. Ain't no muthafuckin' way."

"That's an actual fact," Snot Box reasoned with him. "And it's mo' to the story than what the homies think it is. I wasn't supposed to say nothing, but now that the crab done climbed out the basket, I guess it really don't matter no mo'. This nigga Rahmello on some fuck shit, Blawd. All that big money, monkey shit he was kicking about it's a new day and a new time, and that he'll make us all millionaires if we profess our loyalty to him and make all of his enemies ours, he was indirectly talking about Sonny. This fuck-nigga think he's slick, Blawd. He ain't come right out and say it, but he done already made a move to take over Sonny's whole shit. And because this nigga knew he needed an army behind him," he held up his Block Boy chain, "he flew the homies out here to Philly so he could get us to do his bidding. Ol' mark-ass nigga. But little do he know, I'm already up on game, you feel me?"

"Oh, yeah?" D-Day rubbed his chin, still looking up the highway at the two red dots. He was thinking about Rahmello's speech on the upper deck right before the shooting rang out. He didn't catch on then, but it was clear to him now that Rahmello was working angles.

"And what about Sonny?" D-Day looked over the console at Snot Box. "You think the homie know?"

"Hellllllll *yeah*, the homie knows! Shit, that nigga the one who put me on game. He hit a nigga up right befo' the party. Told me what was going down and to link up wit' the lil' homie, Heemy. Matter of fact," Snot Box's voice trailed off when a light bulb flashed inside of his head. He flipped the lid on the center console, reached inside and then pulled out his Samsung.

"Who you calling, Blawd?" D-Day asked him.

"The lil' homie, Heemy," Snot Box replied, while pressing down on Heemy's number. It was locked in his phone under Philly Hitter. "Sonny gave me the lil' nigga's number when he hit me up befo' the party. Hopefully, the lil' nigga answer."

Ring! Ring! Ring!

"Who the fuck is this?" Heemy's voice came through the phone. "And what the fuck is you calling me for?"

"This Snot Box, lil' nigga, balm down. I'm in the Escalade behind you, Blawd. That's me, the one beeping the horn and flashing the high beams. Pull over, so I can bark at'chu."

"*Bark at me*? Nigga, bark, shit! I ain't got no mu'fuckin' rap," Heemy stated aggressively. He was clutching his toolie and looking in his rearview mirror at the only set of headlights behind him. They had to be at least one hundred yards away, blinking on and off just as Snot Box said they were.

"Listen, Blawd, it's some brazy shit going down, and niggas need to come together and move as a unit. After that shit Rahmello pulled at the party, ain't no telling what this niggas fit'nah do next, you feel me? And I'm saying that assuming he's the one who told them niggas to pop off."

"No disrespect 'cause I know you the big fool and all dat, but on some G shit and to keep it one hunnid, nigga, I 'on't know you. For all I know, you in cahoots wit' Rahmello," Heemy's words came out with a little less sting. He was glancing at the headlights in his rearview mirror and cutting his eye at Nahfisah, who's condition hadn't changed one bit.

"No. No. Don't shoot," Nahfisah sobbed and trembled. "No. No. Don't shoot."

"Listen, fam, I'm rapped out," Heemy continued, still clutching his Glock in any event the Escalade was somehow capable of catching up to his Lambo.

"*Blawd?*" Snot Box stated in disbelief. "Is you serious right now?"

"You muthafuckin' right, I'm serious. I seen the way you was acting when Rahmello was talking that bullshit on the upper deck, all hyped up on some Joe shit. And now I'm 'posed to believe that you're out here rydin' for my man? Negatron. And who's to say Rahmello ain't send you to come kill me? Matter of fact, fuck all this talking shit."

Scurrrrrrrrrrrrrrrrrrrrrr!

Heemy down shifted to *neutral*, and then stomped on the brakes while cutting the steering wheel hard to the left. The Lamborghini fishtailed from one side to the other, then spun around 180° before stopping on a dime, engulfed in a thick white cloud of its own smoke.

The driver's side door flipped up and Heemy hopped out the car soaking wet. His rock hard, dark chocolate physique was showing through his wet, white linen. The Glock in his right hand was aimed down the highway at the oncoming Escalade, and the iPhone in his left hand was pressed against his ear.

Snot Box, D-Day and Gizzle were less than sixty feet away when the Lamborghini spun around backwards. The heavy smoke from it's churning tires made it momentarily hard to see. But when it cleared out a few seconds later, the first thing they saw was Heemy. He was walking toward them with a gun his hand. The look in his eyes spelled *murder*.

"These niggas sho'nuf wasn't bullshitting," Snot Box stated aloud, referring to everything he heard about Heemy's gangsta. Nodding his head in approval, he slowed the Escalade to a stop and threw the transmission in *park*.

D-Day chambered a round into his AK-47 and cracked open the passenger's side door. The dome light cut on, but was quickly extinguished when Snot Box nudged him on the arm and told him to close the door. "Gawn and fall back, Blawd. I got this."

"*Fall back?*" D-Day questioned, still looking at Heemy through the windshield. "Yo, you buggin' right now, Scrap. This nigga 'bout to shoot up the truck."

"Just chill, homie. I told you, I got it," Snot Box told him. "Lil' homie, you still on the line?"

"You mu'fuckin' right, I'm still here," Heemy snarled back. He couldn't have been no less than thirty yards away. "Fuck is you still in the truck for? I thought we was having us a mu'fuckin' gangsta party?"

"Yo, Snot, where the fuck is y'all at?" Sonny's voice invaded the airwaves, catching Heemy off guard. He had no idea that Snot Box called Sonny on three-way and merged the call.

"*Sonny?* Heemy stopped in his tracks, questioning his big homie's voice, even though he knew it was him.

"Heem? Snot? Yo, who the fuck am I talking to?" Sonny's voice exuded frustration.

"You talking to both of us," Snot Box clarified. "Me and Heemy both on the line, Blawd. Now, tell this lil' nigga what it's hitting fo befo' he get his ass splattered out this muthafucka."

"Pussy, you ain't splattering shit!" Heemy flamed right back, fierier now that he'd heard Sonny's voice.

"If both of you niggas don't shut the fuck up!" Sonny snapped out. "These bitch-ass niggas kidnapped my mom and the kids!"

"Say what, Blawd?"

"Yo, Sonny, what'chu talking 'bout?" Heemy interjected. "Somebody kidnapped Miss Annie and the kids? *Who?*"

"Them YBM niggas. They got Fat-Fat, my mom and Imani."

"Naw, man. Naw," Heemy said as he shook his head in disbelief. "Yo, I *told*, Rahmello. I told this stupid-ass nigga."

Snot Box hopped out of his Escalade and walked over to Heemy, with D-Day and Gizzle right behind him.

D-Day was clutching his chopper and looking at Heemy, hoping he didn't make a move. He and Sonny went way back, and the last thing he wanted to do was set trip on one of Sonny's pups. Gizzle was different. He was two days over sixteen and thirsty to catch his first homicide, homie or not.

"We down fo' whatever you need us to do, Blawd," Snot Box declared. "Just name it, and we on it. And that's on Pueblo, my nigga."

"Y'all gotta find 'em before it's too late," Sonny's voice cracked. "Especially my mom and Imani, they're the main ones I'm worried about. Fat-Fat is Alvin's granddaughter, so I know he told them niggas not to hurt her. But my mom and Imani, ain't no telling, Scrap. They could fuck around and already be—already be..."

"Fuck, man!" Heemy lashed out when he heard the agony in Sonny's voice. The shit was so deep that Sonny couldn't even bring himself to say the words he was actually thinking.

"Yo, we had these niggas, bro. We fuckin' had him," Heemy continued with tears in his eyes. "Right in our fuckin' hands."

"Had who, Blawd?"

"Them YBM niggas," Heemy said as he wiped away the lone tear that was trickling down the right side of his face. "The nigga I was fuckin' up at the party before the shooting started, was one of 'em. These pussies been runnin' through the city on some shake down shit, knocking off everything moving. The word on the street is they were coming after me and Rahmello. I tried to tell him, but he wouldn't listen. This stupid-ass nigga thinks he's invincible."

"Hold on, back up. The party?" Sonny raised his voice a few octaves. "*Nahfisah's party*? Them niggas shot up my sister's party? Where the fuck is Nahfisah at, Heem? Tell me you got my sister off that muthafuckin' yacht."

"Nahfisah's good, bro, I got her," Heemy quickly confirmed. "She's a little shook up, but she's still in one piece. No thanks to

Rahmello. Fuckin' crab. Bitch-ass nigga left his own sister for dead?"

"A'ight, Blawd, but back to these YBM niggas." Snot Box stated, his intense stare was locked on Heemy as he waited for an answer.

"What the fuck, is you deaf? I just told you," Heemy snapped at him. "The nigga's top I popped was one of the bosses of that shit. Matter of fact," Heemy's eyes lit up like a 5,000-watt bulb, "Sonny, you know this nigga, the ol' head Beaver Bushnut, the one niggas be saying used to run wit'cha pops back in the day."

"Beaver Bushnut? From Richard Allen? You mean the smokah bul, Beaver Bushnut? The nigga I stomped out in front of ya mom's house?"

"Yeah, that's him." Heemy nodded his head. "Fucked me up when I seen him. He got this new dope whammin' in the city called *Nut Shit*. That's what them niggas be out here pressing mu'fuckas to sell for 'em."

"A'ight. So, what do we need to do in order to get a line on this nigga? You know a way to get at him?"

"Yup." Heemy bit down on his bottom lip, then he slowly raked his teeth across it. He was thinking about Keeno and his old head, Smitty. "I know just the way to track this nigga down, and if not him, then the niggas he be running wit'. Just gimmie a couple of hours and I got'chu."

"Say that," Sonny replied. "And another thing, I think this nigga, Grip, got his hands in this shit. To what extent? I'm not exactly sure, but he's definitely involved. So, just be careful and stay on point. The less people who know, the better. 'Cause the last thing I need is the cops getting involved. They get to showing pictures on the news, and them niggas might panic. Fuck around and do sum'n that they never intended."

"We got'chu, Blawd, and for the record, tell this lil' nigga who I be. So that way, he ain't gotta have his guards up around me and the homies."

"Aye, yo, Heem, Snot Box is official, you heard me? He's dedicated to the team one thousand percent, straight up and down, no ice, no chaser. And besides you, he's the only nigga I trust. He's good money, bro, believe that. And this is coming straight from me."

Snot Box looked at Heemy, and Heemy gave him a nod.

"A'ight, Sonny, yo' momma and the kids, we gon' get 'em back for you, homie. Safe and sound, believe dat."

"Nah, bro. I 'on't believe shit," Sonny tersely replied. "Not until I *know* they're okay. 'Til then, just hit me back at the top of every hour, or as soon as y'all find sum'n."

"Trust me, Blawd. We got'chu."

"Nah, homie, don't *got me*, get me."

Click!

Snot Box looked over to say something to Heemy, but Heemy was already climbing inside of his Lamborghini. So, after debating on whether or not he should call out and say something to reassure he had the young gun's back, he just gestured for D-Day and Gizzle to hop back inside of his Escalade. The situation was well beyond words. It was time to put on. It was time to show and prove, and ride out for the homie.

Chapter Five
Back At La Casa Moreno

I knew it had to be this nigga! Rahmello's teeth began to chatter. He was propped up on his right elbow and peering through the smashed in frame of the broken windshield. About thirty feet out, quickly approaching the car, were the silhouettes of two men. The first silhouette was much larger than the second, and both men were stepping in stride. Rahmello knew without question that the voice belonged to Grip, but it wasn't until the silhouettes came a little closer that he first saw his grandfather's face.

After scowling at Grip, he set his visage on the oversized, black man who was walking right beside him. He was big and bulky and blacker than night. His lumpy, bald head was shiny and slick, and his big, poppy, yellowish eyes had him looking like a young Bill Duke.

Calmer now, Rahmello closed his eyes and sucked in a deep breath. He was silently calling on God, asking The Most High to forgive him for his sins and have mercy on his girl and son, who he assumed was already dead.

"Hurry up before it blows," Grip said, as he came to a halt. He gestured for Pierre to keep moving, and then stepped off to the side about four feet away from the car.

The reality that Rahmello had taken sides with the enemy was something Grip would have normally deemed indelible. But because he knew his enemies were working in overdrive to disunite his family, and using Rahmello to do it, he was willing to make things right. But only if Rahmello was willing to do the same. Grip decided he would give Rahmello two options: either kill Olivia to send a message to their enemies, or die right beside her. The choice was his.

Clonk! Clonk! Crash!

The sound of Pierre kicking out his passenger's window forced Rahmello to pop his eye back open. He spat out a few more drops of gas, and then cracked up laughing.

"You ready to die, muthafucka?" He showed Pierre the lighter.

"Wait. No."
Flick!
Boom!
The Lamborghini burst into flames, as Pierre went flying through the air. His massive frame collided into Grip, and the two men went stumbling backwards. The only thing they heard was Rahmello screaming. He was flapping around the front seat and banging his hand against the door, frantically trying to force his way out. His gasoline-soaked body was engulfed in flames, lit up like a big, red fireball with sizzling red sparks flying out of his mouth.

"It's burning! It's burning! It's fucking burning! Somebody get me outta here! Pleeeeeeeeeeeaaaaasssssssse!"

Hearing his grandson burning alive incited in Grip's heart, a feeling he hadn't felt in nearly forty years. The twisted, eerie feeling was a combustion of love, disappointment and pain all rolled into one. The last time he remembered feeling that way was when he sanctioned the murders of Angela and Russell.

Angela was his baby sister, and Russell was his best friend. They were both killed in cold blood. Not because Grip wanted them dead, but because he needed them dead. In addition to going behind his back to cut a side deal with Big Angolo, they were working with the federal government in an effort to put him away for good. The only difference between now and then, was back then, Grip did what he had to. But this time around, he sincerely wished things would have turned out different. It was bad enough he dropped the ball when it pertained to Easy, so now that he finally had the opportunity to fulfill and further his legacy through the advancements of his grandsons, he hated Rahmello was in this grave predicament.

Aaaaaaaagggghhhhhhhhh! Get me out! Get me out of here, please! Griiiiiiiiiiiiiip! Get me outta this fucking car!

No longer capable of taking what he was seeing, Grip hopped back to his feet and attempted to save him. He took a step forward, but was pulled back to the ground when Pierre snatched him by his leg.

Ka—Boom! Pow!

A secondary explosion lit up the night, as the Lamborghini lifted off of the ground.

Wham!

It came back down with a crackling thud, sending fiery embers whooshing into the cool night air.

Rahmello's gut-wrenching wails were no more.

"What the hell was that? What happened?" Alexis said, as she ran over with a crying Omelly pressed against her bosom. Her intense glare moved from Pierre to Grip, and then further down the driveway where Alejandro was limping over with a gun in his hand.

"Oh, my God." Her eyes grew wide when she realized the Lamborghini belonged to Rahmello. "Nahfisah? Is Nahfisah in there, too?" She moved toward the car, but Pierre reached out to stop here.

"She no in dere, only 'e," Pierre spoke in his broken English.

"But what the hell happened?" Alexis covered her nose and mouth to abate the smell. The black smoke rising from the car was a chemical combustion of burnt metal, melted rubber, and well-done human flesh.

De mon *postal!*" Pierre stated with Caribbean flare, moving his thumb as if he were sparking a lighter. "Gwan blow up de car when Pierre reach out fa save 'im. Send Pierre *far* way pon de sky!"

After taking another look at the burning car, Alexis looked toward the house to see if Gangsta was coming. Seeing that he wasn't, she turned back around to face Grip.

"Here." She handed over Omelly. "So now that Gangsta's not around, can you *please* tell me whether or not you were able to get Miss Annie and the girls?"

"I did," Grip finally confirmed as he stood there looking over his great grandson for the very first time. Omelly's Moreno blue eyes and curly black hair brought a quick smile to the old man's face. "Well, actually, I sent one of my guys, Delaware Fats to go get 'em. That was over an hour ago. He hasn't contacted me as of yet, but I'm expecting his call any minute now. I told him to take Annie and the kids back to their old house on Reese Street. I figured that's the last place anyone would go looking for them."

"Damnit, I feel so much better hearing that," Alexis said. Up until then, she was under the impression that Grip was on some bullshit. "And just so you know, it wasn't my intention to ask about it in front of Gangsta. I had just finished watching the video from Nahfisah's party, and I was so overwhelmed that I wasn't thinking clearly. That fuckin' Juan. I just hope Nahfisah's still alive."

"I feel the same way," Grip calmly replied, even though he already knew that his granddaughter was safe.

Prior to being tortured and killed, Shabbaz and Aziz, acting on Grip's orders, secretly planted tracking devices in the dashboards of the two Lamborghinis that Rahmello had shipped in earlier that morning. The tracking devices were equipped with wide range cameras that covered the interiors of both vehicles.

Conveniently, Grip had been monitoring Rahmello's actions since earlier that afternoon, from La Casa Moreno to North Philly and then back to La Casa Moreno. The last time he checked on the cameras was when his three-vehicle caravan arrived at his front gate.

In the first Lamborghini, he saw that Rahmello was seated behind the steering wheel. He appeared to be crying, and was looking back and forth between the road and his hand. The tracking device, according to Alejandro, indicated that he was only ten minutes away from La Casa Moreno. So even though Grip was well aware of Rahmello's whereabouts, when he asked Alexis, he was only doing so in order to keep her off balance. It was all a part of his new strategy to stay ahead of the game, knowing that if he sat back and studied the thin line between loyalty and treachery, he could easily determine who was with him and who was against him. The same rules applied to what he knew about Nahfisah.

After watching the video footage of Rahmello, he switched over to the footage in the second Lamborghini. Right away, he was looking at the dark-skinned young man who Alexis referred to as *Heemy*. He was leaned back behind the steering wheel with a mug so mean that the old man smiled. In the leather seat beside him, Grip's cold blue eyes settled on his granddaughter for the very first time. Her condition pained him. She was curled up in a ball, shivering and shaking and mumbling under her breath so lowly that it was hard for Grip to hear. He couldn't help but to wonder what preceded her condition. So now that he knew about what happened at the party, it relieved him to know that his granddaughter safe. And even then, despite seeing that Alexis was genuinely concerned, Grip decided it was best to keep what he knew to himself.

"So, back to Gangsta," the old man digressed, rubbing Omelly's back because the little boy was still crying. He'd been whining non-stop since Alexis awakened him from his sleep. Grip caressed him around his neck and shoulders and the little boy cooed, resting his face on his great-grandfather's chest.

"I already know," Alexis began, but was quieted when Grip shushed her.

"Don't you tell that muthafucka shit, not a goddamned thing. There's a lot about that boy isn't right, he's been acting quite strange lately. He's calling himself trying to hide it from me, but he can't. I'm way too sharp for that shit."

"My mother already told me," Alexis tried to explain. "I only tell him whatever I—"

"*Listen*," Grip held his hand out to stop her, "Just listen. Whenever he's around, just be careful and keep your eyes open. We've got thirteen days until it's time for Sontino to come home, and I don't want any more waves, not a muthafuckin' ripple. You understand?"

"Kalamè!" The huskiness of Touissaint's voice grabbed their attention. They looked up the driveway where the massive sized Haitian was trooping down from the far side of the house. Olivia's long black hair was tightly clutched in his beefy right mitt. She was swinging her arms and kicking her feet, but there was nothing she could do to stop Touissaint from dragging her like a caveman ready to mate.

"No! No! Let me go!" Olivia cried out. "Get off of me!"

"*Kalamè!*" Toiussant roared even louder, commanding her to calm down in his native Creole. But when Olivia refused and bucked even harder, his heavy left palm shot up in the air and came down hard across the bridge of her nose.

Whack!

"Huurrrrrrrrmmmm!" Olivia whimpered.

Satisfied that he'd made his point, Toiussant drug her into the grass where Grip, Alexis and Alejandro were standing about fifty yards from the burning Lamborghini. He tossed her body and she thrust forward, her chin and cheek crashing into Grip's wing-tipped Stacy Adams.

Grip looked at her and gritted his teeth. She was naked from the waist up, sobbing and moaning. Her bare, butterscotch skin was bloody and spliced from the sharp slices administered by Toiussant's machete, and her swollen left eye was colored in a purplish hue.

"Here, Alejandro," Grip said as he held out Omelly. "Take him down to the van and hand me your gun. I dropped mines over there beside the car."

"Si, Señor." Alejandro nodded his head. He handed Grip his Glock .50, then accepted Omelly with both hands.

"No!" Olivia's head popped up when she realized they were talking about Omelly. She was so dazed out from being beaten and tortured that she didn't even peep the little boy was sound asleep in his great-grandfather's arms.

"Give him to me back!" Her Colombian Spanglish spewed out loud. "Give him to me back! Give me my baby!"

She swiped at Alejandro's leg, but he was already limping away. She attempted to crawl after him, but a swift kick in the ass left her stretched out flat. Grip kicked her once more, then he reached down and grabbed the back of her jeans.

"Get'cha ass over here." He drug her across the lawn.

"No!" Olivia screamed out, seeing that Grip was pulling her toward the Lamborghini. She was hunched over and scrambling on all fours. "Get off me! Lemme go!"

"Not at all, bitch. You're gonna see this shit here," Grip snarled at her. He rammed her face into the passenger's side door and then tossed her aside.

Still clutching the Glock in his right hand, he dropped to one knee and reached inside of the car with his left. He didn't even care that his hand was burning. He just gritted his teeth and forcefully yanked Rahmello through the busted-out window.

Rahmello's flaming hot body was still burning. His gooey, red skin was blistered and charred, and on the left side of his face, from the nose down, he was sizzled to the bone. His contorted mouth was stretched wide open, frozen from his last scream, and dangling out the side like a Cajun hotdog, was his crispy black tongue.

"Look at him, you fucking bitch! Look at what the fuck you did! This shit is because of *you*!"

Grip grabbed Olivia by the back of her neck and tightened his squeezed. He was forcing her to look at Rahmello's face.

"No!" Olivia's head was twisting every which-a-way. "I no wanna! No!"

"Goddamnit! Bitch, I said *look*!"

He mashed Olivia's face so hard against Rahmello's that when he let go and Olivia pulled back, Rahmello's gooey hot flesh was melted into hers.

"Ay dios mio!" Olivia cried out, frantically wiping the goop from her nose and mouth. "Ay dios mio! Ay dios mio!"

"Stinking-ass bitch, now it's your turn." He towered from behind and aimed the Glock at the back of her dome.

Boca!

Olivia's body jerked forward, slamming against the car about a millisecond after her brains did. She twitched a few times and then fizzed out with the squishy sound of her bowels being released.

Enraged was an understatement. Grip was so hot that when Alexis walked up behind him, he spun around with his finger on the trigger ready to bust a muthafucka's head.

"Calm down," Alexis rambled off fast, with her palms in the air. "It's just me."

She looked down at Olivia, who was sprawled out beside Rahmello, and then brought her attention back to Grip. His chiseled, tan face was illuminated by the fire's red glare, reminding Alexis of Lucifer himself.

"So, what's next?" Alexis asked, as she took a step back. "What do you want me to do?"

"Chop her the fuck up, and leave her on the courthouse steps."

"The courthouse steps? Don't you think that's a little too much?"

"Not at all," Grip shot back quick. "Them muthafuckas wanted a witness, so give them their goddamned witness. And besides, I'm sick of playing these fucking games. I want Sontino out of there, and that's that. He could have easily turned rat, but he didn't. He stood tall, so that's the end of it. And if any of the bosses from the roundtable don't agree, then tough shit. My father's not around anymore to play peacemaker. I'll bury those sonofabitches."

"Alright, well speaking of Sontino, for his sake and ours, I really think it's best that you speak to him before I do. There's so many questions that I simply can't answer, and because things are already so complicated, the last thing I want to do is complicate them any further."

"I agree," Grip replied, as he slowly lowered the Glock. "I'll give him a holler the moment I touch down in Cuba. And speaking of which," he glanced at the time on his David Yurman, "I really need to get going. I never intended to be here this long."

"But wait a minute," Alexis called out when Grip took off toward the front gate. She walked over beside him, and Grip came to a halt. Alexis did the same.

"Hurry up, Alexis. What is it?" Grip spoke urgently. He cut his eye at the Sprinter Van and the two Suburbans, and then settled his gaze back on her.

"What about Nahfisah?"

"What about her?"

"Shouldn't we be doing something to find her? At least, so you can tell Sonny whether or not she made it out safe?"

Grip looked at her and caressed his goatee. He was thinking of a way to throw her off without necessarily lying to her, knowing it was more than likely she would speak to Sonny before he did. "That young kid, Heemy, if he's everything you say he is, then I'm sure Nahfisah's gonna be just fine."

"If you say so." Alexis sighed. "But what about Miss Annie and the girls? Do you want us to go get 'em?"

"*Us?*"

"Yeah." Alexis nodded her head, innocently. "Me, Pierre and Toussaint."

"That's a negative," Grip shot her down. "As far as I'm concerned, they're already safe. Nobody's going to ever suspect they're right back in the heart of North Philly. Not to mention I told Delaware Fats to provide them with around-the-clock security."

"And you trust that?" Alexis questioned. "That was over an hour ago, and you just stated yourself, that he still hasn't contacted you yet. Don't you think that's kinda strange?"

"Listen," Grip replied in a slow, stern voice, increasingly growing more pestered by the second. "My guy's solid. Trustworthy. So, as long as Annie does what he tells her and she stays out of sight for the next couple of weeks, her and the girls should be just fine. And when Sontino comes home, I'll leave it up to him to make the final decision as to where he wants them to be, either naked and vulnerable here in the States, or safe and secure, relaxing down in Cuba with me. The choice is his."

Once again, Grip turned to walk away and Alexis called out behind him.

"There's one more thing." She stepped in closer. "What about Gangsta?"

"What about him?" Grip shot her a perplexed look. "I done already told you, don't you tell that muthafucka shit, not a goddamned thing. Especially when it pertains to Annie and the kids. He's still needed for now, so I'll tolerate him. Just don't do or say anything that will alert him to my suspicions. You got that?"

"I got'chu." Alexis nodded her head. "But what about my mother? Does she know about what's going on between you two? You and Gangsta, I mean?"

"*Does she know?*" Grip's eyelids shrank tightly. "What do you mean does she know? She's the one who pulled my coat to him."

"Oh. Okay," Alexis slowly replied, wondering if she'd given up more information than she intended to; or even worse, more information than she was *supposed to.*

An awkward silence filled the air between them, with neither one necessarily trusting the other. Grip had his reasons, and Alexis had hers. But even then, ultimately, their aspirations were the same: for Sonny to come home and be crowned as The Boss of all Bosses. So, after giving one another a mutual nod, they each went their separate ways.

Alexis, Pierre and Toiussant headed up toward the mansion's west wing, while Grip, stepping slow and calm, headed down the driveway toward the iron front gate.

Chapter Six

Approaching the passenger's side of his first Chevy Suburban, Grip looked to his left where his Sprinter Van and decoy Suburban were parked right behind it. The headlights on both vehicles lit up brightly, indicating they were ready to move out on his signal. Grip nodded his acquiescence, then he cracked open the back-passenger's side door and climbed inside of his SUV. Alejandro, who was seated up front, reached back and handed Grip his iPad.

"Dominic, do exactly as ju say, Señor," he stated in his thick Cuban accent. "De tracking devices wit' de cameras included have been attached."

"On both vehicles?" Grip questioned as he sank down into his leather seat, looking at his iPad screen.

"Si, Señor," Dominic answered from behind the steering wheel. He was halfway turned around in the driver's seat, looking at Grip.

Dominic, like many Afro-Cubans on the island, saw in Grip a much-needed escape from a poverty stricken, third world Cuba that was stagnated in a time warp reminiscent of the 1950's. And with all of Grip's wealth and power, his influence and prestige, they saw a champion; one of their own who returned to the island and was now giving them the opportunity to make a better life for themselves and their families.

In return, they professed to Grip a sacred vow that in addition to their undying loyalty, if or whenever necessary, they would gladly sacrifice their lives to assure the safety of him and his family. Their pledge of allegiance was something Grip had taken to heart, especially where it pertained to men like Dominic, who's Moreno last name and African bloodline were the same as his.

"Gracias, Dominic. You did good," Grip praised the young man who was growing fonder of him by the second.

"Si, Señor." Dominic smiled at him. He settled back in his seat and looked straight ahead, eager for the next opportunity to show Grip how true he was.

"Alright." Grip sighed, as he carefully examined his iPad screen. "Let's see what we've got here."

He clicked on his tracking app, and a virtual grid of La Casa Moreno appeared on the screen. At the top of his driveway, where the cobblestones looped around his Greco Roman brick fountain, he saw a blinking blue dot. A second dot was blinking about a quarter of a mile down from the west wing of his mansion. Its color was light green.

"Okay," Grip said as he looked up from the screen and locked eyes with Alejandro. "The blue dot, being as though it's blinking from exactly where the water fountain would be, I'm assuming that's a simulation of Gangsta's Yukon."

"Si, Señor," Alejandro confirmed with a slight nod.

"And the green dot blinking down the road, that's a simulation of Alexis' vehicle?"

"Si, Señor."

"Alright. Now, for what reason are the dots blinking?" Grip scratched his head.

"Oh, dat's nothing." Alejandro waved him off. "Dat jus' means de cars are no moving. But when dey do," his bushy eyebrows shot up, "de blinking jus' stop, it no more. Dat's how ju know de difference from dey stop and when dey go."

"I see," Grip slowly replied, still not fully aware of exactly what he was looking at. "And how do I keep track of both vehicles? You know, whenever they're too from apart to appear on the same grid?"

"Ju see dat arrow in de top left corner? Press it."

Grip did as Alejandro told him, and the screen split down the middle displaying both dots in their own individual vicinities.

"Ju see?"

"I see," Grip replied, still looking down at his iPad screen. The blue dot was blinking on the left, and the green dot was blinking on the right. "Now, what about the tracking grid and the camera inside the Lamborghini that my granddaughter's riding in, the one I was looking at when we first arrived? How do I go back to that, and how do I track it?"

"Lemme see." Alejandro reached for the iPad.

Grip handed it to him, and Alejandro pulled up exactly what he asked for.

"Dere ju go," Alejandro said as he handed the iPad back to Grip. "De grid ju see is exactly where dey at and where dey moving to. Dat's de reason de yellow dot no blinking, jus' moving. And de box in de top left corner, dat's de video ju ask for. It shows dem both, ju granddaughter and de friend she wit'."

Looking at the screen, Grip noticed the tracking grid was a virtual simulation of Interstate 95. The yellow dot simulating Heemy's Lamborghini was slowly moving northbound from Penn's Landing to Willow Grove, heading toward the town house that Rahmello purchased for Nahfisah a few days earlier. It was mentioned to Grip by Shabazz and Aziz the day before in their briefing report.

"Rock solid," Grip said as he handed the iPad back to Alejandro. "Now, pull up the camera and tracking grid that was placed inside of Gangsta's Yukon."

Alejandro pulled it up with one swipe, then he passed the iPad back to Grip.

"Dere ju go, Señor."

"Gracias." Grip nodded his appreciation.

After swiping back and forth from one tracking grid to the other, Grip clicked out of his tracking app and logged into his Gmail account. He scrolled through his latest received emails, and then stopped on the one he was looking for. After clicking it open, he pressed down on the attachment. The information contained therein had been provided by U.S. Marshal Wayne Mitchell, Big Angolo's go-to-man back at ADX Florence.

Big Angolo would have never imagined that Wayne Mitchell was a double agent secretly working for Grip. At the cool rate of $250,000 per year, Mitchell's task was to keep a close eye on the waning mafia don and report back to Grip all of his phone calls and visits. Even the cell phone he gave Big Angolo was secretly provided by Grip. An illegal version of a Title lll wiretap was attached to the phone, affording Grip unlimited access to every one of Big Angolo's phone conversations. The conversations were converted into transcripts every first of the month, and then sent via email to Gregory Johnson, Grip's best friend and consigliere. GJ would vet the information, and then pass along to Grip whatever he deemed relevant.

Unfortunately, a little over eighteen months ago, the transcripts stopped coming. It wasn't because Mitchell didn't send them, but because GJ and his wife, Alicia, were found murdered in the basement of their Upper Darby estate. In addition to that, because he was on the run from a federal indictment, the last thing on Grip's mind were the missing transcripts. He never even questioned the reason they stopped coming. It wasn't until late yesterday afternoon that the transcripts once again became relevant.

After entertaining his guest and retiring to his study to undergo some serious thinking, Grip received an out-of-the-blue email from Madam François. The email had been forwarded from Mumar Khalifi to The Madam, who for her own personal reasons, forwarded the email to Grip. According to the email, Big Angolo's dead body was discovered in his prison cell the night before, and was currently in the process of being flown back to Philly. There was also an attachment consisting of two full years of Big Angolo's phone transcripts.

Initially, given his new leverage within The Conglomerate, Grip's notion was to nix the information all together. He figured there was no need to beat a dead horse. But after reflecting back to the conversation he had with The Madam, he decided he would give the transcripts a rudimentary look. It was a good thing he did. Because in addition to learning about the secret allegiance between Big Angolo and Joaquin, he also learned about the critical role Gangsta played in breaking the Sinaloa jefe out of a Mexican prison camp.

"And these muthafuckas had the nerve to act as though they had never met one another," Grip mumbled under his breath, referring to the day before when he introduced Gangsta to Joaquin. *"These stupid sonofabitches must'a lost their minds."*

Satisfied that he covered all bases, Grip reclined back in his plush leather seat as Dominic pulled away from the front gate. The Sprinter Van and decoy Suburban were close behind, following at an arms' length distance. The three-vehicle convoy tracked up the hilly road, and then slowly cruised down the other side. The Sprinter Van was safely situated in between.

"To where next, Señor?" Dominic questioned, as they came to a halt at the main road below. "Back to de airport in Teterboro, or no?"

"Not yet." Grip shook his head *no*, referring to the private airport in northern New Jersey. It was there that his ten-man crew of Cuban banditos were lined up and down the clear port securing the two private jets they arrived in three hours earlier. "First, we need to make a quick detour."

"A detour to where?" Dominic was looking at him in the rear-view mirror.

"We need to swing past and collect my granddaughter," Grip clarified the matter. He then blurted out Nahfisah's address for the OnStar system to hear. "1661... Willow Grove, Pennsylvania."

Still reclined back in his buttah leather seat, the Black Mafia don closed his eyes and thought about The Madam. He appreciated Geraldine for spilling the tea on Gangsta, but still he was uncertain as to whether or not he could trust her. So, in order to gauge her so-called loyalty, he decided the best way to do it was through Alexis. If the blue dot simulating Gangsta's Yukon traveled to Annie's North Philly residence, it would prove once and for all that The Madam was working against him. But if it didn't, Grip reasoned it would solidify The Madam's assertions that her organization would plank his unyielding efforts to assure that Sonny inherited his rightful position as The Conglomerate's head chair.

All he had to do now was sit back and watch. It was match point, advantage Moreno. The next move was hers.

"Patterns, my old friend. Patterns."

Askari

64

Chapter Seven

"Damnit, Lorenzo. Answer ya fucking phone," Gangsta demurely stated with his shifty, brown eyes scoping the front door looking to see if Grip or Alexis was coming. He was leaned against the refrigerator in the kitchen of the pool house behind La Casa Moreno. His compact Glock .9mm was resting on the counter, and his cell phone was pressed against his ear. He knew the phone calls he'd been making were an unnecessary risk, but he couldn't help it. He needed confirmation on whether or not his men were successful in kidnapping Annie and the kids and securing the three hundred kilos of raw that Olivia told Juan were stashed inside of the house. The anticipation was heightened the moment he realized Rahmello had somehow made his way back to La Casa Moreno. The YBM was supposed to had kidnapped him the second he left Nahfisah's party. So that way, in any event Olivia's information was incorrect, they could torture Rahmello until he told them where he hid the three hundred keys. Then after that, they would kill him.

Ring! Ring! Ring! Ring!

"These niggas is killing me right now with this not answering the phone shit," Gangsta complained as he disconnected the call and redialed Lorenzo's number.

Prior to calling Lorenzo, Gangsta called The Reaper a total of nine times, searching for answers as to how he and his men allowed Rahmello to slip through their fingers. Strangely, though, The Reaper declined all of his calls, and now Lorenzo was doing the same.

Ring! Ring! Ring! Ring!

"The Boost Mobile subscriber you are calling is not available," the automated answering services stated in Gangsta's ear. *"If you would like to leave a brief message, press—"*

"This fucking Lorenzo," Gangsta lamented, shaking his head in frustration. "I gave this nigga one job, *one*, and he can't even do that right. For all that, I should've kept his ass in jail. In-the-way muthafucka."

Gangsta stuffed his iPhone down in his front pants pocket, then he grabbed his gun from the counter and moved from the kitchen to the living room.

Laying on the floor burrito-wrapped in two blue tarps, were Shabazz and Aziz. The blue tarps covered their dead bodies from the head down, stopping about an inch or so above their ankles. Their bound together feet were sticking out from the bottom, swollen and bloody and staked through the middle with the railroad spikes that Rahmello used to nail them against the wall.

Gangsta returned his Glock to his hoody pocket, then he reached down with both hands and grabbed Aziz around his ankles. He drug his body a few inches closer to the door, but released his hold when an incoming call vibrated his pants pocket. He quickly removed the phone and fixed his eyes on the screen. The caller was Lorenzo.

"Where the fuck are you? I've been calling you nonstop for the past five minutes," Gangsta spazzed at him.

"We're parked outside of Grip's warehouse on Delaware Avenue, just like you told us," Lorenzo replied as he sucked in a drag from his Newport. He was seated behind the steering of a black Crown Vic, parked outside of the second garage door that lined the front of the warehouse. A few doors down, parked in a white U-Haul, were his two cohorts, police officers Dan McKinney and Marvin Brown.

Not even ten hours earlier, Lorenzo and his men were sitting in the county jail, detained for being persons of interest in the murders of District Attorney Seth Willis and his secretary, Michelle Drayton. But now that they were back out, courtesy of Gangsta and his federal connections, they were anxiously awaiting the million-dollar payday that Gangsta promised them over a year and a half ago when they executed the raid on Sonny's night club. Their last order of business was to kidnap Annie and the girls and secure the three hundred bricks that were stashed inside of the house. Unfortunately, they failed on both fronts.

"So, what's up with Sonny's mom and the kids?" Gangsta asked Lorenzo. "Did you guys go out and get 'em?"

"Yeah, we went out to the house, but we didn't get 'em."

"And why the fuck not?"

"Because there was no one there to get. The entire house was a goddamned bloodbath."

"So, you're telling me they're dead?"

"Not exactly, because technically I can't. Aside from all of the blood, the only body we found was a chubby, black guy on the back patio. There was a goddamned Rottweiler feasting on him, like literally chomping down on his fat ass face. The fuckin' dog must'a heard me standing there, because the next thing I know the motherfucker was on me. I shot him a few times and he was *still* trying to bite me. Eventually, I just blew out his two front legs and then went back to searching the house for the shipment. Oh yeah, and there's one more thing," Lorenzo said as he took another drag on his Newport. "You remember Jorge Dominguez, the Sinaloa captain that Joaquin and Chatchi left in charge when they fled down to Brazil?"

"Of course, I remember him. I was just at a meeting with Joaquin and Chatchi yesterday down in Cuba. But what does Jorge have to do with any of this?"

"We found his driver's license in the living room, Terry. It was lying in a pool of blood. Now, when you add that to the fact that Sontino's family is missing, what do you get?"

"*Sonofabitch*!" Gangsta shouted into the phone, realizing his plan was falling apart right before his very eyes. He looked out the front door to see if anyone was coming, and then continued speaking in a much lower tone. "But nothing you're telling me is making any sense. Why the fuck would the Sinaloa's kidnap Annie and the kids?"

"That's not for me to answer," Lorenzo said as he took another pull on his Newport. "All I know is that sonofabitch was here, Terry. It's up to you to take it for what its worth."

"Gangsta's brow began to sweat, as everything Lorenzo told him was slowly beginning to make sense. He knew from talking to Big Angolo that Joaquin had given his word that for the sake of the roundtable, he was willing to let bygones be bygones. But now that Big Angolo was dead and there was no one around to curb his anger, the Sinaloa Jeffe had forsaken his oath and was now seeking revenge for the kidnapping and murder of his son, Roberto. But even then, it was hard for Gangsta to wrap his mind around Jorge's driver's license being left at the scene.

Was it left there intentionally? Did someone want it to be known the Sinaloa's were involved? And if so, who?

"That fucking Grip!" Gangsta's eyes lit up the Las Vegas strip.

"What about him?" Alexis asked, as she stepped into the pool house. "What are you talking about, Terrance? And who are you talking to?" She pointed at the phone in his hand.

"Nobody," Gangsta lied. He pulled the phone from his face and stuffed it back down inside of his pocket.

Alexis looked at him strangely. Her brown eyes scoured the room, then stopped on Shabazz and Aziz before settling back on Gangsta. She folded her arms across her chest and tilted her head slightly.

"Rahmello's dead, Terrance. That explosion, I'm sure you heard, was him. He blew himself up."

"So?" Gangsta shrugged his shoulders. "What the fuck is you telling me for? I hope it hurt."

Alexis scowled at him.

"What the hell is wrong with you, Terrance?"

"What the hell is wrong with what?" Gangsta shot right back, hoping his aggressive attitude would avert any additional questions about the nature of his phone call. He looked behind Alexis at Pierre and Toiussant, who were holding post directly outside of the front door. Their wide, muscular backs were blocking his view of the back yard, so much that he could barely see the moonlight shining down on the veranda.

"What the fuck is you talking about, Alexis?" Gangsta spoke more aggressively.

"What am talking about? I'm talking about *you*." She pointed at him. "You've been acting weird as fuck lately. And that bullshit you pulled back at the house, it was fucking stupid. The only thing you're doing is making Grip suspicious."

"And I'm supposed to give a fuck?" Gangsta stretched his arms out wide. "Fuck Grip. That nigga killed my peoples."

"Are you shittin' me right now?" Alexis looked at him like she wanted to smack his ass. "Can't you see there's a bigger picture in all of this? This isn't a fucking game, this shit is serious shit. My muthafuckin' life is on the line, *yours too*! And you really got the nerve to be stuck in your feelings like some punk-ass, pussy-ass bitch. Really, Terrance? Really?"

"Yo, who the fuck you think you talking to?"

"Nigga, I'm talking to you!"

Hearing the two of them arguing, Pierre spun around and stuck his head through the door. He saw that Gangsta was slipping his right hand through his hoody pocket slit, so he stepped inside of the house and unsheathed his machete.

"Nigga, now what the *fuck* is you looking at?" Gangsta stepped forward and whipped out his burner. The dangerous look in his eyes was daring the Haitian to make a move.

"Pierre, no," Alexis said as she stepped in Pierre's path. Speaking in Creole, she pointed at the front door and commanded him to leave. "Alè."

Pierre's nostrils began to flare. He looked down at Alexis with his bottom lip quivering; his rage-filled eyes begging her for a one-time chance to stomp a bone out of Gangsta's ass.

"*Alè!*" Alexis raised her voice. "Go. Now." She shooed him away with the flick of her wrist.

Pierre sucked his teeth and shot Gangsta the look of death. Slowly nodding his head, he did an about-face and stepped back outside on the veranda.

Alexis turned back around to face Gangsta.

"Come on, Terrance, you know what Big Angolo said, nothing we spoke about is supposed to happen until Sontino's out of there. So, if you choose to not respect anything that I'm saying, then at the very least respect Big Angolo. We've only got thirteen more days. Just thirteen more days, and that's it."

Gangsta gritted his teeth and looked away. He knew that he was moving way too reckless, but not for the reasons that Alexis assumed. Because in all actuality, only he and his old friend, Alvin Rines, knew the *true* master plan that was now in effect, one in which that didn't involve Alexis, her mother, nor the remaining five bosses who had already professed their loyalty to Grip.

"You know what, Alexis, fuck this shit. If you and your mom wanna keep catering to Grip, then that's on y'all. From here on out, I'm doing this shit my way."

"Terrance, wait, don't go. We still need to talk about this," Alexis pleaded as Gangsta hurried his way toward the door. He stepped over the blue tarp that shrouded Aziz, and then shoulder checked Pierre on his way out.

"Stupid ass. He's gonna fuckin' ruin everything." Alexis shook her head. She stepped down on the veranda prepared to go after him, but stopped short when her cell phone began to vibrate.

Vrrrrrrrm! Vrrrrrrrrm! Vrrrrrrrrm!

Alexis pulled the phone from her back pocket and saw the caller was Heemy. "Damnit!" She let out a frustrated groan. She wanted to go after Gangsta, but figured that talking to Heemy was much more important. At least that way she could find out what happened to Nahfisah and then pass it on to Sonny the next time they spoke.

"Raheem, what the hell happened at the party? Is Nahfisah safe? Did she make it off the yacht?" Alexis' words came out faster than a speeding bullet.

"Yeah, I got her, she's still in one piece. But I think she's suffering from shock, though," Heemy put her up on game. He looked over at Nahfisah, who was still shivering and shaking. "These niggas really got my baby sitting here schized out on some other shit," he spoke in a low voice, gently caressing Nahfisah's face with the back of his hand.

"But she's not hurt?"

"Physically, she's not. But mentally and emotionally?" Heemy shook his head and sighed. "That's a whole 'nother story."

Pressing the phone against her shoulder, Alexis snapped her fingers at Pierre and Toiussant. The two Haitians turned around to face her.

"Potè." She pointed down at the two blue tarps, gesturing for each man to grab one. She then stepped into the kitchen and continued talking to Heemy. "Alright, so, where are you?"

"We're in Willow Grove, just now pulling up in front of Nahfisah's house," Heemy said as he cut off the engine.

"And who the fuck is *we*?"

Instead of replying, Heemy climbed out of his Lambo. He tossed the house key that Nahfisah had given him the night before to Snot Box, and then quickly moved around the front of his car.

"*Raheem*?" Alexis' voice roared through his phone. "Who the fuck is *we*?"

"Yo, Lexi, who the fuck is you yelling at?"

"Just answer the question, Raheem. Who the hell is *we*?"

"It's me, Nahfisah, and a couple of the homies that Rahmello flew in from out of town," Heemy said as he lifted up the passenger's side door.

"And you're telling me you trust these niggas, even though they were flown in by Rahmello?"

Heemy's forehead wrinkled. "What'chu think I'm on some other shit?"

"Did I accuse you of being on some other shit?"

"Well, what the fuck is you asking me that for?"

"I asked you that because there's a lot of shit going on, and it's hard for me to decipher who's who. So, do you trust these motherfuckers or not?" Alexis cut to the chase.

Heemy anxiously bit down into his bottom lip. He looked up on the porch where Snot Box was opening the front door, and then looked over his shoulder at D-Day and Gizzle. The two goons were leaning against the Escalade's chrome front grill. D-Day's choppa was clutched in his right-hand lingering at his side, and Gizzle was standing right beside him twisting up a blunt.

After locking eyes with D-Day for a brief second, Heemy looked down inside of his Lambo where he'd inadvertently left his toolie between the driver's seat and the center console. His breathing intensified.

"Do you trust them or not?" Alexis persisted.

"I mean, not at first," Heemy spoke the truth. "But after talking to Sonny, and him telling me they were cool, I'm basically just rockin' off of that."

"Hold on, wait a second. Are you saying that you spoke to Sontino? And if so, when?" Alexis' voice became suspicious and jealous. She was wondering how Heemy was able to speak to Sonny, and she wasn't.

"Like, ten minutes ago," Heemy replied, remembering what Sonny told him about keeping under wraps what he knew about Miss Annie and the girls. He figured that if Sonny wanted Alexis to know, he would have told her already.

"So, does he know about what's going on out here? Does he know about what happened at the party?"

"Yeah," Heemy answered as he gently pulled Nahfisah from the car. She melted into his chest and he pulled her in close. "I told him the whole shit, how it all went down. He just wanted to make sure Nahfisah was safe. I told him she was, and that's the reason I'm calling. Sonny's got some business he needs us to handle, and I ain't comfortable with leaving Nahfisah here by herself. I was hoping you could come through and hold her down, at least until the morning. Hopefully, everything will be good by then."

"Yeah, I can do that. But tell the truth. Sonny knows, doesn't he?"

"Knows, what?" Heemy played it off. He had just entered the house, with Nahfisah close on his hip. He laid her down on the sectional, and then moved over to the window. Looking through the venetian blinds at D-Day and Gizzle, he continued talking to Alexis. "Sonny knows what? What'chu talking 'bout?"

"The business he needs y'all to handle? It's about Miss Annie and the kids, isn't it?"

"How the fuck you know about Miss Annie and the kids?" The tone of Heemy's voice changed. He turned away from the window and locked eyes with Snot Box. "Yo, who the fuck told you that?" He switched the call over to speaker, allowing Snot Box to hear everything that Alexis was saying.

"Calm down," Alexis replied, noticing the change in his demeanor. "It's not what you think."

"Well, what the fuck is it, then?" Heemy's nostrils began to flare. "'Cause to me, dat ass is looking suspect right about now. How the fuck would you know about Miss Annie and the kids missing, unless you had sum'n to do wit' it?"

"Raheem, just listen to me, please," Alexis pleaded with him. "I know this may seem a little fishy, but it's not. Miss Annie and the girls are safe, I can promise you that."

"*Safe?*" Heemy screwed his face up. "*You can promise me?* Man, fuck all dat. Where the fuck is my man's folks at?"

"I wish I could tell you, but I can't," Alexis slowly replied. "For their safety, it's better that no one knows."

"Aye, yo, Lexi, dig right. You can miss me wit' all these fuckin' word games. The big homie's in there stressed the fuck out thinking the YBM kidnapped his folks. So, if you know sum'n different, then I'd suggest you spit it the fuck out, and fast."

"The YBM?" Alexis repeated, thinking about what Shelly told her when she called up to the county jail.

"You heard what the fuck I said. Them niggas violated, and now they gotta see me," Heemy declared. "*All of 'em!* Every last one of them muthafuckas!"

"Listen, Raheem, I'm on my way. Don't leave or do anything else until I get there."

"Yeah, a'ight."

"I'm serious, Raheem."

"I said, a'ight."

"Alright," Alexis snuck in the last word before disconnecting the call. She headed out of the door and caught the attention of Pierre and Toiussant, who were standing on the veranda with Shabazz and Aziz' tarp wrapped bodies pivoted on their shoulders.

"Don't worry about them," she gestured at the two blue tarps as she hurried past. "Just leave them here and hurry up."

"What's de rush now?" Toiussant asked, flinging Shabazz' body from his shoulder like a price of lint. "Kibo nou alè?"

"We're going to North Philly to pick up Miss Annie and the girls," Alexis answered while speed walking toward the far back gate. The wooded area on the other side led to the small road where her Navigator was parked.

"And you know where dey at?" Pierre asked, as he walked up behind Alexis and gave her a boost.

"I do." Alexis nodded her head. She gripped the railing with both hands, pulled herself up, and kicked one of her legs over the ten-foot-high gate. She climbed down on the other side and then gestured for her men to do the same.

"Grip told me they're stashed away at their old house in North Philly. He also said for me to keep away, but I can't. There's something in my heart telling me that none of this is right. I just don't trust that motherfucker."

"But what 'bout yah manman?" Toiussant questioned, as he climbed over the gate and came down on both feet. He was referring to Madam François, knowing that she was working in conjunction with Grip. "Maybe she no wan' fa you doing wha' he say no do."

"Mommy will understand, she knows my love for Sontino," Alexis replied as she backed up a few steps giving Pierre enough room to climb down from the gate.

"And as far as Grip, who gives a fuck? My loyalty is to Sontino, not him. And if Sontino knew exactly what was going on, this is what he would want me to do. There's no way I'm leaving his family in the middle of the fucking hood at a time like this. I'm just not doing it. Especially with Terrance's unpredictable ass roaming around, planning only God knows what. I'm beginning to not trust his ass either."

She took off walking, with the twin towers close behind. Pierre looked at Toiussant and shook his head. He was hoping his older brother would talk some sense into Alexis. But instead adhering to his brother's silent request, Toiussant just shrugged his shoulders and looked away. He loved Alexis like a baby sister, and right or wrong, come hell or high water, he was determined to have her back. Even if the outcome was death.

Chapter Eight
Twenty Minutes Later

"Where the fuck is this so-called around-the-clock security?" Alexis asked Pierre when he made a right turn on the corner of Reese and Dauphin Streets and slowly cruised down the block toward Susquehanna Avenue. She was hunched forward in the passenger's seat, looking around for any signs of the men that Grip claimed he had stationed there. She noticed that a handful of young hustlas were hugging the corner at the top of the block, but that was it. She saw nothing to indicate that the last house at the bottom of the block was being monitored and secured.

"I know this motherfucker *did not* leave Miss Annie and them kids all alone in the middle of the goddamned hood. Especially at a time like this, and with *no protection?*"

"Either daht, or 'im soldjahs abandoned dey post," Toiussant spoke up from the back seat. He was looking out of the window at the filthy, dilapidated block with a smug expression.

As a small child from the heartless streets of Port-au-Prince, born and raised in a clay brick hut with an earth dirt floor, he always thought of America as *The Land of Milk and Honey*, which was exactly what he saw while they were back at La Casa Moreno. But here, in the Bad Landz section of North Philly, the only things he saw were the cracked sidewalks, the graffiti covered walls, the rodent infested, trash filled vacant lots, and the cramped row houses that were lined up and down every street they drove past. It was nothing close to the impoverished life he left behind back in Haiti, but even still, it was a far cry from the grandiose illusion that America presented to the rest of the world.

"Ralanti," Alexis said to Pierre, telling him to slow the SUV. "Suspenn," she told him to stop as they slowly approached the house.

The first thing Alexis noticed when she climbed out of her Navigator was the old Chevy Tahoe that was parked out front. Its tireless frame was covered in dust, and the rusted-out rotors were propped up on cinder blocks. The driver's side door was still smashed in from when Monster and Lil' Buggy sideswiped Riri, and scribbled on the window with a sad face drawn underneath, were the words: *Well Damn Nigga Wouldja Wash Me!*

"Eske se kay la sa?" Pierre questioned as he approached Alexis from behind.

"Yeah." Alexis nodded her head, as she looked at him over her left shoulder. "This is definitely the house."

"Eske ou kwè sa?"

"Of course, I'm sure. I still remember the first time Sontino brought me here to meet Miss Annie. I remember it like it was yesterday," she replied in a somber tone, looking at the house with a blank expression.

As far as she could tell, the house was abandoned. The rusty mailbox beside the door was spilling out mail, and directly above it, covered in dust, was a burnt-out lightbulb. The curtains were pulled closed in every window and on the left side of the house, in the small yard where Sonny used to keep his pit bulls, the overgrown weeds were so high, they toppled over and pushed through the wire fence that surrounded it.

"Me nah like wah me feel," Toiussant said as he unsheathed his machete and looked down at Alexis. "Me *know* ya wan fa save 'em. Me know daht. But *look*." he gestured toward the ran down house, "deys nobody 'ere."

Alexis' eyes began to water. She looked away from Toiussant and set her sights on the paint-chipped front door. She wanted to believe that Grip was right, that Annie and the girls were inside of the house, safe and sound. But it just didn't seem that way. Her gut feeling was telling her the opposite.

After wiping away the lone tear that trickled down the right side of her face, Alexis turned around slowly. She was just about to head back to her Navigator when Pierre stepped forward with an inquisitive look on his face.

"Me see sum'tin'."

"You see what?" Alexis asked him.

"Daht." Pierre pointed his machete at the living room window.

Alexis squinted her eyes and stepped in closer. A flickering orange light was glowing in the window's bottom right corner. It sputtered on and off, and then lit up steady, illuminating the curtains from the other side.

"There's somebody in there," Alexis said as she ran up the stoop and began banging on the door.

Bunck! Bunck! Bunck! Bunck!

"Miss Annie, open the door! It's me, Alexis!"

Bunck! Bunck! Bunck!

"Miss Annie, *please*!" The emotion in her voice escalated to a loud shriek. "If you can hear me, open the door! It's Alexis! I came to get y'all, so I can take y'all somewhere safe!"

Bunck! Bunck! Bunck!

"Alè lot bo," Pierre commanded she move out of the way. He nudged Alexis aside, and then rammed the door with his shoulder.

Crack!

"Yo, what the fuck?" the young hustla inside of the bando shouted when the front door came flying in off of the hinges. When he first heard the commotion on the other side, he assumed it was a family member coming to get their dope fiend relative. But now that he saw Pierre's big ass standing in the doorway, he assumed it was jack move. He leapt up from the dining room table and reached for his gun, but it was no use. Pierre's machete was already tumbling through the air.

Thwap!

It dug into the young hustla's chest and flipped him over the chair where he previously sat.

The two dope fiends seated on the mattress beside the window screamed when they saw it. They jumped up and made a dash for the kitchen, not even caring about the spoonful of dope they'd just finished cooking.

Pierre was on point. He grabbed the two men by the back of their necks, pulled them in close, and then forcefully mashed their heads together.

Wham!

He tossed the first fiend to the floor and focused on the fiend who was still clutched in his grasp. Squeezing his neck with both hands, he snapped the man's head to the left and then yanked it back to the right, tugging so hard that his cracked spine burst through his ashy gray skin.

"Mouri," Pierre whispered death in his ear. He tossed the man's dead body on the pissy mattress beside the window, then he towered over his friend. He grabbed the man by his neck, prepared to give him the same fate.

"Pierre, don't," Alexis said when she stepped into the house with Toiussant behind her. "They're not even here. This is a god-damned trap house. Look." She pointed at the fifty or so dope needles that were scattered around the floor, and then nodded toward the stairs where a young, Spanish woman was slumped forward, slobbering on herself with a needle stuffed in her arm.

"That punk-ass, no good sonofabitch set me up."

"What'cha mean 'bout daht?" Pierre looked at her strangely.

"That fucking Grip. He's been tracking us the entire time. Toiussant show him."

Toiussant stepped forward and held up the tracking device he discovered while she and Pierre were standing at the front door. He knew all along that coming to the house was a bad idea. But it wasn't until he saw the house was abandoned that he realized they'd been set up by Grip. It was then, he discovered the tracking device in Alexis' Navigator. The small, black box was attached to the bottom of her rearview mirror. It was easy for him to identify being as though it was the same model and make he and Pierre used whenever The Madam sent them on a mission.

"'Ere," Toiussant said as he handed Pierre the tracking device. He then walked over to the dining room table and pulled Pierre's machete from the young hustla's chest.

"But why 'im would do daht?" Pierre questioned, looking over the small black box. He looked down at the two men he just killed, then he looked back and forth between the Spanish woman and the first dope fiend who was still knocked out cold. Had Alexis not stopped him when she did, he would have certainly murdered them, too.

"Me nah no wah fa 't'ink." Pierre brought his gaze back to Alexis. "Why 'im would say a t'ing like daht? 'Bout she and petits? Daht dem '*ere*?'"

"He did it to test me," Alexis slowly replied. "Everything he told me, it was all a goddamned test. He was testing me to see if I would tell Terrance."

"Either daht, or ta see if yah do wha' 'im say no do," Toiussant chimed in.

"*That sneaky sonofabitch*," Alexis cursed under her breath. She was thinking about the Sprinter Van that was parked between his two Chevy Suburban's back at La Casa Moreno.

"He had them all along," she shook her head in disappointment, "right under my fucking nose. That's the reason he kept stopping every time I followed his ass over to the gate. He was trying to keep me from asking him about that goddamned van."

She glanced around the living room one last time and then stepped outside into the cool night breeze.

"Come now," she called out over her shoulder as she headed back to her SUV. "I need to call Mommy. I've gotta tell her what happened before Grip does."

***

At an Undisclosed Location

"Mimom, I'm scary," Keyonti whined as she nestled her chin into Annie's lap. "I wan' go home-home."

"Me, too," Imani chimed in. She was seated on Annie's left-hand side, with her right cheek rested on her grandmother's shoulder. "I want my mommy."

"Ssshhh," Annie consoled them while kissing Imani's forehead. She kissed Imani once more, and then gently traced her fingertips along the length of Keyonti's back.

"Y'all be quiet now," Annie continued in a low voice, carefully watching the two men who were seated up front. The handle of her

.357 Sig was sticking out from underneath her right leg. Her fingertips were less than an inch away from it. One wrong move, and the two men would surely learn the word *hesitation* was one in which she failed to comprehend the meaning.

"Mimom's right here," Annie consoled them some more.

Struggling to keep herself from crying, she gazed out of the window and wiped her tears away with the back of her bloodstained sleeve. She was thinking about the tragic events that led them to that point.

***

Four Hours Later

"Yaaayyyyy! Mimom got us pizza!"

"Say what, now?" Annie questioned the sound of Keyonti celebrating. She had just finished taking a bath and was stepping out of the bathroom when she heard it. She tied the belt on her bathrobe and took off walking down the hallway. "Pizza? I didn't order any pizza."

"No, Fat-Fat, don't open the door," Imani said to her baby cousin while peeking through blinds in the living room window. "Mimom said for us not to open the door. Only she can open the door."

"But it's pizza!" Keyonti protested, super excited to know she was about to eat her favorite food. She was standing at the window beside the door and looking up at the man who was standing on the other side. The Papa John's pizza box he held in his hands was making her mouth water. "Look, Mani. It's Papa Johnny's."

"I don't care who it is." Imani folded her arms across her chest. "Mimom said for us not to open the door. So, you better not."

But it's Papa Johnny's." Keyonti pouted. "Papa Johnny's good. You like Papa Johnny's."

"Nope." Imani shook her head, as Keyonti tried to convince her.

"Cheesy-Cheesy."

"Nope."

"Shroom-shrooms and ronis."

"Ahhhhhhh. Nope!"

"Maniiiii?" Keyonti whined, as she stomped her feet into the carpet.

Imani cracked up laughing. "I don't care how much you try to convince me, you're still not opening the door. We gotta wait until Mimom comes."

"Mimommmmmmmm!" Keyonti shouted, unaware that Annie was walking up behind them.

"Stop all that shouting, girl. I'm right here," Annie said as she approached the door. She looked at the pizza man through the peep-hole, and then looked down at Imani.

"Mani, did you order this pizza?"

"Uhn-uhn." Imani shook her head. "Me and Fat-Fat was sit-ting in the dining room playing with our toys, then the next thing we knew, we heard somebody knocking on the door. We looked out the window, and that's when we saw the pizza man. I thought you or-dered pizza for us. I thought you were try'na surprise us."

"Surprise you?" Annie placed her hands on her hips. "Eight o'clock at night with some dag-gone pizza?"

"I 'on't know." Imani shrugged her shoulders.

Knock! Knock! Knock!

"Papa wit' de John's pizza," the man stated in his thick, Span-ish accent. "We bring de pizza ju ordered for."

"Y'all gawn upstairs and get ready for bed," Annie told the girls while once again looking out the peephole. She studied the man from head to toe, noticing how strange he looked. His red hat and tan shirt as well as the Papa John's logo appeared to be on point. But what struck Annie as odd, was his iced-out Rolex, his cashmere slacks, and the shiny, green, Alligator boots he wore. The shit didn't add up.

"A pizza man wearing a Rolex?" Annie questioned out loud, still sizing him up. "What pizza man can afford a Rolex? Cashmere pants and some brand-new gator boots? Yeah, fucking right."

"Papa wit' de Johns pizza!" the pizza man raised his voice, pounding on the door so hard that its vibrations pushed Annie's face away. *"We bring de pizza ju ordered for!"*

Knock! Knock! Knock! Knock! Knock!

Still looking at the man's face, Annie followed his eyes when he looked to the left. He nodded his head, and two men emerged from the shadows beside the porch. Both men, each clutching a gun, flanked him at the door.

When Annie noticed the girls didn't follow her instructions to go upstairs, she said, "Mani, go in the kitchen and grab Mimom's phone." *She backed away from the door.* "I left it on the island."

"But, why? What's wrong? What happened?" Imani asked her.

"Damnit, girl, just do what I told you!" Annie snapped at her. *"Keyonti, come here."* She grabbed the little girl by the hand. She led Keyonti toward the closet beneath the stairs, and then pulled open the door. *"You stay here and don't come out until Mimom tells you. You understand?"*

"Umm-hmm." Keyonti nodded her head. *"Like hide and seek-seek?"*

"Yes, baby, just like hide and seek-seek." Annie's eyes began to water.

Ka-Whack!

The loud sound of the door being kicked in, caused Keyonti to scream. Annie flinched.

"Mimom, I'm scary," Keyonti began cry. *"I want my daddy."*

"Ssshhhh." Annie gestured for the little girl to keep quiet. *"Everything's okay, we're just playing a game. Now, gawn and hide in the closet. I'll come back to get you."*

"Mimom, what's that noise?" Imani called out from the kitchen. She had just grabbed Annie's cell phone and was moving through the dining room when she heard it. *"Mimom?"* She stopped walking and looked to Annie for an answer. *"Did you hear me? I said what was that banging noise?"*

Ka-Whack!

Boom!

"Mani, run!" Annie shouted when the front door came flying in and dangling at the hinges.

The Mexican disguised as a pizza man barged inside of the house and tackled Annie to the floor. His two cohorts stormed into the house behind him. The second man snatched Keyonti by the waist, while the third man ran after Imani.

Imani spun back around and hauled ass into the kitchen. The loud wails of her grandmother and little cousin screaming made her tremble and shake. Crying hysterically, she looked around for safe place to hide.

Wham!

The sound of a loud thump made her tremble even harder. She looked towards the back of the kitchen where the thumping continued. It was Rocko. He was standing on the other side of the patio door going crazy, ramming his head against the glass and desperately trying to force his way inside.

Uuuggrrrrrr! Urf! Urf! Urf! Uuuggrrrrrr! Uuuggrrrrrr!

The Mexican chasing behind Imani barged into the kitchen, as she took off running towards the patio door. He reached out and swiped at the back of her shirt, but he missed it by inches.

"Aaaaaggggghhhhhh! Leave me alone!" Imani screamed, as she stumbled against the door. She hit the floor and then popped back up, reaching for the door handle. She snatched back the lever and slid the door back wide enough for Rocko to stick his head through the crack. Rocko sprang through the crack and jumped up in the air, just as the Mexican was raising his gun.

Boca!

The bullet blew away Rocko's left ear, but he still kept coming. He slammed into the Mexican, fangs first, knocking him backwards. They crashed onto the floor, with Rocko yanking and twisting like a Pit bull in a death match.

Uuugggrrrrrr! Uuugggrrrrrr! Uuugggrrrrrr!

"Agggggghhhhhhhh!" the Mexican cried out, as Rocko's fangs sank deeper into the right side of his face. "Ay dios mio! Ay dios mio!" He flailed his arms and kicked his feet, but his movements *were useless. Rocko's powerful body was slamming him around like a ragdoll.*

In a final attempt to free himself from Rocko's attack, he pressed his Glock into Rocko's right shoulder and pulled back on the trigger.

Boca!

Rocko squealed like a pig, but instead of releasing his bite, he bit down harder; his thousand pounds of jaw pressure crushing the Mexican's jaw bone and eye socket. Blood splattered everywhere.

Imani, thinking fast, ran over to the knife rack and pulled out the closest knife to her. She then ran back into the living room, where her grandmother and little cousin were being attacked. The Mexican standing over Annie was leaned forward and choking her. Keyonti was kicking and screaming and clawing at the face of the Mexican who was carrying her towards the door.

"Get off my mimom!" Imani screamed, as she ran up to the Mexican and stabbed him in his ass.

"Ju filthy little bitch," the Mexican groaned as he turned around to face her. He released his hold on Annie, then he reached back and pulled the knife from his back side. He tossed the knife on the floor, and then smacked Imani with the back of his hand.

Whack!

She flew into the dining room and came down hard on the table, cracking it down the middle.

Crash!

The Mexican holding Keyonti tossed her aside when he heard the commotion behind him. Seeing Annie reaching for the knife that his cohort tossed on the floor, he aimed his .9mm at the back of her head.

Boca!

Annie heard the gunshot and turned around fast. The Mexican standing beside the door dropped to his knees with his eyelids blinking. His gooey, hot brains were leaking from his forehead, pouring out of a lemon-sized exit wound. He toppled over landing on the carpet face first. The gun in his hand discharged a single round, blowing a hole into the flat screen hanging on the wall.

Annie looked up at the face of the man who shot him. He was standing in the doorway with a smoking gun clutched in his hand. Standing outside on the porch behind him was another man. His HK-MP5 was aimed at the Mexican disguised as a pizza man. He was running through the dining room calling out for the third Mexican, unaware that his dead body was being ripped apart by Rocko.

Bdddddddddddoc!

The gunfire rang out, flipping the Mexican forward, right into the kitchen where Rocko wasted no time feasting on him. The two dark skinned men ran into the kitchen behind him, and the loud sound of gunfire echoed throughout the house.

Annie hopped up from the floor, seeing the opportunity to make an escape. She grabbed Keyonti by the arm, and then ran into the dining room to pick up Imani. The little girl was covered in the Mexican's blood. Annie reached down to pick her up, then snatched her car keys from the coffee table before running out of the house. She hopped down from the porch and made a beeline straight to her Benz.

Beep! Beep!

She popped the locks and deactivated the alarm.

"Hurry up, Mani, hop inside." She motioned for Imani to climb in the back seat. She was just about to toss in Keyonti when the sound of a female voice spoke out from behind her.

"If you want to live, you need to come with me."

***

Back to the Present

Annie wiped the tears from her eyes, then looked back down at her babies. Shaking her head, she looked into the front seat where the two men who saved them sat quietly. Returning her gaze to the window, she closed her eyes and fought hard to keep from breaking down.

Askari

Chapter Nine
At Grip's Warehouse on Delaware Avenue

Click! Clack!

That was the Godforsaken sound Lorenzo heard when the cold steel from The Reaper's sawed-off shotty sent shockwaves rippling down his Puerto Rican spine. The double barrels were pressed against the left side of his dome, jammed so hard that the right side of his face was mashed against his shoulder.

"Who the fuck is you?" The Reaper snarled at him, still turned up from the drama back at the yacht.

"You must be Rayon?" Lorenzo nervously replied. He was pressing down on his brake pedal to signal with his taillights for McKinney and Brown in the U-Haul truck behind him to stand down.

"Bitch, you got about five seconds to tell me who the fuck you is, and why the fuck you parked outside of this muthafuckin' warehouse. And if whatever you say don't tickle my muthafuckin' fancy, this lil' sexy ass bitch of mines gon' twist ya muthafuckin' cap off. Now, talk!"

"I—I—I'm with Terry," Lorenzo stammered.

"Who?" The Reaper nudged his shotgun more forcefully.

"*Gangsta!*" Lorenzo buckled under the pressure. "His name is Terry, but on the streets you all refer to him as Gangsta."

"And what about him?"

"Goddamnit." Lorenzo cringed when he caught a glimpse of the U-Haul truck in his rearview mirror. There were two shooters dressed in all-black posted on both sides. Their assault rifles were aimed at McKinney and Brown through the halfway rolled down windows.

"Muthafucka, I said what about him?" The Reaper nudged him even harder.

"*Okay!* Okay. Just take it easy," Lorenzo shot back quickly, beginning to feel nauseous. "I'm his inside man at the PPD. I've been working with him for years, most recently on the Sontino Moreno case. He said the two of you go way back, and for me and my men to meet him here so he could formerly introduce us to you. I'm telling you, man, I'm just here to assist you. That's it."

"That's it, huh?" The Reaper nodded his head, looking at Lorenzo as if he didn't trust him. He glanced up and down the dark alley that separated the two warehouse buildings, then he brought his scowl back to Lorenzo.

"For Christ sakes," Lorenzo pleaded, "I just finished telling you who we were. Now, can you please get your gun out of my fucking face," his words spilled out calm and polite, yet firm and direct, each syllable laced with the sarcastic undertone of a police officer on the wrong side of a gun.

Slowly, The Reaper did as Lorenzo requested. He then whistled across the alley for Killah Kye and Murda Mont to fall back. Both men did exactly that. Simultaneously, they lowered their choppas and stepped away from the U-Haul truck. But even then, they were watching McKinney and Brown, daring either one to give them a reason to start blasting.

"So, y'all the crooked cops Gee was telling me about?" The Reaper said when he looked back down at the Crown Vic's driver's side window. "Lorenzo, right?"

"Well, I wouldn't exactly put it like that," Lorenzo replied with a nervous grin. "But, yeah," he stuck his hand out the window to shake The Reaper's, "I'm Tony Lorenzo."

The Reaper looked at his hand, but refused to shake it.

"So, let's get this straight," The Reaper said as Lorenzo pulled his hand back inside of the car. "Fuckboy's mom and his kids? That's them over there in the U-Haul truck wit'cha peoples?"

"Hold on, wait a second." Lorenzo's head jerked back in disbelief. "You mean Terry didn't tell you?"

"Tell me what?"

"Everything that happened at Sontino's mother's house?"

"Fuck is you talking 'bout?" The Reaper's pupils began to dilate. "Gee ain't told me shit. The last time we spoke was earlier today, and the only thing he said was what I already knew. That me and my crew were to kidnap Rahmello, and that you and yours were to kidnap Fuckboy's family and at the same time, secure the three hunnid keys that was stashed inside the house. Then after that, bring everything back to me until further instructions came down from Alvin.

"So, again," The Reaper clutched his shotty with both hands, "where the fuck is they at?"

The Reaper's scowl, coupled with his sawed-off shotty, was more than enough to convince Lorenzo that his life was in danger. Trembling like a vibrator cranked on high, he sneakily reached behind his back with his right hand feeling around for the .9mm that was laying on his center console. His fingertips brushed over the handle, but before he could palm it, the click clacking of Kia's .45 made him freeze like a crackhead taking his first blast.

"Pussy, I wish the fuck you would," Kia dared him. She was standing on the passenger's side of his Crown Vic with her Fo' Pound aimed at his face through the window.

"*Damnit!*" Lorenzo cursed under his breath, kicking himself in the ass. Had he not been so focused on The Reaper's shotgun, he would have noticed Kia creeping up beside his car.

"Get'cha hands on that muthafuckin' steering wheel," Kia commanded. "Matter of fact," she aimed her Fo' Pound at his nickeled-out Nina, "gimmie that fuckin' gun, and *then* put'cha hands on the steering wheel."

Lorenzo hesitated.

Kia scoffed.

"Don't make me tell ya stupid ass again," she issued a final warning.

Begrudgingly, Lorenzo did as Kia commanded. After handing over his pistol and curling his fingers around the steering wheel, his body became tense when The Reaper's shotgun was jammed back against the left side of his grill. His breathing intensified, and his eyelids began to flutter. The stench of his fresh, warm piss invaded the car when he soiled his sack.

"Listen, man, what I'm about to tell you is the God's honest truth," Lorenzo spoke slowly, choosing his words carefully. "We drove out to the house to get 'em, but we couldn't find 'em."

"And what the fuck is that supposed to mean?"

"It means they were already gone," Lorenzo insisted. "We slashed open every goddamned bed and every couch cushion. We even pulled the carpet back searching for a trap door, and you know what we found? Zero. Zilch. Not a goddamned thing. The shit wasn't there, and if it was, someone else must have taken it."

"What'chu talking 'bout? *The work?*" The Reaper's left eye began to twitch. "Nigga, I 'on't give a fuck about that shit! My main concern is that bitch and them kids. Now, where the fuck is they at?"

Lorenzo was confused, yet relieved at the same time. For the past two hours he'd been worried sick, assuming that Gangsta and The Reaper would go bonkers when they learned about the missing shipment. He figured it was more than likely they would accuse him of taking it, rather than believing it was never there. But now that he knew The Reaper was more concerned with the kidnapping of Sonny's family, it felt like a weight had been removed from his shoulders.

"Oh, well, now that's an easy one." Lorenzo perked up. The color returned to his face, and the tone of his voice was more confident. "When we arrived at the house, they were already gone. The Mexicans had already taken 'em."

"The Mexicans?" The Reaper shot him an incredulous look. "What Mexicans?"

"The Sinaloa Cartel. The Alvarez brothers, Joaquin and Chatchi."

As Lorenzo relayed everything he and his men discovered when they arrived at the house, the only person The Reaper could think about was his older brother, Alvin.

The initial plan between Alvin and Gangsta, was for Gangsta and the YBM to annihilate Grip's entire male bloodline all the way down to Omelly. In turn, that would leave Gangsta as Big Angolo's last living male descendent, the inheritance that was once designated for Sonny could be passed down to him.

But first, in order for that to happen, Alvin and Gangsta knew they would need two things. The first thing they needed was for Big Angolo to die. Then after that, the Roundtable's full support, which at the time was evenly split down the middle between Big Angolo and Grip. One half supported Big Angolo and his professed intentions to appoint Sonny as the Boss of all Bosses, while the other half supported Grip and his sole ambition to take over as The Conglomerate's head chair with Sonny and Rahmello flanked at his side.

It was only a matter of time before Big Angolo's cancer got the best of him, so naturally the former was much easier than the latter. Therefore, the only thing standing in their way, was the Roundtable itself.

After deep contemplation, Alvin and Gangsta reasoned that the best way to garner the Roundtable's full support was convincing Sonny to rat out Grip. If successful, they knew the Roundtable would come together for one common cause—to eradicate Sonny. That's when Gangsta, playing the role of a mediator, would step in and murder Sonny, thereby currying the Roundtable's full support. Then finally, and with the lane wide open, he could take over as the Boss of all Bosses. Alvin would serve as his second-in-command.

Their master plan was set in motion a year and a half earlier, on the same night Lorenzo and his men invaded Sonny's nightclub. After leaving Sonny a voicemail claiming that Grip and Muhammad were coming to kill him, Gangsta reached out to Lorenzo and offered him a million dollars to conduct a raid on Club Infamous. Lorenzo agreed and the rest was history.

The police officers Sonny killed in the process was exactly what they needed to place him in a corner, assuming that because he was facing the death penalty, he would rat out Grip in exchange for his own freedom. But when Sonny refused, and the Commonwealth's case began falling apart at the seams, they were forced to come up with a new plan.

It was then, they decided to take advantage of Big Angolo's orders to have Sonny released from custody. But not until they kidnapped his mother and children and made it seem as though Grip was responsible. If it was one thing they could count on, it was Sonny's hot temper. They knew the second he learned about his missing family and that Grip was the one who'd taken him, the moment he was released, he would seek out and murder his grand-father. So, whether ratting out Grip or killing him, Sonny was the key.

Initially, their intentions were to kidnap Annie and the kids and keep them at a safe location until Sonny killed Grip. But unfortunately, all of that changed when Sonny violated AJ and sent the video to Alvin. At that point, the situation became personal. Fuck business. Alvin wanted Sonny to hurt the same way he did. So earlier that night, after contacting The Reaper and sending him the video, Alvin gave him specific orders to torture Annie and Imani in the same manner that Sonny done to AJ. But under no circumstances was The Reaper, nor anyone else, to bring any harm to his granddaughter, Keyonti. So now that Keyonti was *truly* in danger, kidnapped by the Mexicans, The Reaper knew Alvin would surely flip his lid when he found out. He also knew that his brother's propensity for violence so vicious and unpredictable that even he, himself, could possibly have to pay for the mistakes made with this own life.

"And you're saying that Gee knew about this shit?" The Reaper squinted his eyes at Lorenzo. "That the Mexicans kidnapped Fuck-boy's family?"

"You're damn right he knows," Lorenzo asserted, mistakenly believing that if the heat was aimed at Gangsta it was less likely to scorch him. "I told him all about it, and that's the reason I was so surprised when you said you didn't know. I just assumed he would have contacted you by now. That was almost an hour ago when I spoke to him."

The Reaper was pissed. He was thinking about the missed calls that came in about forty minutes earlier, not too long after his shotgun blew Diablo's ass clean off the yacht. But because he was so busy searching around the pier for Diablo's dead body, which he never found, he completely disregarded the calls. Not to mention the fifteen or so police cars and the three ghetto birds that arrived on the pier. In that instance, his only objective was making a clean getaway. Fuck a phone call.

"I know one thing," The Reaper said as he once again removed his shotgun from Lorenzo's face, "ya ass better not be lying."

After giving Kia the head nod to keep her eyes on Lorenzo, The Reaper dug down inside of his pants pocket and pulled out his Samsung. He looked at the screen, and sure enough there were a total of twelve missed calls—nine of the missed calls came in from Gangsta, while the remaining three came in from Alvin. The last call from Gangsta came in about fifteen minutes earlier. He pressed down on the *call back* button.

Askari

Chapter Ten

Gangsta's last minute flight to Miami was scheduled for takeoff in less than hour, and he still hadn't heard anything from The Reaper. They were supposed to be carrying out the next phase of their plan. But, unfortunately, due to a recent change of events, Gangsta figured it was best that he fly down to Miami so he could link up with Juan. He needed to make sure their alliance was still intact, and even more important, he was hoping Juan could shed some light on the meeting he was required to attend the following night down in Cuba. He knew it was more than likely the meeting was convened for the purpose of discussing Big Angolo's death and the shift of power that was sure to follow. But even then, his guilty conscience was telling him that something was wrong, that Grip had somehow learned about the secret plot between him and Alvin.

If there was one thing Gangsta learned as a detective for five years and a federal agent for another seven, was that coincidences didn't exist. So, being as though Grip was back in the States at the same time Annie and the kids went missing, and that Alexis knew about it, but didn't tell him, was a coincidence that simply did not wash. Another thing that rubbed him the wrong way was Jorge Dominguez' driver's license being left at the house. The Sinaloa Cartel was a billion-dollar operation, and for the time being, Jorge was at the helm. So, why would he personally be involved in a kidnapping so minuscule? It didn't make sense. The only logical conclusion that Gangsta could think of was Grip. There was no other way to explain it. How else could the old man manage to thwart his advancements at every turn?

Damn, I hope that's not the case, Gangsta thought to himself as he pulled into the parking lot of the Philadelphia International Airport. *But if it is, then who the fuck could'a told 'em? It couldn't have been Alexis and The Madam. Because as far as they know, I'm still moving according to Big Angolo's original plan, to kill Grip and see to it that Sonny's appointed as the next boss. I don't know, man, maybe I'm just trippin'. But what if I'm not?*

After pulling into the first available parking space, he threw the transmission in park and then grabbed his overnight bag from the back seat. He was just about to kill the ignition when the ringing of an incoming call came through the truck's speakers. He looked at his dashboard and saw it was The Reaper. He pressed down on accept.

"Yo, Rayon, what the fuck?" Gangsta's voice channeled The Reaper's eardrum. "Where the fuck are you? I've been calling you for damn near an hour now."

"First of all, nigga, lower ya fuckin' voice when you talking to me," The Reaper checked him off the rip. "Fuck you think this is? I ain't one of ya lil' bitch-ass flunkies. Better get that shit straight."

Gangsta paused for a brief moment to calm himself down. He knew if he didn't, it would lead to the two of them going for the other one's jugular, which was something they'd been doing since they were teenagers back in the late eighties, back when Grip first commissioned the emergence of the YBM.

"Alright, man, whatever," Gangsta spoke in a tone that was more civil. "Where are you?"

"I'm where the fuck I'm supposed to be, at the old warehouse on Delaware Avenue. I got'cha man, Lorenzo, wit' me. According to him, some Mexicans kidnapped Fuckboy's fam, and that you knew about it. So, why the fuck you ain't say nothing?"

"Nigga, that's the reason I was calling you," Gangsta replied. "But the Mexicans aren't the ones who grabbed 'em. It was Grip."

"*Grip*?" The Reaper retorted, looking down at Lorenzo when he said it. The nosey muthafucka was tuned in, listening to his every word. "And what makes you say that? Because everything Lorenzo said is pointing at the Mexicans."

"I already know. I spoke to him earlier and he told me the same thing. But that's too easy, it's too obvious. I'm telling you, Ray, it's that fuckin' Grip. That tricky, old bastard knows more than what he's letting on. Exactly what? I can't say. But he definitely knows *something*. I can feel it. I know this muthafucka like the back of my hand."

"Well, this is what *I* know," The Reaper shot back. "Alvin's gonna be pissed when he finds out. He wanted that bitch and them kids. This shit is personal now. I wasn't supposed to say nothing, but..."

The Reaper stopped talking and looked down at Lorenzo. He then looked across the car at Kia. The both of them were staring at him and listening to his every word.

The Reaper knew what he had to say was strictly confidential, so he backed away from the car and strolled down to the bottom of the alley, about two feet away from the rusty fence that lined the far end of the warehouse.

"Listen," he continued in a low tone, even though he was too far away for Lorenzo and Kia to hear what he was saying. "I spoke to Alvin, and he told me that a few things needed to change. Not to the point that we still can't do what we need to do, it's just that his intentions are a little bit different now."

Gangsta's face turned sour.

"Who the fuck does Alvin think he is, that he can modify something that was already agreed on? This nigga don't run shit! I'm the boss now! It's the blood in my mu'fuckin' veins that got us in this position. Without me, don't none of this shit move. What'chu niggas forgot?"

"Nah, Gee, it ain't even like that."

"Well, what the fuck is it like, then?"

"If you cool out for a second and let me talk, I can tell you," The Reaper simmered his tone, remembering then that Gangsta was indeed the new boss. "All I'm saying is that shit got a lil' funky in the past few hours. Right before we left out for the party, I got a call from Alvin. Well, actually, he sent me the video first."

"The video? What video?"

"The Reaper went silent. He was contemplating on whether or not he should tell Gangsta about the video that Sonny sent to Alvin. He knew how embarrassing it was to his brother. It was even to the point that when Alvin first sent it to him, he made him promise he would never show it, nor speak about it to anyone ever. But without mentioning the video, how else could he justify and explain Alvin's new intentions?

"Listen, Gee, this is some serious shit I'm 'bout to lay on you. So, you gotta keep it between us, you dig? You can't tell nobody that I told you this shit, not even Alvin. *Especially, Alvin.*"

"Alright, fam, I got'chu."

"I'm serious, Gee."

"Nigga, I said I got'chu."

"A'ight, so this is the situation. You know them crackas done transferred AJ back down to the county to be resentenced on that Juvenile Lifers shit. So, while he was down there, he somehow ran into Fuckboy, and the two of them niggas went at it. I'm assuming it was over Daphney."

"But Sonny didn't have anything to with that. That was the Sinaloa's striking back for what him and Rahmello did to Mexican Bobby."

"Come again." The Reaper's face grew tight. "You're saying that you *knew* about this shit? That them Mexicans killed my niece, and ya ass ain't never say nothing?"

"That was Big Angolo's call, not mine," Gangsta spoke unapologetically. "I wanted to say something, but the old man told me not to. He said it would have been bad for business. The Sinaloa's hold a seat at the Roundtable, and because there was already so much hostility between the bosses, he wanted things to calm down a bit. So, instead of dwelling on the blood that was already spilled, the old man said it was more important that we focus on Sonny, who we both know is the key to what we're try'na do."

"I hear what'chu saying, but that's still some fucked up shit. How you gon' know about sum'n like this, and never tell us? Especially after everything we been through? My brother's been up top for damn near twenty-five years, and all because he'd rather take his fall like a man, than go out like a bitch and tell on his comrades. *You* included. And *this* is how you do him?"

"Listen, fam, I don't know what else to tell you," Gangsta remained firm. "It's just like Big Angolo said *it would have been bad for business.*"

"Yo, that's crazy, Gee, straight up. All this time, me, Alvin and AJ were thinking it was Fuckboy who done it, or at the very least sanctioned the hit. Especially when he changed his mind after telling me and the young bul to kidnap Daph. Talking 'bout he wanted us to drive out to some pig farm in Bucks County, so we could get ready for what he had planned for her. But you know the story and how the shit went down. I smoked the young bul, and then double backed and drove out to Upper Dublin, so I could scoop up Daph. And then, that's when I found her. That's when I found *him*."

"Who you talking 'bout? Diablo?"

"I don't know his name, but he's a scrawny ass, lizard looking muthafucka. Creepy as shit. He's got fangs like a vampire and two lumps on his forehead like it's devil horns try'na pop out."

"Yeah, that's him," Gangsta confirmed. "They call him Diablo. He's a Sinaloa hitman, the one they originally sent to hunt down Sonny."

"Well, then, that's the muthafucka who killed Daph," The Reaper added, subconsciously feeling the fang wounds at the base of his throat where Diablo nearly crushed his windpipe.

"It was all beginning to make sense to The Reaper. For the past year and a half, not a day went by where he didn't think about the Mexican monster he encountered on that fateful night he drove out to Sonny's Upper Dublin estate. *Who was he? Where did he come from? Who sent him?* So, now that he knew the truth, he couldn't help but to wonder if Lorenzo was right.

"And you're sure the Mexicans ain't the ones who snatched 'em?" The Reaper questioned, still caressing the fang wounds at the base of his throat. "Because that nigga, Diablo, was definitely back in the city. I ran into him while everything was going down at the boat party. And I know it was him, because I shot his ass."

"Trust me, fam, I know what I'm talking about," Gangsta assured him. "Now, back to Alvin. You said that his intentions are a little bit different now. His intentions pertaining to what?"

"Pertaining to Fuckboy. Being as though we all thought he had sum'n to do with what happened to Daph, earlier today while AJ was down the county, he stepped to this nigga. But instead of

Fuckboy squaring up and giving AJ a fair one, him and some young niggas did my lil' nigga dirty, Gee. They fucked him up so bad that we could hardly recognize him. They even broke a broomstick off in his ass. But even worse, them niggas filmed the whole shit, and then sent the video to Alvin.

"So, that's when Alvin hit me up and told me about his new plans. He said that he wanted us to do to Fuckboy's fam what he did to AJ. He also said he wanted us to record it, so he could send the video to Fuckboy. Nah mean? So, that way he could show the nigga how real shit can get. And you know how Alvin is. Once he's got his mind set on doin' sum'n, it ain't no stopping him. That niggas like a pit bull locked on a milk bone.

"And the reason I didn't tell you is because I knew you would'a tried to stop me. So, what was I 'posed to do? Tell this nigga no? Not follow his orders, and then end up wit' a broomstick broke of *my muthafuckin' ass*? That shit ain't happening, fam. It ain't happening."

Gangsta, who was leaned back in the driver's seat with the back of his head pressed against the rest, was internalizing everything The Reaper had just told him. He knew about the beef between Sonny and AJ, because he was standing in the foyer when Alexis told Grip. And even though he felt some type of way about Alvin going behind his back, it was actually the furthest thing from his mind. His main concerns were centered around Grip.

How the fuck is this nigga so far ahead of me? he thought to himself as he cracked his knuckles one at a time. *I just don't get it. How the fuck is he five steps ahead of me, when he's supposed to be two steps behind? How the fuck is this shit even possible?*

"Yo, Gee, what's up?" The Reaper's voice came through the speakers, snapping Gangsta out of his thoughts. "You got quiet on me just now? You good?"

"Yeah, I'm good. I'm just sitting here thinking," Gangsta told him. "So, what's the status on the shipment? Did Lorenzo and his men secure it?"

"Hell, naw. Lorenzo's swearing up and down that it wasn't there. Them niggas prob'bly tucked that shit," The Reaper accused.

He was gently tapping his shotgun against his right leg, and looking up the alley at Lorenzo's Crown Vic. "I don't trust this pork belly ass Lorenzo, Gee. It's sum'n about this nigga that I'm just not feeling."

"That nigga's irrelevant," Gangsta dismissed. "There's nothing else him and his crew can do for us now, anyway. What we *need* to be focused on is finding a way to get squared even with Juan over those three hunnid keys. Because without the support of him and his cartel, that makes our situation that much harder. And that brings me to another thing. Rahmello. How the fuck did y'all miss?"

"You mean, he's still alive?" The Reaper asked, as he set his sights on Kia. According to what she told him, she caught Rahmello running back to his Lamborghini and lit his ass up something nice.

"But I'm saying, though," The Reaper spoke slowly, "shouldn't that be a good thing? If Rahmello's still alive, then all we gotta do is twist his ass around until he tells us where he hid the shipment."

"Good luck with that one." Gangsta sighed. "Since when have you ever known a dead nigga to talk?"

"But I thought you said we missed?"

"I said *you* missed. *He* didn't. The stupid lil' nigga did his'self."

"A'ight, so let's assume that Lorenzo was right, that the shipment was never stashed at the house. There still has to be a way that we can bring Juan totally on board."

"And you know what? There actually is," Gangsta said, as he caressed his goatee. "I know just the way to do it, and at the same time kill two birds with one stone."

"And how is that?"

"Big Angolo's funeral."

"Damn, that's right. I *did* hear on the news this morning that Big Angolo died. I was meaning to ask you about that. They said he died in his sleep last night, and that his body was being flown back to the city."

"And that's my point. Being as though Big Angolo was the Boss of all Bosses, out of respect for him and his position, the entire Roundtable's gonna be there, all except for Grip and Joaquin. So, this is what I'm thinking—we stage an ambush. We shoot up the funeral, and then spread the word that Grip was behind it. Eventually, when the bosses from the Roundtable find out, they're all gonna want Grip's head, even the ones who currently support him. I'm telling you, Ray, this shit'll be perfect."

"I dig." The Reaper nodded his head and cracked a smile, seeing that Gangsta was on to something. "And since they're all gonna want Grip's head, then all we gotta do is step in and give it to 'em. Chop that muthafucka off and serve it up on a silver platter."

"You feel me?" Gangsta chuckled at his own wit. "And then right before the shit pops off, I'ma reach out to Juan and give him the heads up not to attend. I'm sure that's something he'll appreciate, especially when it's all said and done, and he realizes that we saved his life."

"And what about Fuckboy? How does any of this account for him?"

"That's simple. Our first obstacle was Big Angolo. So, now that he's dead, by staging the ambush, we automatically skip phases one and two, making Sonny's role in the plan obsolete."

"That's not what I meant," said The Reaper. "What I'm saying is that we still need to kill him. 'Cause if we don't, who's to say he won't step up and claim his position?"

"Whoever said anything about not killing him? That muthafuckas a dead man walking. But in order to make it clean and quiet, and not draw any suspicious looks from the Roundtable, our best option is to switch over to Plan B."

"But Alvin said he wasn't feeling that," The Reaper reminded him, referring to Alvin's apprehensions about testifying against Sonny before a federal grand jury.

It wasn't for the sake of having Sonny convicted, but for the sake of having his case placed under the federal court's jurisdiction. So that way, because Gangsta was a federal agent, he could arrange to have Sonny murdered during a transfer from one federal prison to another. The only downside to the plan was Alvin. A large part of his street legacy was that he never he told, even after Clavenski offered him a get-out-of-jail-free-card in exchange for his testimony against Grip and his entire organization. So, after twenty-five years of standing on his own principles, chest out with his chin up, the last thing he wanted to do was tarnish his name and legacy by becoming a rat. Even if it was only for show.

"Listen, fam, I dig where Alvin is coming from and I understand why. But at the same time, what other choice do we have?"

"But why we can't just let him come home, and then body his ass the second he leaves the courtroom?"

"Nah, man, Sonny's too sharp for that. He'll never allow us to get that close."

"You're giving this nigga too much credit, Gee."

"See, that's the problem. Muthafuckas don't ever wanna believe shit stinks until they step in it. I keep telling you and Alvin no matter how much y'all don't agree or refuse to believe it, Sonny's not a fuckin' joke and he definitely doesn't play any fuckin' games. So, if we gotta hit him, then it's best that we do it while he's still on the inside. Because the second he touches down and has enough time to reorganize and regroup, that's a whole 'nother problem. A *major* fuckin' problem at that."

"If you say so," The Reaper replied sarcastically. "To me, his lil' punk ass ain't shit. If he was, then why the fuck was he out here calling on me whenever shit got hot? That nigga's over rated, if you ask me."

"Who the fuck said I asked you?" Gangsta snapped at him. "Nigga, I'm *telling you.*"

"Yeah, whatever," The Reaper downplayed his last remark. "But other than that, what's our next move?"

"Our next move is that we still need to account for those three hunnid keys. I'm not sure if I told you this, but Juan's whole thing was to keep Sonny and Rahmello quiet about the role he played in Roberto's murder.

"Roberto? Who the fuck is Roberto?"

"That's Mexican Bobby, the nigga I was telling you about."

"The nigga that Fuckboy and Rahmello killed?"

"Exactly. And that's the reason Juan wanted 'em dead. He was afraid they would reveal to the Sinaloa's that he and Poncho paid them niggas to do the hit. Rahmello's already a done deal, so that's one down and one to go. And I'm pretty sure that when we kill Sonny, that'll be worth more to Juan than his missing shipment. We just need to make sure that we stay on point. No more fuck ups. We done already struck out twice. There's no room for a third."

"And what about these bitch-ass, pork belly ass cops? You said we don't need 'em no more, right?"

"Nah, we don't need 'em," Gangsta said as he killed the engine and climbed out of his Yukon. He closed the door and triggered the alarm.

"Go 'head and rock them niggas to sleep, 'cause they definitely ain't getting that mil' ticket we promised 'em," he continued in a low voice, casually making his way toward the double doors that led into the airport's lobby. "And don't worry about Alvin. I'll give him a call as soon as I touch down in Miami."

***

Back at Grip's Warehouse on Delaware Avenue

After disconnecting the call, The Reaper stepped out into the middle of the dimly lit alley.

"Ay, yo, Keys!" he called out and waved his hand in the air, eliciting Kia's attention. "Gawn and tell them niggas I said lay down."

"Lay down?" Lorenzo questioned when he turned back around to face Kia. "What the hell is he talking about? Lay down what?"

His questions were answered the second Killah Kye and Murda Mont lit up the U-Haul truck.

Boc! Boc! Bdddddddddddoc! Bdddddddddddoc! Boc! Boc! Bdddddddddddoc!

"Oh, my fucking God!" Lorenzo cried out when he saw the damage that was done to the truck. It's busted out windows and peppered up frame was engulfed in smoke. McKinney's dead arm was dangling out the window.

"For the love of God. Don't kill me, please?" Lorenzo said when he returned his attention to Kia. His quivering lips were moving, but his words were inaudible. *"Please?"*

Kia just looked at him and shook her head slowly.
"YBM, baby."
Boom! Boom! Boom! Boom!

Askari

Chapter Eleven

If Sonny were wearing a mood ring, the color would have been stuck on *fuck it.* The pain in his chest was begging for ease, and the two Backwoods he'd just finished smoking was the only thing that seemed to help. He didn't even care the funky aroma was flowing out of the bottom of his cell door, stinking up the entire cell block. Because truth be told, whether staff or inmate, it really didn't matter, whoever tried to stop him from getting his blaze on had better been prepared for war. The shank in his left hand was his only warning. Whoever wanted it, could get it.

Sparking up his third Wood, he continued pacing back and forth from one side of his jail cell to the other. He was waiting on Heemy to hit him back with whatever information he could gather out on the streets. But in the meantime, to settle his thoughts, he was listening to Yo Gotti's *Momma* on repeat. The music was bumping through the ear buds attached to his iPhone. The lyrics were so real, that his heartbeat increased every time Gotti said the word "Momma".

"Momma told me fuck ya loses, just keep moving on. If you caught, just never snitch, one day you coming home. Momma gave me the game, and for Mother's Day, I spent a million and a half on you prepaid. And you the owner, I'm the worker. This shit yours, do what you want 'cause you deserve it, Momma."

As the music looped on repeat, Sonny removed his iPhone from his back pocket and then plopped down on his bottom bunk. Staring up at the bunk above, he wiped the tears from his eyes, and then slowly ran his fingers through the length of his beard. The only thing on his mind was Annie and the girls.

"Damn, Mommy, I should'a listened." Sonny broke down crying, once again looking up at his wall full of family pictures. "All them times you told me to leave this shit alone, and I didn't. I was only try'na make you smile. Try'na make shit easier for you. I wanted to give back everything you ever gave me. All the shit we lost when Pops got fucked up on that shit. The crib, the cars, your jewelry and clothes. I still remember all the nights you used to cry ya'self to sleep 'cause you ain't have nothing to eat. Try'na play it off like you already ate, knowing that if you didn't, I wouldn't have eaten not one bite without you. I bubbled in the game, and for what? To lose everything that I was hustling for? To lose everything that ever-meant sum'n to me? My heart and my soul? And on top of that, these niggas got my baby and niece?" His waterworks streamed down harder. "What the fuck, yo? What the fuck I done did to my mu'fuckin' family?"

He closed his eyes and massaged his temples, not even realizing moments later, he drifted off to sleep.

***

Alejandro and Dominic sat quiet in the front seat, while Grip was reclined in the back. He was puffing on a Cohiba cigar and thinking about the live stream video he'd just finished watching of Gangsta. He was well aware of Big Angolo's secret plot, but what he didn't know was that Gangsta had been working on a plot of his own. This was yet again something the old man would have never seen coming, especially where it pertained to Alvin and the YBM. His once prized protégé was a man of respect, a devoted soldier who had proven without a doubt that his loyalty was unmatched. But now that Grip knew different, that Alvin and Gangsta had teamed up against him in a brash attempt to come for his crown, he was determined to meet their aggressions head on.

"Well, I know one thing," Grip said to himself as he blew out a thick cloud of cigar smoke, "that sure enough is a helluva plan, nephew. A *helluva* plan. Witty and cunning, so slick that I couldn't have planned it better myself. But what you and Alvin fail to realize is that men more capable have tried, and not one of them mutha-fuckas succeeded. And neither will y'all."

Still looking down at his iPad screen, he swiped to the left so he could pull up the tracking grid on Alexis' Navigator. But instead of a tracking grid, the only thing that popped up was a blacked-out screen.

"Deactivated?" Grip read the caption that appeared on the screen. "What the hell is wrong with this thing?"

"What's dat, Señor?" Alejandro turned around to face him.

"This." Grip held up his iPad. "It was working a few seconds ago, but now it's not."

"Lemme see. Give it to me back," Alejandro said as he reached for the iPad. Grip handed it to him, and Alejandro quickly began troubleshooting. He logged out of the app, and then logged back in. Seeing that Alexis' tracking grid was still blacked out, he clicked on Gangsta's and then clicked on Heemy's. Both grids were working just fine.

"Ju do to it what jus' now?" Alejandro asked when he returned to the blacked-out screen.

"I didn't do shit," Grip replied with an attitude. "I just switched over from one tracking grid to the other."

"Well, den we have us a problem, Señor. De device must'a been deactivated," Alejandro said as he cut his eye at Dominic.

Dominic, who was leaned back and whipping the Suburban with one hand, took it as though they were coming for him. He could literally feel Alejandro staring him down.

"Dat's no my fault," the young Cuban spoke aggressively, giving Alejandro a cautionary look not to fuck with him. "I do exactly what'chu say me to do. Dat's it."

"So, basically, you're telling me they found it?" Grip's icy stare moved from Dominic to Alejandro. "And that these muthafuckas know I've been tracking them?"

"Si, Señor." Alejandro nodded his head. "Dat's de only thing dat could have happened. But if ju want, I can bring up de location dey was at last."

"Well, you do that and then hand it here," Grip said as he sucked in another pull from his stogie. He hit the Cohiba until the cherry crackled and then tossed what was left out the window.

"Dere ju go, Senor," Alejandro said after bypassing the system and pulling up Alexis' last documented location. He handed Grip the iPad, then explained to him exactly what he was looking at. "Dat's de location dey was at when dey do it."

Grip looked at the screen and gritted his teeth. The green dot simulating Alexis' Navigator was blinking in the one location where he told her not to go—Annie's row house on Reese Street.

Vrrrrrm! Vrrrrrm! Vrrrrrm!

"Now, who the fuck is this?" Grip snarled through his clenched teeth. He removed his iPhone from his front pants pocket, and then closely examined the screen. The caller was Madam François.

"You've got a lot of goddamn nerve calling me!" Grip barked into the phone when he accepted the call. "I should have known better. I should have known not to trust your bourgeoisie, French-nigger talking ass!"

"I understand that you're upset right now, so I'm going to let that slide," The Madam replied in a calm manner. "I'm just calling, so I can explain what happened. Obviously, I'm referring to Alexis."

Grip's anger had him ready to tear into The Madam with his words. But instead, he calmed down, knowing that if he said the wrong thing, it would jeopardize the validity of their allegiance.

"Alright, Geraldine," he spoke with a controlled temper, "you go 'head and speak. Say whatever it is you need to say. I'll make my point when you're finished."

"My daughter is in love, Gervin. That's the *only* reason she did what she did. It wasn't because she was working angles or deliberately overstepping her bounds. She was only doing what we *both* know Sontino would have wanted her to do, based on the information that was provided to her. And before you ask me, the answer is *no*. I did not tell Alexis the full extent of our plan. As far as my daughter's concerned, we're still working with Terrance in accordance with Big Angolo's plot to make an example out of you before the Roundtable. She has no idea that you and I are working together, nobody does."

"And how can I be so sure?" Grip's octave exuded frustration.

"Well, for one thing, the information I passed along should speak volumes. And secondly, when you make it back to the airport, you'll see that I was right about Joaquin and Chatchi. That bullshit they were spewing about Diablo going rogue and coming to kill

Sontino's family was just that, *bullshit!* I tried to tell you, but you wouldn't listen. So, when I left your compound, instead of flying back to Miami, I flew back to Philadelphia. And when me and my men arrived at Sontino's mother's house, Jorge and two of his soldiers were already there."

"Oh, yeah?" Grip replied in a nonchalant tone, sparking up another Cohiba to calm his nerves. "So, what happened?" he spoke the words through a thick cloud of smoke.

"I think you know me well enough to know what happened," The Madam asserted like the boss bitch she was. "I handled my business, and it's a good thing I did. Because God only knows what would have happened to Sontino's mother and children had I done anything different."

"And what about Delaware Fats? Are you saying that he didn't handle his? He was supposed to have been there by eight o'clock."

"First of all, that fat motherfucker arrived too late. And when he *did*, he was asking so many goddamned questions that my only option was to leave him there. You know my motto: No eyewitness. No evidence. No case. I figured he would have only been an unnecessary witness. So, I, personally, shot him in the face and left him for the dog to eat. I haven't heard a man scream that loud in years. The shit kinda turned me on, truthfully."

Grip was only partially satisfied, he needed more. He needed the opportunity to access The Madam's energy in contrast to Gangsta's, and the five bosses from the Roundtable who claimed to be in support of his movement. Only then, could he make his final determination as to whether or not The Madam's loyalty was true.

"It's going on a quarter after one," Grip said as he checked the time on his watch. "I've got one more stop to make, then after that we're heading back to the airport in Teterboro. You can expect us somewhere around three-thirty."

"And Gervin," The Madam slid in another statement before she disconnected the call. "Above all else, the main thing that solidifies our allegiance, is the new life that's growing in my daughter's womb. So, be sure to keep that in mind."

Click!

Thinking about The Madam's last statement, Grip looked down at his iPad. He swiped to the left and brought up the tracking grid on Gangsta's Yukon. According to the locator, it was parked outside of the Philadelphia International Airport. The time digits in the bottom right corner displayed that it been there for the last ten minutes, and because he knew Gangsta was flying down to Miami to link up with Juan, this was something he could use to his advantage.

Grip sucked in another pull from his Cohiba, and then tossed it out the window. Slowly releasing the smoke, he downloaded the video footage of Gangsta reclined back in his SUV talking to The Reaper. He then clicked out of his tracking app and logged into his Gmail account. After clicking on the attachment that Madam François sent him the day before, he forwarded the information to Sonny. He also sent him the video footage from Gangsta's SUV.

"Dominic, how far away are we from my granddaughter's house?"

"De OnStar says we're just a block away," Dominic replied while looking at the screen on the dashboard.

"Alright, well, just circle her block a few times," Grip instructed, while going through his phone and pressing down on Sonny's number. "The last time I checked, that young kid, Heemy, is still with her. If he's anything like they say he is, then he's sure 'nough gonna give us a problem. I'd rather have Sontino on the line when we pull up. At least that way, I can have Sontino talk to him in any event things go left. The less attention, the better."

Chapter Twelve
Back at The County Jail

Vrrrrrm! Vrrrrrm! Vrrrrrm!

The vibrations from Sonny's iPhone awakened him from his sleep. Assuming it was Heemy calling back with some vital information, he picked it up quickly. It threw him for a loop when he saw it was an incoming email, rather than an incoming call.

"What the fuck is this?" Sonny groggily stated when he clicked open the Gmail envelope, seeing the email had been sent to him by Grip. The information read:

To: Sontino Moreno
From: Gervin Moreno
Date: July 5th, 2015
RE: Some shit you need to know. (See Attachments)

Steaming like boiling water whistling from the spout of a teapot, Sonny sat up on his bunk. He pressed down on the paperclip, and the attachment popped up on his iPhone screen. It appeared to be a document of some sort. He scrolled down the pages, and then scrolled back to the beginning. After reading the first line of Page One, his cell phone alerted the presence of a newly arrived email. He clicked open the envelope and squinted his eyes. It was another email from Grip. The only difference between the first email and the second, was the information detailed in the reference line. There, it read:

RE: Video Included (See Attachment)

"This nigga got me fucked up. What, he thinks this shit a game?" Sonny flexed his jaw muscles. He clicked open the attachment and saw it was a still shot video of Gangsta. He was leaned back behind the steering wheel of his SUV. His shoulders and chest were blotted out by a white *Play* button.

Vrrrrrm! Vrrrrrm! Vrrrrrm!

Sonny's iPhone vibrated once more. This time, it was an incoming call. The caller was Grip.

"Pussy, where the fuck is my folks at?" Sonny lashed out when he pressed down on the *Accept* button. "I know ya grimy ass the one who got 'em."

"Well, goddamn, a thank you would have been nice," Grip spoke with an arrogant tone of authority.

"A *thank you*? Nigga, I'ma blow ya fucking head off."

"Sontino, would you knock it off? I'm calling to let you know that your mother and the kids are safe. I got 'em back at the airport in Teterboro, New Jersey. I'm currently in the process of picking up your sister, and as soon as I do, I'm gonna fly 'em all down to Cuba."

Sonny was at a loss for words, not sure if he should curse his grandfather, or do what the old man suggested and thank him.

"Did you hear me? I said I've got your mom and the kids. They're safe."

"Yeah, I heard you," Sonny replied slowly. "But when you say *safe*, you mean safe from what? Rahmello, and that fuck shit he was up to?"

"I hate to be the one to tell you this, Sontino, but Rahmello's dead. He blew himself up in his Lamborghini. I guess he was calling himself trying to kill the both us. But in the end, he only managed to hurt himself. It was never my intention for any of this to happen, but it did. And there was nothing I could do to stop it."

"Damn," Sonny said as he shut his eyes tightly and bit into his bottom lip. His anger toward Rahmello had boiled over to the point he was prepared to kill him if need be, but now that he knew his brother was dead, and even worse, dead from his own volition, it tapped into the love that was there all along, regardless of the way Rahmello stabbed him in the back.

"I know," Grip's voice cut through the silence. "It was worse than it sounds, seeing him go out like that. But the good thing is that we got rid of that snitching ass bitch of his. She's the reason Rahmello was so confused, doing the shit he was doing."

"But how?" Sonny spoke with a cracked voice. "There's no way Olivia could have known about the facts of my case. I didn't even know Poncho when that shit went down. Somebody must'a put her up to it."

"Who knows? Maybe it was Rahmello, maybe it wasn't. Either way, that stinking ass Olivia was the only evidence they had against you. So now that I've finally got her out the way, these next two weeks should fly by in a breeze. And when you *do* come home, the two of us are gonna sit down and talk. There're a few things I need to bring to your attention. Namely, our position at the Roundtable, who's with us and who's against us."

"Here you go wit' this Conglomerate shit." Sonny sighed. "I never asked for it, nor did I want it. I'm good where I'm at."

"*Nonsense*." Grip stated with more aggression than he intended. "You didn't have to ask for it, you were *born* for it. This shit is your destiny. Embrace it."

After a brief moment of silence, Sonny returned to the topic of his family. He was wondering if Grip knew about the beef between him and Alvin.

"But you still didn't answer my question. What was it that my mom and the kids needed to be safe from? You're talking about that faggot-ass Alvin, ain't you? You know about the shit between me and AJ."

"Actually, I do. Grip was forced to admit. "I heard about it from Alexis. I can't exactly say why it happened, but knowing you," the pitch of his voice was accusing, "I'm pretty sure you only did what you had to."

"So, then you know about Alvin sending them YBM niggas to snatch up my mom and the kids. That's the reason you flew back to the States to get 'em."

"Well, not exactly," Grip spoke carefully.

"Fuck you mean, *not exactly*? If it wasn't for that, then why else would you fly back to the States to make sure they were safe? Who the fuck else they needed to be safe from?"

"Some information was passed along that gave me reason to believe they were possibly in danger."

"Information like what?" Sonny gritted his teeth.

"Information pertaining to the Sinaloa Cartel. More specifically, that goddamned Diablo."

"Who the fuck is Diablo?"

"He's Joaquin and Chatchi's number one killer. They sent him back to the city, so he could settle the score for what you and Rahmello did to Roberto."

Hearing Rahmello's name sent a chill down Sonny's spine. It was still hard to accept that his younger brother killed himself.

"I didn't hear about what happened between you and Alvin until a few minutes ago," Grip continued speaking, "which brings me to my next point. I've recently discovered the existence of a new problem, one that has the potential to be more dangerous."

"Oh, yeah? And what's that?" Sonny's nostrils began to flare.

"It's your cousin, Gangsta. He and Alvin teamed up to take us down. They're also working with Columbians, and whoever else from the Roundtable they may have already swayed. Now, what's good is that I'm ten steps ahead of this shit. When you view the attachments to the emails I sent, you'll understand why."

Again, Sonny was at a loss of words. The entire time, since learning about his missing family, he assumed the worst about Grip. But now he was beginning to realize that through all of the hatred and hostility, the lack of trust and the bad blood between them, his grandfather was actually his closest ally. It was something he would never forget.

"Aye, yo, Grip, man, thank you. Straight up. Whatever you need me to do, fam, I got'chu."

Grip smiled. It was something he'd been hoping to hear for years now.

"Don't even sweat it, kid. You're my grandson, it's only right that I make sure that *we*, as a family are good. Now, with that being said, there's *definitely* something I need you do for me."

"Just let me know, and it's done."

"That lil' soldier of yours, Heemy. I need you to get him on the phone. I just drove past your sister's house, and two of his guys were posted out front. I'm pretty sure you heard about what happened at her party back at the pier."

"I did. My lil' nigga told me about it when he called."

"Well, just so you know, that was Juan's people who done it. They were more than likely sent by Gangsta and Alvin. So, clearly, your sister isn't safe. Not here in the States, anyway. It's better that I fly her down to Cuba with the rest of the family. My only problem is this young kid, Heemy. There's no way he's gonna allow me to take her without putting up a fight, and obviously that's the last thing I need. These crackas would love nothing more than to see me locked away in a cell next yours."

"Say no more, I'm on it," Sonny assured him. "I'ma hit him up right now. And, Grip, thanks again, man. I really appreciate it."

"Rock solid," the old man replied. "Rock solid."

Askari

Chapter Thirteen
Back at Nahfisah's House

"I told you I got'chu, and I meant that shit," Heemy said to Nahfisah as he gently removed her Coogi dress and G-string. They were all alone in her bedroom, standing at the foot of her California King. Her fluffy, soft Chanel bathrobe was draped over his right shoulder, and his left hand was holding her steady. He removed the bathrobe and wrapped it around her body, gently pushing her arms through the sleeves one at a time. Softly, he kissed her on the forehead.

"Real shit, Nah, I'd rather die than to let sum'n happen to you. And for whatever it's worth, I apologize for what I said to you earlier. I conducted myself less than a King, and I own that. I should'a never accused you of being a distraction. 'Cause to keep it a bean, had I been out there wit' Shorty Rock and Yahyo, instead of laying up wit' you, I might'a fucked around got smoked right along wit' him. So, if anything, you saved me."

Nahfisah just stood there quiet and calm. The three Xanies he gave her when they first arrived at the house were kicking in quickly. Her catatonic ramblings had simmered to a meek, mild demeanor. Her hysteric cries were reduced to a low, light sniffle and her glossy, blue eyes were staring into the widows of his soul.

"Promise me you'll never let me go," she stated with a sniffle. "Promise me you'll never leave me."

"Baby Love, you got a nigga for life," Heemy said as he pulled her in close. He kissed her once more, and she melted into his arms. Squeezing him tightly, she held onto the muscular grooves of his back.

"Promise me, I said."

"I promise."

Satisfied that her heart was secure, she buried her face into his chest.

"Aye, yo, Blawd!" Snot Box called out from the bottom of the stairs. "The homies got some lady out here talking 'bout she wanna come inside to see ya girl!"

"Heemy made a move toward the door, but Nahfisah wasn't having it.

"*No!*" She vehemently stated, squeezing him even tighter. "You promised you wouldn't go."

"I'm just going down there to see what's up. It's probably Alexis."

"I don't care." Nahfisah sniffled. "You promised me."

"A'ight, Nah, just calm down." Heemy sighed when she leaned in against him "I'm right here wit'chu. I ain't going nowhere."

Still holding Nahfisah close, Heemy looked up at the ceiling and shook his head slowly. The longer he was there, the longer it would take him to do what he promised Sonny.

"Yo, you heard me, Blawd?" Snot Box called out some more, this time a little bit louder. "The homies got—"

"I heard you the first time," Heemy cut him off. "Tell them niggas I said let her in."

"Fa'sho," Snot Box said as he stepped outside and relayed Heemy's message.

D-Day and Gizzle let the woman through.

Heemy's focus returned to Nahfisah, who was yawning and telling him how tired she was. He kissed the top of her head and then gently caressed her back through the fluffy, soft fabric. Nahfisah's nipples stiffened.

"Umm, excuse me," Miss Mary stated from the hallway.

"Who the fuck is you?" Heemy looked back quickly. He was expecting to see Alexis, but standing before him was a thick and curvy, middle aged, Latina woman. The look she gave him was a strange one. His smooth, chocolate face was identical to the man's she'd just finished watching on the news. There were no mistakes about it. *It was him.*

"I'm, umm. My name's Mary Santiago," the woman announced, fidgeting with her hands when she said it. She was thinking about the video footage that was captured at Nahfisah's yacht party. Apparently, the video had gone viral. Not only on social media, but media networks nationwide. Heemy's face was at the center of attention. Even Kirk Cuomo, the correspondent for CNN, had described him as the number one suspect in what he referred to as *The Philadelphia Fourth of July Massacre.*

"Miss Mary?" Nahfisah questioned the name and voice. She pulled away from Heemy and looked out into the hallway. Her sniffles turned to tears when she saw Miss Mary standing there. "Oh, my God. Miss Mary." She broke down crying like a scared little girl, whose mother had just come to save her.

Miss Mary wasted no time running toward her. She wrapper Nahfisah in her arms and held tightly, the same way she would have done to Riri, had her daughter still been alive.

"I'm here, baby, just gawn and let it out," Miss Mary spoke through her own tears. She guided Nahfisah over to the bed and sat her down gently.

"Miss Mary, I can't get her out of my head." Nahfisah cried. "I see her every time I close my eyes. It's sorta like it's playing on repeat. I keep seeing what he did to her."

"I'm here now, baby. I won't let him, nor anyone else hurt you," Miss Mary said, as she sat down on the bed beside her. She guided Nahfisah's head into her lap and gently caressed the back of her neck. "Go ahead and tell Momma Mary what happened. You gotta let it out, baby. That's the only way to move past it."

"It was Flo," Nahfisah sobbed. "That man with a shotgun killed her. He blew her head off right in front of me. She was standing beside me so close that the wetness of her brains splashed me in the face. She didn't even scream when he did it. She didn't cry out, or nothing. She didn't even ask the man not to shoot her. Just *bang!* Just like that, and now she's dead. Oh my God, I can't. I can't, Miss Mary. I can't."

"It's okay, baby, just let it out," Miss Mary cooed, steadily bouncing Nahfisah's head in her lap and caressing her at the same time. It was almost as though she were holding Riri, instead of Nahfisah. The thought, alone made her thump. "That's all you gotta do, Riri. Just let it out," she slipped up and stated her daughter's name.

"I'm trying." Nahfisah yawned, too traumatized to realize Miss Mary just called her Riri. "But it's still there. Every time I close my eyes, I can see it."

Heemy heard what Miss Mary said, but he brushed it off. To him, the name *Riri* didn't mean a goddamned thing, especially since he didn't know Sonny around the time Riri was killed. He was more focused on the issue at hand. And now that Nahfisah's was drifting off to sleep, it was the perfect opportunity to make his move.

Thinking about Keeno and the YBM, Heemy walked over to the bedroom closet. He reached up on the top shelf and parted the stack of jeans that occupied it. The Glock .40 he stashed there the night before was propped against the back wall. His thirty-shot ladder was laying right beside it. After removing both items, he stuffed the magazine into the butt of his gun, and then cocked back a live round.

Click! Clack!

"Aye, yo, Blawd? *Blawd?* We got us a muh'fuckin' issue out here," Snot Box called out once again. "I don't know who the fuck they is, but niggas just drove past this muh'fucka two times now. It's a Sprinter Van and two Suburbans. All three of them muh'fuckas was jet black and smoked out."

Heated beyond words, Heemy hurried down the stairs two at a time. He stepped outside on the front porch and looked down at D-Day.

"Which way them niggas came from?"

"They came through from down there." D-Day aimed his chopper down the street.

"And they drove through twice?"

"Yup." D-Day nodded his head in the affirmative. "That's a fact."

"How long in between?"

"About a minute or so. They fuck around and spin the corner any second now."

"So, what'chu think, Blawd?" Snot Box asked when he stepped outside into the cool night air. "You think it's the boys?"

"I doubt it," Heemy said as he hopped off of the porch and stood beside D-Day and Gizzle. "Not out here, anyway. It's more than likely them YBM niggas. They prob'bly coming to get Nahfisah, too. That's the reason they were at the party."

Snot Box's face turned to stone. Being as though he was born and raised in the Pueblo Del Rio housing projects in South Central, he had never heard of the YBM. And even if he did, it wouldn't have mattered. Them niggas violated Sonny, so they violated Pueblo.

Reaching behind his back for his .50 caliber Dessey, Snot Box set his sights on D-Day and Gizzle.

Gizzle was on his wild cowboy shit, two guns up and ready to wet whatever. D-Day was right beside him standing strong. His stockless, AK-47 was dangling at his side. Both men were looking down the street waiting on the three vehicles to turn the corner. They didn't have to wait long. A set of headlights slowly moved around the bend, followed by a glowing set of two more.

"There them niggas go right there!" D-Day exclaimed. Gripping his chopper with both hands, he looked at Heemy, who had his Glock .40 gripped tightly. He then looked to his left at Gizzle. The baby face killah was looking down the street with a murderous rage in his eyes.

"Real shit, Ike. I'm ready to spank sum'n." Gizzle told him, as he moved toward the sidewalk. Two guns strapped, he was ready to show niggas how the Steel City got down.

The four-man crew spread out around the front of the house. Heemy ran out into the middle of the street, while Snot Box stood beside the porch. D-Day held his ground in the middle of the front lawn, while Gizzle ran down and held his own at the curb. All eyes were looking down the street at the oncoming convoy.

The three vehicles came a little closer, and then stopped on a dime. Not even two seconds later, the ringtone from Snot Box's cell phone filled the air. The song was *Gang Signs*, by The Game.

When them gang signs go up/ You see ya life flash right before ya eyes, and you know what? That's how it is on the West Side when them gang signs go up.

Snot Box knew from the ringtone the caller was Sonny. He grabbed the phone from his front pants pocket, then he looked over at Heemy. "Yo, this the homie calling me, Blawd."

Heemy was so zoned out that he didn't even look his way, let alone respond. He was miles beyond the talking point. It was time for niggas to die, and if he died along with them, then so be it.

Snot Box shook his head. There was need to say anything else, so he accepted the call and placed the phone against his ear.

"Tell Heemy I said stand down," Sonny's voice came through the phone. He already knew from talking to Grip that Heemy was standing in the middle of the street, and he was hoping his young bul didn't do anything stupid.

"Blawd, it ain't no barkin' at this nigga. He on his goon shit right now," Snot Box replied, looking at Heemy when he said it.

"Put him on the phone."

"Blawd, this nigga standing here rocking from side to side like a linebacker on fourth and goal. I ain't walking up on this nigga."

"Well, put me on the speaker, then."

Snot Box did what Sonny told him, then he held the phone up for Heemy to hear.

"Aye, yo, Heem, fall back. Them niggas wit' us," Sonny's voice permeated the airwaves.

The sound of his big homie's voice snapped Heemy out of his zone, but only momentarily. He cut his eye at the Samsung, and then looked back at the first Suburban. Still ready for war, he tightened his grasp around the Glock's rubber-grip handle.

"*Aye, yo, Heem!*" Sonny spoke louder. "Fuck is you deaf, nigga? You ain't heard what the fuck I said? Stand down. Them niggas wit' us."

A lone tear trickled from Heemy's left eye. He wiped it away, then he walked over and grabbed the phone from Snot Box. "Yo, Scrap?"

"Them niggas is rydin' wit' us," Sonny spoke more calmly, relieved that Heemy didn't do anything stupid. Especially when considering that fifteen of Grip's banditos were lurking in the shadows, barreling down from four different angles. They'd been there ever since the first time they circled the block. They hopped out the Sprinter Van and decoy Suburban on the next street over, cut through the back yards that surrounded Nahfisah's, then covertly moving under the cloak of darkness, spread out on both sides of the street. The only thing they were waiting on was Grip's signal. The homies would have never seen it coming.

"That's my grandpop in the first Suburban," Sonny added, still speaking with his voice on chill. "He came to get Nah, so he can fly her down to Cuba with the rest of my fam."

"But I thought you said this nigga was the enemy?" Heemy questioned. "The last time we spoke, you said he kidnapped ya mom and the kids, and now you want me to hand over Nahfisah to him?"

"I know what I said, but I was wrong," Sonny felt the need to clarify. He knew if he didn't, things would only become more complicated than they already were. "He didn't kidnap 'em, he came back to save 'em. Them YBM niggas is working wit' my cousin, Gangsta, to put me under. They'll use whatever they can to get to me, my family included. So, that's the reason Nahfisah's not safe. I gave my grandpop the green light to go get her, so don't do nothing to step in his way."

"Not just him, but the other three as well," Grip's voice came through the speaker. Sonny had him on the three way when he called. "I don't want any bullshit," the old man stated for clarity. "I just wanna get in, and get out."

"Y'all heard what he said?" Sonny stated for everyone to hear. "Fall back and let him do what he came to do. Don't start no shit."

No sooner than Sonny said it, the blue and red lights on the first Suburban's front grill lit up bright, signaling Grip's banditos to move in. A second later, they spilled out from behind the shadows and ran toward the house. Each man was strapped with an M-16 and wore black camouflage from head-to-toe.

The first five barged through the front door and ran up the stairs. The remaining ten held post on the front porch. Not a single word was spoken between them. They just stood erect and stared straight ahead, looking at three vehicles rolling down to the house. The first Suburban came to a stop, and the two vehicles behind it did the same. The back-passenger's side door cracked open and a thick cloud of cigar smoke wafted into the air. Grip climbed out slowly and smoothly began walking toward the house. Dominic was a few steps behind him.

D-Day, and Gizzle looked at one another in disbelief. The caliber of drama the old man was capable of bringing was something they weren't prepared for. The only thing they could do was shake their heads and silently thank God that Sonny called them when he did. Because had he not called, they would have been wiped out in an instance.

Snot Box, on the other hand was madder than a muthafucka. It was one thing hearing the voice of the man who killed his little cousin, Mook. But to actually see Grip, live and in living color, had him heated to another degree. It infuriated him even more to know that Sonny was rocking with him. Certainly, this was something he would call Sonny out on.

How the fuck this nigga banging wit' the same nigga who killed his big homie? Snot Box thought to himself, ice grilling Grip as the old man strolled toward him. *Typical East Coast shit.*

Seeing that Snot Box was grilling him, Grip looked at him in the same manner a Pit bull would do a barking Chihuahua. He blew a cloud of smoke in his face, then he walked up the front porch's steps and disappeared inside of the house.

"Yo, Heem, you still there?" Sonny's voice sliced through the silence.

"Yeah, I'm here," Heemy replied, looking at the phone in Snot Box's hand. He was so taken aback by the way Grip rolled through, he momentarily forgot Sonny was on the line.

"Grab the phone from Snot Box and take me off the speaker," Sonny told him.

Heemy reached out for the phone, and for the first time noticed the way Snot Box was looking at him.

"Nigga, what's up?" Heemy stepped in closer. "Fuck is you staring at me like that for?"

"Ain't nothing, Blawd. Ain't nothing at all," Snot Box said as he handed over the phone and walked away, mumbling under his breath.

"Who you was just talking to?" Sonny asked when Heemy took him of the speaker.

"Ya man, Snot Box. This nigga was looking at me on some other shit. Fuck around and get his dumb ass parked out this mu'fucka."

"So, how we lookin'?" Sonny asked, disregarding Heemy's last statement. He already knew the reason Snot Box was mad, so talking about it to Heemy was useless. He would have much rather spoken to Snot Box in person, which was something he planned to do at his first opportunity.

"I mean, I guess we good." Heemy looked down the driveway, where Snot Box was talking to D-Day and Gizzle. "Ain't nobody try to move, or nothing. We did exactly as you said."

"That's good," Sonny replied. "I know shit prob'bly seem a lil' brazy to you, but trust me when I tell you, everything I'm doing is for a reason. I'ma break it all down you as soon as I'm outta here. For now, I just wanna focus on my case."

"And what about the YBM?"

"What about 'em?"

"Them niggas violated, bro. They killed Shorty Rock and Yahyo, and that sucka-ass Keeno tried to smoke me while we were back at the pier. I ain't letting that shit ride, bro. I'm not."

"And I don't want you to," Sonny gave him the green light to get busy. "Give them niggas all the smoke they can handle. And whatever you don't clean up, I will. I'm running down on niggas the first chance I get, believe that."

Heemy was so thirsty for wreck that his trigger-finger was itching. He was expecting Sonny to tell him to fall back. But now that he knew his big homie was back on his murder shit, he was ready to set the tone.

"The first nigga I'ma holla at is my ol' head, Smitty," Heemy began laying out the plan he devised when he first left the pier. "Them niggas was leaning on him to move that Nut Shit for 'em.

127

So, if anybody can give me a line on these niggas, it's Smitty. I just hope he don't try to talk me out of it, or do nothing stupid. It's bad enough I killed my real pops. I'd hate to have to kill Smitty, too."

"I hear you, my nigga. Whatever you need to do, do it. Just keep in mind that whenever money's involved, niggas gon' follow that bag, you feel me? And I know the ol' head, Smitty. That nigga's damn near just as crafty as my grandpop. So, if he's fucking wit' the YBM on some money shit, then you should already know where his loyalty is. Don't trust that nigga no further than you can throw him."

Heemy was just about to explain to Sonny the full extent of his and Smitty's relationship, how Smitty had always been there for him like the father he never knew, but he never got a chance. He was too busy looking at Grip and his soldiers emerging from the house. The young Cuban who followed Grip inside was carrying Nahfisah. She was knocked out cold, and her limp body was cradled in his arms.

Heemy's nostrils began to flare. The sight of another man holding his woman had him ready to snap.

"Hey, uh, young fella," Grip addressed Heemy, seeing the way he was looking at Dominic. "You mind giving me a few ticks. I just wanna rap wit'cha."

Heemy held up his index finger, signaling for Grip to wait a second. He then turned his back to him and continued speaking to Sonny. "Yo, ya grandpop talking 'bout he wanna holla at me."

"Go 'head and holla at him, it's cool. Just remember what I told you. The most dangerous thing you could ever do in the streets is give a muthafucka more credit than they deserve. Don't never forget that. Big business."

"Business as usual," Heemy sent the love back. He disconnected the call and then turned back around to face Grip. Looking the old man square in his eyes, he said, "A'ight, Ol' Head, what's up?"

Grip sucked in a long, heavy drag on his Cohiba cigar, then he opened his mouth so the smoke flow out.

"First, let me start by saying that I know who you are, and I respect you being there for my granddaughter. I also know what you mean to Sontino. For that reason, I'm willing to allow you to fly down to Cuba with us. It'll be better for you."

"Better for me?" Heemy's eyelids shrank. "What'chu mean by that?"

"They're coming for you, kid. There's no doubt about it."

"I'm cool wit' that. I'm coming for them, too."

"You're not understanding. I'm not talking about just anybody, I'm referring to the feds. The shit that happened earlier tonight at my granddaughter's party. If I know about it, you can rest assure they know about it, too. It's only a matter of time before they come and get you. They're probably kicking in your mother's front door as we speak."

"I appreciate the offer, Ol' Head, but I'm straight," Heemy said as he stuffed his Glock .40 down in his waistband. "The only thing you can do for me is keep my girl safe. As far as myself, I can hold my own. And that's pertaining to the feds, the YBM, or whoever else that wanna test this shit here. *I'm fit.*"

"Suit yourself." Grip shrugged his shoulders, then flicked his cigar in the grass. "But if you find yourself in a position where you need to get ghost, my offer still stands. You contact Sontino, and then have Sontino contact me. I'll have a private jet waiting for at the airport in Teterboro, New Jersey. It'll fly you down to Cuba with me and the rest of the family."

Heemy didn't speak, he just nodded his head.

As he turned to walk back to his Lamborghini, he looked to his right where Miss Mary was walking down the front porch's steps. Her glossy, wet eyes locked on his, then she lowered her head and walked away, crying.

Askari

Blood of a Boss 5

Chapter Fourteen
An Hour Later

Smitty was sitting up in his bed with his bare back pressed against the suede headboard. His young girl, Somayah, was laying between his legs topping him off, sopping so good that he could barely keep his focus on the late-night news. He looked down at his slick, wet dick going in and out of her mouth, and then reached over and grabbed the remote control from his nightstand. He aimed the remote control at his 60" plasma and turned up the volume.

"According to my co-host and guest, Sebastian Phoenix, from Philadelphia's East Homicide Division, the young man in the video we just finished showing has been identified as Raheem McDaniel's, a nineteen-year-old drug dealer and reputed hitman for the Moreno Crime Family," Kirk Cuomo announced. The middle aged, clean cut Italian was situated on the left side of the screen. He was broadcasting live from the CNN building in downtown Atlanta, while Detective Phoenix, situated on the right side of the screen, was broadcasting live from a mobile unit parked on the corner of Delhi and Cumberland, directly up the block from Treesha's house.

"Raheem McDaniels is considered armed and dangerous," Detective Phoenix stated with caution, his brown eyes staring into the camera. *"We strongly advise everyone who's watching, namely the citizens of Philadelphia, if you see Mr. McDaniels, or have any information pertaining to his whereabouts, report him immediately. You can either contact your local authorities by dialing nine-one-one, or place an anonymous call to the one-eight-hundred hotline number that's posted at the bottom of the screen. But under no circumstances, ladies and gentlemen, do not approach him. I repeat, do not approach him."*

"What the hell?" Smitty's body went tense when a mugshot of Heemy appeared on the screen. "Hold on now, Sugar Love." He tapped Somayah on the shoulder. "Wait a second. I need to see this."

Somayah heard what he said, but instead of stopping, she gunned him even faster, slurping so loudly that if Smitty didn't

131

know any better he would have sworn she was mopping up a plate of spaghetti.

Slurrrrrrrrrp!

"Sugar Love, I'm serious." He tapped her on the shoulder once more. "Cool out. I need to see what the hell is going on."

Somayah lifted her mouth from his dick, and then rolled over to see what her man was talking about.

"Oh, damn." She looked at the television in disbelief, seeing Heemy's mugshot was on full display. "This ain't even the local news, this is CNN."

"See what I mean?" Smitty looked at her with a raised brow.

"But what happened? What are they saying he did?"

"I don't know," Smitty replied as he turned the volume up a little bit louder. "I'm trying to find out now."

The CNN telecast switched back to the split screen between Kirk Cuomo and Detective Phoenix. Kirk Cuomo was talking.

"Alright, now the video we're about to show was taken a little while earlier. It involves content of a sexual nature and explicit language. So, viewers be advised. Okay, Sandy, cue us in."

A few seconds later, the video footage of the PPD executing their search warrant at Treesha's house appeared on the screen. A plethora of Swat Team members from Units One and Two were lined up and down Delhi Street. It seemed to be at least twenty of them, half were holding bulletproof shields, and the other half were strapped with M-16 assault rifles. The Unit One Swat Team leader was standing at the front door with a battering ram clutched in his hands. The Unit Two leader was standing on the stoop directly behind him. Both units were dressed in all-black with black ski masks covering their faces from the nose down.

The Unit Two team leader glanced up and down the dimly lit block, and then signaled for the two men closest to him to take post at the rear of the house. Using his index and middle fingers, he pointed at his eyes, and then pointed at the vacant lot to the right, gesturing for his three men standing on the sidewalk to be on the lookout for a runner. Satisfied that both units were strategically positioned around the house, he slowly began his countdown.

"On three. Two. One!"

Ka-Boom!

"Get on the fucking ground! Get down!" The Unit Two team leader shouted, as the front door went flying off the hinges. He pushed his partner with the battering ram out of his way and stormed inside of the house with his M-16 cradled in both hands. His partner with the battering ram tossed it aside, then he pulled out his handgun and barged into the house behind him. An additional six officers were right behind him. All guns were aimed at Treesha and Young Papi, the fifteen-year-old crack dealer from Marshal Street, who's dick she was sucking for a dime rock. Young Papi's dick and balls were blurred out for the sake of the camera, but even then, it was clear from the video that Treesha was sucking him off. Not only was a stringy glob of spit dangling between her bottom lip and his blurred-out pelvis, his blue and white, 76ers breakaway warm-ups were pulled down and bunched around his ankles.

"Ahn-ahn! Just who and the fuck you muthafuckas think y'all is running up in my goddamned place?" Treesha screamed at the eight, armed-to-the-teeth Swat Team members. She was seated on the arm of her couch with her blurred out titties dangling from the bottom of her pulled up T-shirt. Her twitching jaw bone and blood-shot eyes were a clear indicated that she'd just finished boomping. The smell of her crack smoke was still in the air.

"Goddamnit! I said get on the fucking ground!" The Unit Two team leader growled at her, aiming his M-16 at the bridge of her nose.

"Kiss my whole ass, muthafucka! I ain't doing shit!" Treesha screamed back at him, too spaced out to realize that if she made one wrong move, it could prove to be fatal.

Young Papi, thinking about the thirty bags of crack in his front pants pocket, slipped one of his legs free and took off running toward the back door.

Bdddddddddoc!

A hail of gunfire peppered the back of his shirt and decorated the wall in front of him with his own insides. He staggered a few steps forward, then toppled over dead as a door knob before he hit on the carpet.

Treesha hopped up from the couch screaming. *"Black lives matter, muthafucka! Black lives—"*

Wham!

The Unit Two team leader cracked her upside the head with the butt of his rifle, cutting her off mid-sentence. She crumbled to her knees, then was quickly pinned down and placed in handcuffs.

"Search this muthafuckin' house from top to bottom," The Unit One team leader ordered his men.

As they scattered throughout the house, some running up the stairs while a few others stormed the kitchen and basement, he reached down and forcefully grabbed Treesha by the hair. He yanked back and slung her down on the couch.

"Raheem McDaniels. Your son. Where the fuck is he?"

"What? What'chu said to me just now?" Treesha looked at him in a daze. The gush of blood pumping from her forehead was trickling down the left side of her nose. It looped around her top lip, slid down the sides and then dotted the front of her dingy white Tee. Still woozy from the blow, she stirred around with her eye lids fluttering. She looked to her right, where Young Papi was laying on the floor hunched forward with his ass in the air, then she brought her gaze back to the questioner. *"Rah-Raheem, what?"*

"Where the fuck is he?" The Unit One team leader nudged his pistol into her left cheek. *"He's wanted for murder."*

"Oh, hell to the muthafucking naw!" Treesha's eyes popped wide open. It was then, she was beginning to realize what all of the fuss was about. *"All of this is because of him?"* She leaned forward shaking her head in disbelief. *"Ain't that about a bitch! I done been told you muthafuckas that boy wasn't shit! He killed his own goddamned daddy right in front of me, and you muthafuckas ain't did a damn thing to him! So, now that he killed somebody else, y'all wanna pull this shit? What about my goddamned man? What about my Pooky? Y'all knew that goddamned boy killed him! No! Ahn-ahn, no! Y'all should'a locked his ass up the last time! I ain't telling you muthafuckas shit!"*

The CNN telecast switched back to the split screen between Kirk Cuomo and Detective Phoenix. Kirk Cuomo had a bewildered look in his eyes.

"Now, Detective Phoenix, the woman in the video was Raheem McDaniels' mother, am I right?"

"You are." Detective Phoenix nodded his head. He was leaned back in his chair with his fingers locked together. *"We've identified her as Treesha Grimes."*

"Okay." Kirk Cuomo nodded his head. *"And according to Miss Grimes, this isn't the first time your suspect, her own son, Raheem McDaniels murdered someone? In fact, she's claiming that he murdered his own father, for crying out loud. She's also claiming that she witnessed the entire incident, and that she contacted the local authorities, but nothing was ever done. Are any of these claims true, Detective Phoenix?"* The look on Kirk's face was skeptical and accusatory. *"Because if that's the case, then clearly if something were done, we wouldn't be sitting here today talking about this Fourth of July Massacre. I'm pretty sure that everyone viewing would appreciate some clarity."*

"Well, ah, some of what she said is actually true," Detective Phoenix stated with an uneasy voice, feeling as though the integrity of his badge was being called into question. He cleared his throat, and then leaned forward slightly, slowly unlocking his fingers. Looking into the camera, he carefully revealed what he knew about Heemy and his connection to the Moreno Crime Family.

"In December of Two-Thousand-and-Fourteen, we received information from Miss Perkins pertaining to the murders of Raheem McDaniels, the suspect's father, and another individual by the name of Jamar Christie. The information she provided ultimately led to the arrest of her then, sixteen-year-old son, Raheem McDaniels.

"Unfortunately, in the process of building a case against Mr. Daniels, we ran into a few problems. The first problem was the missing bodies of Mr. Daniels and Mr. Christie, which until this very day have never been found. The second problem was that our district attorney at the time, Seth Willis, deemed Miss Perkins to be

an unreliable witness, given her extensive criminal background. Another problem we ran into was the suspect, himself. As a result of not having any physical evidence linking him to the crime, we were pretty much hoping the we could get a confession."

"And I'm assuming that didn't happen," Kirk Cuomo interjected.

"Not at all." Detective Phoenix shook his head. *"He flat out denied any knowledge of the crime, essentially leaving us with our hands tied. There was nothing else we could use to officially hold him, so we were forced to let him go."*

"I see." Kirk Cuomo nodded his understanding. *"So, how would you describe the current status of the case? Is it open? Is it cold?"*

"Well, officially, the case is still open," Detective Phoenix stated with a frustrated sigh. *"We're currently in the process of looking into a few developments that could possibly bring us closer to an indictment. But so far, we haven't been able to make any arrests."*

"And based on these new developments, would you still consider Mr. McDaniels your number one suspect?"

"Well, technically, Kirk, I'm not at liberty to say," Detective Phoenix replied with a slight chuckle. *"But what I will say is that one thing we know now, that we didn't know then, is that our suspect, Raheem McDaniels, is heavily affiliated with the Moreno Crime Family. In addition to being one of their top enforcers, for the past year or so, he's been appointed as their number one drug distributor, trafficking of cocaine from Philadelphia to Richmond, Virginia."*

"Alright, now the Moreno Crime Family, for those of our viewers who don't know, could you please explain exactly who you're referring to?"

"Sure thing." Detective Phoenix gave him a slight nod. *"The Moreno Crime Family, also known as The Black Mafia, is an extension of the Italian Mafia here in South Philly. It's leader and founder, Gervin 'Grip' Moreno, is the son of Angolo 'Big Angolo'*

Gervino, the protégé and criminal heir to the Boss of all Bosses, Mr. Charles 'Lucky' Luciano.

"This international crime syndicate is rumored to be a faction of a secret society known as The Con—"

"You know it's funny you mentioned Big Angolo," Kirk Cuomo interrupted, deliberately raising his voice, so that Detective Phoenix couldn't finish his sentence. *"Immediately prior to the breaking news new coming in out Philadelphia, we were actually in the process of doing a story about his recent death. According to the prison officials at ADX Florence, where the hundred-year-old Mafia don was serving a life sentence, his dead body was discovered in his prison cell late yesterday afternoon. They're saying he died from cancer."*

"That's an actual fact," Detective Phoenix stated. *"But before we delve too deep into Big Angolo's death and the criminal mystic surrounding him, I would rather keep the focus on Mr. McDaniels and his connection to the Moreno Crime Family."*

"By all means," Kirk Cuomo gave him a cautionary look, *"proceed."*

"Earlier today, just a few hours before the yacht party, which we now know was a birthday celebration for Nahfisah Thompson, Gervin Moreno's granddaughter, Mr. McDaniels paid a visit to Gervin's grandson, Sontino Moreno, at our county jail here in Philadelphia. We can't prove it, but we strongly believe that Sontino was previously made aware of a potential ambush at his sister's party, and that he gave the order for Mr. McDaniels, his top street lieutenant, to do whatever necessary to keep his sister safe.

"There are numerous elements to this mass shooting, many of which we believe stem from a power struggle between a number of criminal organizations, international and nationwide. All of them fighting for a piece of the power pie that Big Angolo left behind. The Moreno Family, we believe, are dead smack in the middle of it. We further have information that Gervin's grandson, Sontino Moreno, the acting boss of the Moreno Crime Family, is next in line to take over as The Conglomerate's head chair. A position that was handed

down from Lucky Luciano to Big Angolo Gervino, and is now being handed down to him."

"Allow me to interject," Kirk Cuomo stated while holding up his right hand, gesturing for Detective Phoenix to slow up a bit. He attempted to speak over him, but Detective Phoenix wasn't having it. He snatched out his earpiece and continued saying what he had to say.

"It's been rumored for decades, dating all the way back to the end of World War Two, that a worldwide criminal organization, green lighted and supported by the CIA, has been—"

Zip!

"What the fuck happened to the TV?" Smitty questioned, looking at the blacked-out screen. Checking to see if his television was still working, he held up the remote control and pressed down on the click-back button. The previous channel he was watching popped up and appeared to be working just fine.

"Alright, now ESPN is still good. So, what the hell is going on with CNN?"

He clicked back to CNN and noticed right away that the channel was back in. Only this time, instead of a split screen, he was looking at a close-up of Kirk Cuomo. Detective Phoenix was no longer on the air.

"Sorry for that, ladies and gentlemen. We appear to be having some type of malfunction on Detective Phoenix's end. But for the time being, and for those of you who just tuned in, we're going to switch back to the video footage that was taken earlier tonight at Penn's Landing in Philadelphia, Pa. This video contains graphic images and explicit language, so viewers be advised. Alright, Sandy," he nodded his head at the producer behind the screen, *"cue us in."*

The telecast switched over to the yacht party, with a clear image of Heemy setting it off with his first shot.

Boca!

"Dang, Papa, it's a good thing you didn't let me go to that party, huh?" Somayah said, as she nibbled on Smitty's earlobe. She was propped up on her knees at the foot of their bed, where Smitty was seated at the edge. Her 44 Double D's were pressed against his back, and her fingertips were softly caressing his shoulders. "You think it'll be a long time before they catch him?" She whispered in his ear and then kissed him on the neck.

Smitty didn't reply, as he sat there watching the video, quietly thinking of all the variables that could possibly lead to his downfall. He caught a glimpse of The Reaper, and knew it was only a matter of time before they identified him as the man with the shotgun. The Reaper's arrest would ultimately lead back to Alvin and the YBM, and then eventually back to him. There was also the possibility that Heemy, with his dropping off money bags every first of the month, may have unintentionally pulled him into an indictment.

"*Damnit, young blood!*" Smitty mumbled under his breath, thinking about Detective Phoenix and everything he said about Heemy. He figured that if Detective Phoenix knew as much as he claimed he did, then nine times out of ten, they must have had Heemy under surveillance. And if that were the case, then certainly they had him on camera dropping off money at the Doo Drop. The thought, alone, was enough to make the old man sick. So sick, that he was already making plans to speak to his attorney first thing in the morning.

"*A picture's worth a thousand words, and perception is a muthafucka,*" he remembered a valuable jewel that he once passed down to Easy, many years earlier when he first put him on to the robbery game.

Ironically, the same advice he gave Easy was the same mistake that could land him in jail for the rest of his life. Because the second the video was shown to a jury, coupled with the slick talking of a well-seasoned prosecutor, his forty years of playing the background, dibbling and dabbling and stacking his fetty were pretty much over.

"Papa?" Somayah nudged him on the shoulder when he failed to reply. "*Papa?*" She nudged him a little bit harder. "Are you even listening to me right now?"

Smitty turned his head to the side, looking at Somayah who was leaned over his left shoulder. He gritted his teeth, then he turned back around and continued watching the news. He knew the game and how bitches got down the second they caught a whiff of an indictment. Somayah, like every other hustla's wife, the second he went to jail, would be bouncing on to the next nigga's dick no sooner than the handcuffs were locked around his wrist. It was so common that he couldn't even knock her. All he could do was charge it to the game.

"Pew." Somayah screwed her face up, as she crawled off of the bed. "You over here acting all stank and whatnot. You ain't gotta talk to me, I was just about to get on the Gram, anyway. I know it's prol'ly lit right now."

Standing in the middle of the room, she looked around for her cell phone, but didn't see it. She usually kept it on the dresser, but for some reason it wasn't there. Patting her weave to stop it from itching, she moved toward the closet where her Birkin bag was hanging on the door knob. She zipped it open and peeked inside. The charger was there, but her phone wasn't.

"Papa, you seen my phone?" She asked Smitty when she turned around to face him. "Well, *did you*?"

"No, Sugar Love. I didn't," Smitty slowly replied, wanting so bad to tell her to kick rocks, or sit her dumb-ass down somewhere. Couldn't she see he was going through a crisis? That his life as a free man was possibly coming to an end?

"Papa, you sure?"

"Yes, Sugar Love, I'm sure."

Well, where the fuck I left it, then? Somayah thought deeply. She retraced her steps, going all the way back to when they first returned home from Atlantic City. It was then, she remembered she left the phone inside of his Bentley. The entire ride home, she was taking selfies and talking shit on Snap Chat and Facebook Live. Her cell battery died about ten minutes before they pulled into the driveway, and because Smitty's charger was already hanging from the socket, she used his instead of her own, leaving the phone on his center console.

"Papa, gimmie ya car key." She patted her weave once more, and then held her hand out toward him.

"Give you my car key for what?" Smitty looked at her hand like it was covered in shit.

"Say whahhh?" Somayah's head leaned to the side. She was so used to having Smitty wrapped around her fingers, that it caught her off guard when he questioned her request.

"I said, give you my car key for what?"

Oh, no the fuck this old muthafucka didn't! Somayah's eyelids shrank tightly. She folded her arms across her chest, and then shifted her weight to one side. "Are you serious right now? Really?"

"Humph." The old man gave her a funny look, knowing his feelings for her were already suppressed. It wasn't his fault; it was just his nature. He'd been taught by the game to never love a thing he couldn't turn his back on at the snap of a finger. Somayah fell into that category.

"All I wanna do is get my cell phone," Somayah said with her feelings hurt. "I left it on your charger and forgot to get it when we came inside the house."

"Alright," Smitty said as he stood to his feet and began walking toward the closet. "I'll go down and get it for you."

Somayah was speechless. His stern, hard demeanor was nothing close to the pussy-whipped, thrilled-to-be-with-a-young-girl, old man, that she was used to. It rattled her brain trying to figure out what turned him so cold. For the past two hours, they'd been making love, kissing and sucking on one another; laughing at each other's jokes, and then making love all over again. But now, and for reasons she couldn't explain, he was treating her like a pussy-popper picked from a strip club.

Was it something I said? Something I did? Was the pussy wack and the head not good? He never complained about it before? Why the hell is he acting like this?

Attempting to smooth things over, she stepped in his way when he tried to brush past her. She wrapped her arms around him, and kissed him on his chest.

"Papa, what's the matter? Why you acting like this?"

Smitty pushed her away and continued making his way toward the closet. He stepped inside and then closed the door behind him.

The front half of the closet belonged to Somayah, and the second half belonged to him. He removed one of his bathrobes from the rack and slipped it on slowly. He then stepped into a pair of his silk-lined, suede and leather house shoes.

Ready to go, he reached up on the top shelf and carefully removed the Prada box that was slightly hanging off of the edge. He sat the box on his watch stand, flipped it open and reached inside. Stashed beneath the paper, was his nickel-plated .38. He grabbed the gun from the box, and then placed it in his bathrobe pocket.

"Papa, can you at least say something?" Somayah asked when she slipped into the closet.

Her flush, red face and glossy wet eyes were making Smitty's heart hurt. He wanted to believe she would stand by his side when push came to shove, but he knew better. So, instead of replying, he just shook his head and eased right past her.

Chapter Fifteen

The city was too hot for Heemy and the homies to be riding around in the same vehicles they had back at the pier, so after driving across the bridge to Camden, New Jersey, where they switched rides at Heemy's apartment, they drove out to Delaware County to see Smitty.

They were parked up the block from the cul-de-sac, where Smitty's house was situated at the bottom. Their headlights were turned off and their engines were quietly running. Heemy and Gizzle were tucked behind the 30% tint in Heemy's F-250, while Snot Box and D-Day were parked right behind them, blowing on a Wood and leaned back in the buttah leather seats in Heemy's Impala SS. The four men could have easily piled into one ride, but having niggas seated behind him in the back seat was a no-no in Heemy's eyes. It was a horror story waiting to happen, too easy for a muthafucka to leave him with his brains splashed against the windshield and dash.

"Damn, Scrap, that's ya moms going in on you like that?" Gizzle stated when Heemy handed over his cell phone. The news segment from CNN was all over Facebook, and everybody Heemy knew was tagging him in the video of Treesha throwing him under the bus. It didn't surprise him. He knew the way his mom got down. He was just wondering whether or not he was wrong for thinking about killing her. He figured if it was so easy for Treesha to throw her only son's life away, then why should it be so hard for him to take hers?

Vrrrrrm! Vrrrrrm! Vrrrrrm!

Heemy's cell phone vibrated in Gizzle's hand, and Gizzle handed it back to him. Looking at the screen, Heemy saw it was Treesha calling. He started to block her, but for reasons he couldn't explain, he accepted the call.

"What'chu calling me for?"

"Heemy Boo, where you at?" Treesha called him the nickname she gave him as a child. "I need a lil' sum'n, sum'n. And before you say *no*," she rambled off fast, "this ain't no handout. I got about five hunnid dollars. White Boy Frank just rolled up, and he wanna get the party started. And you *know* how White Boy Frank do, his ass be done ran back and forth to the ATM about twenty damn times before the morning come. I'm try'na get this money, so gawn and lay sum'n on me. I'ma break you off wit'cha cut."

Listening to his mother's voice and knowing she was leading him into a trap, brought tears to Heemy's eyes. Refusing to let his tears fall, he wiped his eyes with the back of his hand and then spoke to her calmly.

"What color you want?"

"Huhn? Boy, what'chu talking 'bout?"

"I said what color?" Heemy growled at her. "Yellow, pink, or blue?"

"Boy, what the fuck is you talking 'bout?" Treesha raised her voice. "I ain't said nothing about no goddamned colors."

"Bitch, I'm talking about the dress I'ma bury you in. What color you want?"

"Oh, hell naw!" Treesha shrieked, looking at Detective Phoenix who was standing at the interrogation room's doorway. "See, I done told you muthafuckas! I told y'all the goddamned boy was crazy! Y'all ain't gon' do nothing but get me killed!"

"Raheem?" Detective Phoenix's voice came through the phone. "This is Detective Phoenix from East Homicide. We need you to come down to police headquarters to turn yourself—"

Click!

Heemy disconnected the call and hopped out of his truck steaming hot. He slammed the phone against the ground and stomped on it until it cracked to pieces.

"*Stankin' ass bitch,*" he mumbled under his breath, while reaching down to grab the chip. He tossed the chip down the sewer drain, and then kicked the remnants of his broken phone across the street.

"Damn, Blawd, what's poppin'?" Snot Box asked when he walked up behind him. "You good?"

"Fuck no, I ain't good." Heemy shot him the look of death. "Them fuckin' boys is on me. They got me on camera from the shootout back at Nahfisah's party. They even playing that shit on CNN."

"Nigga, say hood."

"That's on Fo' Hunnid." Heemy threw up the set. "They even ran up in my mom's spot looking for me. The stankin' bitch just called my phone try'na line me up."

Snot Box looked up and down the street, then returned his visage to Heemy. "Maybe we ought'a be thinking about getting low," he suggested. "The homies that flew in from the ATL is back at the hotel. A few of them niggas ain't make it, but the ones who did is on standby waiting on my next call. We can easily send you down south for a little while. New York is too close, Pittsburgh is still in Pa., and flying out to Bali wit' me would be asinine. With all this heat, you'd never make it through the airport. And you definitely can't stay in Philly."

Hearing the mentioning of an airport, the first thing that came to Heemy's mind was Grip and the offer he made. Maybe flying down to Cuba was the best thing for him. At least that way he would have some time to get his head together and regroup. Even better, it would bring him closer to Nahfisah. Cuba was beginning to sound really good to him, but for now, his only focus was Keeno and the YBM. There was simply no way he was willing to let slide what they'd done to him. If he was locked up in the process, then so be it. Either way, it was time to start chin-checking muthafuckas.

"So, what's poppin'? What'chu fit'na do?" Snot Box asked him.

"I'ma handle my fuckin' business," Heemy said as he took off walking. "Y'all niggas wait here. I'll be back in a few minutes."

***

The weather was a tad brisker than Smitty remembered. He tightened the belt on his bathrobe, then he stepped outside and trucked down his patio steps. The bright lights from his motion-sensor security system came to life the second his right foot touched the pavement. Moving from the patio to the side of his house, where his Range Rover and Bentley were parked in the driveway, his red Doberman Pinscher, Momma Sadie, ran up to the fence that separated the back of the house from the side. She pressed her nose against the fence, and then stood up on her hind legs. Her front paws were propped on the fence's edge.

"Momma Sadie, what'chu doing, girl?" Smitty stopped at the fence. He rubbed the sides of Momma Sadie's neck, gently caressing her brownish-red fur. Momma Sadie panted. She looked at Smitty, then dipped her head to the side when the cracking sound of a snapped twig grabbed her attention. Her pointed, red ears shot up at attention when a shadowy figure moved from the grass patch beside the house and in between Smitty's Bentley and Range Rover.

Uuuggggrrrrrrr! Her pointy, sharp teeth sprang forward like a Great White ready to feast. *Uuuggggrrrrrrr!* She growled even louder, hopping up on her hind legs, trying to make it over the fence.

Smitty, knowing from Momma Sadie's demeanor that was someone was creeping up behind him, reached for his .38, then spun around with his finger on the trigger.

"Who the fuck is that behind my truck?" Smitty questioned with his gun aimed high. "Fuck around if you want, and I'll get to ringing this bitch. *Hollows*! Six of 'em. Turn Miss Piggy's ass into bacon bits *real quick*. Now, go 'head and try me."

Heemy stepped out from behind Smitty's Range Rover with his empty hands in plain view. As soon as Momma Sadie saw him, her intense growling became a tongue-wagging pant. To her, Heemy was just as good as her second owner. Ever since Smitty used to bring her to the Doo Drop when she was only a pup, Heemy would take her for long walks all throughout the neighborhood and hand feed her packs of bologna. She still remembered and loved him for it.

"Goddamnit, young blood! You almost made me shoot your ass," Smitty admonished, as he showed Heemy his gun. "What the hell you doing creeping around my house in the dark for any damned way? You know me better than that, young blood. You know I don't go for the kinda shit. Liked to be done got'cha ya head blowed off. And for what? *A mistake*?"

"You see the news?" Heemy asked, showing no concern for the gun in Smitty's hand, nor the fly shit he was talking. He stepped around him, then reached out and patted Momma Sadie on the head.

"You damn right, I seen the news. Boy, you done boogie-woogied out the frying pan and landed your ass first into the fire. I done told you about that wild cowboy shit. You can't get money and go to war at the same time. The shit don't mix, one is gonna always outweigh the other. It's the money we out to get, young blood. The money. All that other shit is for the birds. I done told you this a million times."

Looking at the young man he loved like a son, Smitty shook his head and sighed. "*Damnit, young blood.* Y'all done went and made the whole city hot. This the type of shit that make the feds come knocking. They might even come knocking for me."

"Oh, yeah?" Heemy gave him an intense stare. "And how you figure that?"

"Them crackas been try'na get ol' Smitty for damn near forty years now. So, you can bet'cha last nickel when my name pops up, they'll be coming to get me. My ass'll be on that indictment sheet right along wit' the rest of y'alls."

Heemy knew Smitty was referring to his affiliation with the YBM, but he wanted to hear him say it. So that way, if Smitty tried to play any games concerning their whereabouts, Heemy could justify in his own mind his reason for smoking him.

"You know it wasn't only you I seen on that goddamned video," Smitty continued. "I saw Rayon's ass, too. So, if they're coming for you, then they're sure as hell coming for him."

"Rayon?" Heemy squinted his eyes. "That's the name of the nigga who had the shotgun?"

"Umm-hmm, that was him." Smitty nodded his head. "Sonofabitch crazier than a bedbug, him *and* his brother, Alvin. Now, dig this here, young blood. I'm glad you were sharp enough to make it off that yacht, I really am. But you're hotter than fish grease in the middle of August, and that type of heat I'm not built for. It's bad enough they probably got'chu on camera dropping off money at the Doo Drop, and that alone could get me on a conspiracy. I can't stand it, young blood. I don't need it, and I can't stand it. So, from here on out we gotta go our separate ways."

"Our separate ways?" Heemy replied, his unresolved abandonment issues kicking in full drive. "What's that supposed to mean? Our separate ways? How?"

"What I'm saying, young blood, is that I gotta turn my back on you. I hate to say it like that, but that's the way it is now. That's the way it *has* to be, every man for himself."

"Just like that?" Heemy chuckled in disbelief. "Nigga, you like a dad to me."

"I don't know what else to tell you, young blood. I gotta do what's best for me, and you gotta do what's best for you. And look at'chu. You ain't even gotta say it, I can see it in your eyes. You're thinking about going after Rayon and his crew."

"Eventually." Heemy shrugged his shoulders, his gangster exterior blocking out the pain within. "But first, I'ma run down on that pussy-ass Keeno. He thought he had me, but he missed. So, now he gotta deal wit' me."

"Then after that, what? You gon' take on the entire YBM by yourself? Them muthafuckas will eat you alive, young blood. Don't be stupid. I raised you better than that. The only thing you need to be worried about is laying low and copping you a top-notch lawyer. Now, I know you been stacking that bread up like I taught you?"

"That ain't none of ya concern no more," Heemy replied in a hurt voice, once again feeling the pain of not having a father. "Ain't that what'chu just said?"

Smitty grimaced. He attempted to smooth things over, but Heemy gestured for him not to.

"Don't even waste your breath," Heemy said as he backed away slow. "It's every man for himself, right? So, do you, and I'ma do me."

"Hey, young blood?" Smitty called out when Heemy turned to walk away. "54th and Kingsessing."

"What?" Heemy said as he turned around, but still moving backwards.

"That's where you can find Rayon and his crew. The third house from the corner. It has a wire fence this high," Smitty raised his hand at shoulder level. "There's a German Shepherd on the other side."

Heemy nodded his head, then turned back around and continued walking.

Smitty trailed behind him, but stopped walking when he reached his driveway. Still watching Heemy as he moved up the block, Smitty pulled out his car key and deactivated the Bentley's alarm. Pulling open the driver's side door, he looked over his shoulder as Heemy was climbing inside of his F-250. The Ford truck pulled away from the curb, and another car pulled out behind it.

"These stupid muthafuckas must'a bumped they head," Smitty said to himself as he reached down and grabbed Somayah's phone from the Bentley's center console. "Thinking they can start a bunch of shit and then bring me down wit' 'em. We gon' see about this shit. 'Cause I'll be damned if I'm going to trial wit' a bunch of broke-ass, good for nothing, co-defendants. Especially these young muthafuckas, they stupid asses get to telling and shit. I ain't doing it," he shook his head defiantly, "ain't happening. I'd rather see 'em kill each other."

He thumbed in the password to Somayah's cell phone, and then called The Reaper.

Askari

Chapter Sixteen
At the YBM Headquarters on 54th and Kingsessing

"Did any of you muthafuckas see or hear anything from Bushnut since we came back from the party?" The Reaper questioned as he knocked down a double-shot of Henny. He was seated at the mini bar in the back corner of the basement, and looking around for somebody to give him an answer.

Kia, who was slouched back on the couch with her legs spread open like a nigga, shook her hard *no*. Killah Kye, who was seated beside her, did the same and Murda Mont, who was stretched out on the love seat beside the couch, didn't say anything at all. His undivided attention was locked on the late-night news. He turned up the volume.

"It was here, in South Philly, at the Penn's Landing pier, just a few hours earlier, where America's most recent mass shooting had taken place," said Roland Rushing, the lead correspondent for Channel 9 News. He was standing at the edge of the pier, about a hundred feet away from the yacht that hosted Nahfisah's party. The tan collar on his Brooks Brothers trench coat was flapping from the wind blowing in off of the Delaware.

"As you can see from the yacht behind me, the bullet riddled, top and lower decks are still smoking. The Fire Department went through great lengths to extinguish the fire, but not a water hose known to man could extinguish the fire that's burning inside the heart of this city, our nation for that matter. Our prayers go out to the victims and their families, the thirteen dead and the forty-two wounded."

Murda Mont was leaned forward, puffing on his Kush-filled Dutch, and hanging on Roland's every last word. The news segment had already showed the video of Heemy shooting at The Reaper, so now Murda Mont was listening closely, praying there wasn't a second video from the parking lot, one that may have possibly shown him.

"So, now of all a sudden don't nobody know shit?" The Reaper lashed out. He was already mad that his face was on the news and because he still had to report back to Alvin and explain everything that went wrong, it pissed him off even more to see that his crew was ignoring him. He tipped over his shot glass and grabbed his shotgun from the bar top. *Click! Clack!* He chambered a round. *Boom!* He blew the television clean off the wall.

Killah Kye hit the floor and then crawled under the coffee table, bitching. Murda Mont hopped up from the love seat covering his ears, and Kia just sat there shaking her head.

"Goddamn, yo! Double R, what the fuck?" Murda Mont complained with his eardrums ringing. He was the closest one to the blast.

The Reaper leveled the shotty at Murda Mont's chest and stepped in to him. He was standing so close, the smoking hot shotty barrel was heating up the front of Murda Mont's shirt. "Do I got'cha attention?"

"Yeah, man, you got my attention." Murda Mont gritted on him.

"Nigga, *fix ya face*," The Reaper snarled with his teeth clenched.

"A'ight, man, I'm good." Murda Mont softened his stance.

The Reaper's nostrils began to flare. He lowered the shotgun and left it hanging by his side. His right hand was still clutching the grip. "Fuck is you smiling at?" He looked at Kia.

"These bitch-ass niggas you got running wit' us," Kia stated without fear. "My pussy got more balls than both of 'em put together. *Look at 'em*," she nodded at Killah Kye, who was climbing back to his feet, "this nigga hiding under the coffee table with his ass in the air, and then you got this nigga," she pointed at Murda Mont, "all shook up and shaking and shit. He prob'bly pissed on himself."

"Fuck you, Keys." Killah Kye ice-grilled her.

"Kye, you couldn't fuck me if you wanted to. Ol' bull-dagger ass nigga. Fuckin' wit'chu, we'd just be bumping pussies."

"Yeah, a'ight, you keep on thinking that."

"Both of y'all shut the fuck up," The Reaper cut the nonsense short. He moved his gaze from Kia, to Killah Kye, and then back to

Kia, whose gangsta he respected more. "I'ma ask you this again, have you seen or heard anything from Bushnut?"

"Nah." Kia shook her head *no*. "The last time I seen him was here."

"And what about you?" The Reaper looked at Killah Kye.

"The same as Keys. I ain't seen the nigga since he came through before the party."

"And Mont?"

"Naw, man, I ain't heard nothing," Murda Mont said as he cut his eye at Kia, still salty that she called him out in front of The Reaper.

Kia gritted her teeth and scowled right back. "*You's a whole bitch*," she mouthed the words so The Reaper wouldn't hear.

"Well, what about Doo Dirty and Keeno?" The Reaper proceeded his interrogation, still looking at Murda Mont. "You seen or heard from 'em since we left the pier?"

"Yeah, I heard from 'em," Murda Mont said as he broke his staring match with Kia. "The lil' nigga, Keeno, got tagged in his shoulder. It wasn't nothing serious, just a flesh wound. I told Dirty to take him to the 'spital."

The Reaper nodded his head, then backed away and returned to the bar. He picked up his Hennessey bottle and drank straight from it. "Ummmm," he groaned when the brown liquor scorched his throat. He gulped down another swig, and then laid his shotgun on the bar counter.

Vrrrrm! Vrrrrrm! Vrrrrrm!

Damn, I hope this ain't Alvin calling me again, The Reaper thought to himself as his Samsung began to vibrate in his front pants pocket. *This nigga ain't blaming me for this shit. This shit is on Gangsta. He's the one who fucked up, so why the fuck should I have to explain shit? Fuck that.*

The Reaper pulled the phone from his pocket, then he exhaled a sigh of relief when he saw the caller was Smitty. He pressed down on *Accept.*

"Fuck is you calling me for?"

"I know you done seen the news, right?" Smitty got straight to the point.

"Yeah, I seen it. So, what?"

"So, what, is they ain't said ya name yet," Smitty quickly replied. "They ain't said it 'cause they can't. They still don't know who you are. But as soon as they get to young blood, it ain't no telling. If he gives up the tapes, we could all be locked up by the morning."

"So, what'chu saying?"

"What I'm saying is that we gotta kill him, we gotta get to him before they do."

"And how the fuck we 'posed to do that?"

"Easy. 221 2nd Street. Apartment A."

"And that's somewhere in the Bad Lands?"

"Not at all, that's over the bridge in Camden. It's the address to the apartment I cosigned for him. He's got a few other spots that I don't know about, but that's the main one. Just lay on him for a few hours. I'm sure he'll pop up."

"A'ight, now gimmie the address again," The Reaper said as he picked up a pen and grabbed a napkin from the shelf.

"That's 221—2nd Street—Apartment A."

"Say that." The Reaper nodded his head.

"And make sure you bring your crew along with you," Smitty stated for good measure. "The last time I seen him, he had a few shooters with him."

The Reaper disconnected the call, then gulped down another swig of Henny. Shaking away the burn, he returned the phone to his pocket, then he grabbed his shotty from the counter.

"Gawn and strap up," he told Kia. "You two muthafuckas wait here until we hear sum'n from Bushnut," he told Killah Kye and Murda Mont. "Come on, Keys, we out."

Kia stood up from the couch with her .45's in each hand. Looking at Murda Mont, she tapped the barrels together and winked at him. "YBM, baby."

***

Back at SCI Graterford

"Why the fuck ain't none these niggas answering the phone? I know they see me calling," Alvin blurted in frustration. For the past hour he'd been calling Gangsta and The Reaper nonstop, trying to figure out if they successfully kidnapped Annie and the kids. He was also pressed to know if his granddaughter remained safe in the process. He hated that his rash decision placed Keyonti in the cross-fire, but on such of a short notice, what other choice did he have? It was better that the YBM kidnap her rather than the Columbians, because either way Sonny had it coming from all different angles.

"These muthafuckas is playing games," Alvin fumed while checking the time on his phone. It was a quarter to three, and the feeling in his gut that something had gone wrong was growing stronger by the minute. In addition to calling Gangsta and The Reaper, he also placed a few calls to Lorenzo. Unfortunately, each one of his calls went straight to voicemail. The stress inside of him, coupled with his thirst for revenge, had him heated to no avail; even to the point he was thinking about placing a hit on his own brother.

"Throw on some hot water to make us some coffee," Alvin said to Bruno, while placing another call to The Reaper.

He was expecting Bruno to hop down and get right to it, but instead Bruno remained silent, completely ignoring him while texting on his cell phone.

"Damn, nigga, what'cha ass went deaf?" Alvin looked up on the top bunk. "You ain't heard what the fuck I just said?"

"Nah, A, I ain't even hear you. I was up here fuckin' wit' this phone."

"I said throw on some hot water to make us some coffee. It's late as hell, and I'm starting to feel tired. I need sum'n to keep me up. These niggas got my blood pressure building."

"Say no more, I got'chu," Bruno said as he went back to texting. "Just gimmie a second, so I clap back at this last message."

"Nigga, fuck ya message!" Alvin snapped at him, irritated and dying to put his hands on something. He hopped up from the bottom bunk and looked at Bruno like he wanted to smash him. "Go 'head and make me show you how these muthafuckin' hands work. Go 'head, nigga, do it. Fuck around and get'cha big ass tossed up in this muthafucka."

"A'ight, fam, you ain't gotta be getting all crazy. I told you, I got'chu," Bruno cowered like a bitch.

"I ain't try'na hear that shit, nigga. Get'cha ass up and do what the fuck I told you."

Bruno climbed down from the top bunk, and Alvin sat back down.

"And make my shit strong," Alvin said, referring to the way he liked his coffee. "John Wayne—no cream, no sugar."

This nigga in his feelings right now, Bruno thought to himself, knowing that Alvin was stressed out to the max. So instead of saying anything that would further provoke him, he let slide the crazy shit that Alvin was kicking to him. And even if he did want to do something, he knew better not to. Fucking with Alvin was like killing your own family and then blowing your own brains out. It was better to roll with the punches and move when the boss said move.

So, that's exactly what Bruno did. He grabbed an empty coffee bag from the sink and filled it up with water. He then placed the bag in the plastic washtub they used as a stinger bucket. The water inside of the washtub was halfway filled to the top, and sticking out of the water was a makeshift stinger. Bruno plugged in the stinger, then he hopped back on his bunk and went right back to texting.

On the bottom bunk, Alvin was stretched out and massaging his temples. He knew there had to be a reason why Gangsta and The Reaper were ducking his calls, and that whatever the reason, it had to be bad. He just hoped it wasn't something they couldn't bounce back from, like fucking up Juan's shipment or doing something to hurt his granddaughter.

"Fuck was I thinking?" Alvin perked up with a new idea. "I shoulda been did that."

"You shoulda been did what?" Bruno asked, still texting on his cell phone.

"Ain't shit, I'm just thinking out loud," Alvin dismissed him, seeing no need to tell Bruno what he was thinking. He picked up his cell phone and saw he had an unread message. Ironically, the message was sent by the very same person he was just about to contact. He read the message, and shook his head slow.

"CNN?" He scrunched his face. "How stupid can this nigga be?"

"It's that shit from the yacht party, ain't it?" Bruno asked him, even though he already knew the answer. "Yeah, man. It's fucking Rayon. They got his dumb-ass nigga on CNN," Alvin hissed back. "Yo, turn the news on."

Bruno did what Alvin told him, and the first thing they saw was Heemy and The Reaper's mugshot. A few seconds later, the CNN telecast switched back to the video footage from the party.

Zap!

The video stopped playing and the screen went black.

"Fuck you turn the TV off for?" Alvin snapped at Bruno.

"I ain't turned off shit. That muthafucka turned off on its own."

"Well, turn it back on."

"It *is* on. For some reason the channel went out."

"Well, turn it to another channel and see if the shit still working."

Bruno turned to VH-1, and Love & Hip Hop appeared on the screen.

"Now, turn back to CNN."

Bruno returned to CNN, but the screen was still black.

"Yo, what the fuck is going on? How the fuckin' channel ain't working?"

"I 'on't know." Bruno shrugged his shoulders. "And look at this." He lowered his cell phone for Alvin to see. "I was just watching the video that Juan posted on Facebook, but now they got it blacked out, too. It's almost like somebody's try'na hide what happened."

Alvin looked at Bruno's phone and then pushed it away from his face. The situation was worse than he thought. The only person powerful enough to shut down the news was the last muthafucka he needed in his business. For that reason, he knew he needed to start cleaning house. Trembling with rage, he thumbed in a reply message to his secret hitter.

Chapter Seventeen

Keeno was a nervous wreck, and for good reason. After checking out of the hospital too soon for the doctor's comfort, he would have sworn the biggest threat to his life was Heemy. But now that he was riding back to Philly on the passenger's side of Doo Dirty's Infinity, he wasn't sure who and what would kill him first: a hot slug fired at him by Heemy, or Doo Dirty's high ass, who was speeding across the Ben Franklin bridge, swerving from one lane to the other and sideswiping the railing.

Wacka! Pop!

Scurrrrrrr!

Vrrrrrm!

"Agh, shit! Yo, Dirt, man? What the fuck?" Keeno shouted in pain when his shoulder mashed against the door panel. He looked down at his blood-stained bandage, and then cut his eyes at Doo Dirty. He didn't know it, but the *Nut Shit* that Doo Dirty been snorting had him higher than Lebron James slam dunking on Jupiter. He was barely conscious, leaned back in the driver's seat, and whipping the coupe with one hand. The last time he said a word was back at the hospital when Keeno asked if he could drive them back to Philly.

"Nigga, you better hop ya ass in on the passenger's side. Sit back and shut the fuck up," Doo Dirty slurred, rubbing his nose when he said it. Since then, he'd been slobbering out the side of his mouth, nodding in and out, and shaking his head with his nose running.

"Damn, nigga, what the fuck you was doing, drinking syrup?"

"Huhn?" Doo Dirty sluggishly replied, looking back at Keeno and wiping the snot from his nose. His droopy, low eyes and sluggish speech had him looking and sounding like Snuffaluffagus from Sesame Street. "Nah, fam, I'm straight."

No sooner than Doo Dirty said it, he nodded back out with his driver's foot mashing down on the gas pedal.

"Hey, yo, Dirt. *Dirt!*" Keeno shouted as he leaned over to grab the steering wheel.

Skirt!

Vrrrrrm!

"Huhn? What happened?" Doo Dirty sprang back to attention, blinking his eyes. He was looking back and forth between Keeno and the two empty lanes up ahead. "Fuck is you doing? Stop touching shit."

"Nigga, wake ya ass up," Keeno snapped at him, steering the coupe back in its own lane.

"Stupid mah'fucka." Doo Dirty slurred, smacking Keeno's hand out of the way. He slurped in the snot string that was dangling from his top lip, and then shook away the dizziness he felt from the dope. "Niggas always wanna be touching shit. *Dickhead.* You ain't gon' do nothing but make us crash."

"*This nigga?*" Keeno mumbled under his breath. "Yo, how the fuck I roll these windows down? It smells like gorilla ass up in this muthafucka." He pressed the button on his door panel, but it didn't work. Doo Dirty had the windows locked.

"Fa'real, dawg, roll the windows down. It stinks in here. I hardly can't even breathe."

Doo Dirty snorted and wiped his nose. He was gripping the steering wheel with both hands and fighting like hell to keep his eyes open.

"The windows, nigga. The windows."

Doo Dirty ignored him.

"Man, fuck this shit." Keeno was fed up. He reached across Doo Dirty to roll the windows down from the driver's door panel, but Doo Dirty pushed him away.

"Nigga, chill." Doo Dirty snorted and rubbed his nose. "I told you: *stop touching shit.*"

"Fuck outta here, nigga. Ya high ass keep nodding off to sleep, 'bout to drive us off the fucking bridge. I told ya stupid-ass to let me drive, and now you done scraped up the side of ya shit. And stop driving so goddamned fast!" Keeno snapped at him. "We coming to the end of the bridge."

"Mah'fucka, I got eyes. I can see."

"Well see that you slow this muthafuckin' car down and stop driving all crazy. You know the boys be in them toll booths, try'na get niggas for DUIs. It's bad enough you looking all high and ugly. They see us speeding and swerving, they gon' fuck around and pull us over. You know we riding dirty."

Hearing Keeno mentioning the cops, forced Doo Dirty to let up from the gas pedal. After slowing the ride, he turned the radio volume to twelve, and then lowered the A/C to 59°. A mechanical sound chimed from the center console.

Zzzzzzzz. Click!

"Yo, Keeno, where ya toolie at?"

"It's under my seat where I stashed it at. Why?"

"Toss that mah'fucka in the box."

"The box? What box? You mean the glove box?"

"Nah, nigga, the stash box under the console." Doo Dirty snorted. "That's where I be stashing all my shit. Double R and Bushnut made us all get boxes when we copped our new whips. It's already open, so just lift up the console and throw ya toolie inside. And hurry the fuck up, we almost at the booth."

"A'ight, nigga, stop rushing me," Keeno snapped back. He leaned forward and reached back with his left hand, wincing when a sharp pain shot up his right arm. After palming the Glock's handle, he pulled it out slowly and leaned back up.

"And grab that sandwich bag of *Nut Shit* I left inside the console," Doo Dirty said as he lowered the windows to let in some fresh air. "Just throw it in the box wit'cha toolie."

Keeno flipped the lid on the center console, then he reached inside and pulled out the sandwich bag that Doo Dirty was talking about. Right away, he noticed something strange. Scattered around the rubber banded bundles of *Nut Shit* were a handful of empty wax bags. Each bag was dusty white from the powdered dope that was once inside. Keeno removed two of the bags and then held them up for Doo Dirty to see.

"Nigga, cut it the fuck out. This the reason ya ass keep nodding out, snorting and sniffing and shit? *You was in here snorting dope?*"

"Huhn? What?" Doo Dirty was caught by surprise, looking at the two empty bags in Keeno's hand. "Nigga, mind ya fucking business. Matter of fact, gimmie my shit." He snatched the sandwich bag from Keeno's lap, and then tossed it down in the stash box.

"You outta pocket, dawg. Straight up." Keeno shook his head.

"Mah'fucka, I said gimmie my shit." Doo Dirty snatched the two empty bags from Keeno's hand. "And better not go running ya fuckin' mouth. I hear one word of this shit, and I'ma kill ya ass my damn self. Now, gawn and try me."

"Yeah, whatever," Keeno said as he lowered his Glock .40 down inside of the stash box. Leaning back in his seat, he fired up a Newport and sat quietly as they rolled up to the toll booth.

***

Fifteen Minutes Later

"Pussy muthafuckas shoulda killed me when they had me. Now, they gotta deal wit' me," Heemy mumbled under his breath, exhaling a thick cloud of Loud smoke. He was leaned back in the driver's seat of his F-250. Gizzle sat quietly on the passenger's side. They were parked at the bottom of Marshal Street, about two houses up the block from Norris Street. Snot Box and D-Day were parked at the top of block, closer to Diamond Street. Keeno's row house was placed in the middle, six houses down from the corner on the right-hand side. All of the lights were turned off except for the porch light beside the front door.

"I'm saying, though, Ike, why we can't just run up in that muthafucka?" Gizzle suggested, so anxious that he couldn't stop his leg from bouncing. "This nigga prob'ly laying in his bed, curled up like a newborn baby. I'm try'na put him to sleep fa'real, Ike. Nephs."

"Naw, Gizz, that nigga ain't in there," Heemy slowly replied, looking at Keeno's bedroom window. It was the first window on the second floor. "The only one home is his grandpop, Mr. Carl. That's his car right there." Heemy pointed at the light blue Corsica that was parked across the street, a few yards down from the flickering street light.

162

"Well, let's send his ass a message, then," Gizzle stated with a thugged out passion. "Who better than his grandpops? I'm down to smoke whatever, Ike. I just don't give a fuck."

Disregarding Gizzle's last statement, Heemy sucked in another drag from his Dutch and inhaled deeply. As the Loud smoke marinated his lungs, he licked his lips and continued watching Keeno's window. The fact that it was still dark supported Heemy's assumption that Keeno wasn't there. Because if he was, then his bedroom window would have been illuminated by the blue ray from his television. What Heemy knew, and what Gizzle didn't, is that Keeno's second hustle, aside from case working on Delhi Street, was selling Tree on the late night from his bedroom window. To alert his customers that he was home and open for business, he would leave the television on. His customers, seeing the blue hue from the television, would alert him by tossing little pebbles at the window. The window would crack open wide enough for Keeno to send down a little Teddy Bear that was tied to a string. His customers would stuff their money inside the slit that was ripped into the Teddy Bear's back, and then Keeno would pull the Teddy Bear back inside the window. After replacing the money with the amount of Tree paid for, he would lower the Teddy Bear back out the window. He'd been doing the shit for years.

I swear to God, I'ma park these niggas, Heemy thought to himself, slowly exhaling the smoke from his nose. He placed the Dutch between his lips, and then cracked his knuckles one at a time. *Every last one of these niggas gotta die. All of 'em. And I ain't stopping 'til they do.* He wasn't only referring to Keeno, but the dark-skinned nigga with the shotgun, who he now knew was Rayon the Reaper. He never had any personal dealings with The Reaper, but the streets talk. He knew The Reaper was about his business, but so was he. May the hardest nigga win.

"Huhn." Heemy hit Dutch super hard, then he passed it to Gizzle. He was just about to step out the truck to take a piss when a pair of headlights turned the corner. He looked down at the burgundy coupe and saw Keeno sitting on the passenger's side. "Yo, that's the nigga right there," Heemy said as he leaned back in the driver's seat, hoping Keeno didn't see him. "Damn, I'm slippin'! I forgot I was riding in this fuckin' truck."

"You think he noticed?" Gizzle asked. His right hand was clutching the door handle, his left hand was flexing into the rubber grooves on his Trè Pound semi.

"I don't know. I don't think so," Heemy replied, still looking at the burgundy Infinity. "Call Snot Box and tell him that's him. Tell him I said to follow the car if it pulls off. If he sees the windows roll down, just start flaming."

"Say that," Gizzle replied while nodding his head. He released his hold on the door handle, then pulled out his iPhone and called Snot Box.

"Bark at me," Snot Box's voice came through the phone. "That's him?"

"Yeah, that's him," Gizzle confirmed. "He might'a seen us, though. If the car pulls off, Heemy said to follow it. If the windows roll down, start blasting."

"Pueblo the fuck up," Snot Box replied, looking at D-Day when he said it. "Get ready, Blawd. Heemy said that's him. We 'bout to have us a real live gangsta party out this muthafucka."

"More or less." D-Day stated with a heartless notion, at the same time snatching back the lever on his AK-47. *Click! Clack!* "Let's get it poppin'."

Seeing the burgundy coupe roll to a stop, Heemy popped open the driver's side door and slipped out slow. He motioned for Gizzle to do the same. Crouched down low, he tiptoed around the front of his truck and slowly made his way toward the Infinity's passenger's side door. Gizzle crisscrossed behind him, slowly making his way toward the driver's side. The infrared beam on his Trè Pound led the way.

***

"Not here, it's two houses up," Keeno directed from the passenger's seat. He pointed out his house and then reached down inside of the stash box, so worried about retrieving his Glock that he failed to notice Heemy's truck when they spun the corner and drove right past it. His egregious oversight would prove to be fatal.

"Don't forget about what I said," Doo Dirty reminded as he slowly eased the coupe to a stop. He pressed down on the brake pedal and shot Keeno a threatening look. "One word about me getting high, and that's a mah'fuckin' wrap. You think what I did to ya bitch-ass homies was sum'n, that ain't shit compared to what I'ma do to you. Believe that."

"Nigga, what I look like telling ya business? I ain't no muthafuckin' rat," Keeno fired back with a screwed-up face. "Hold up! Yo, what the fuck?" His eyeballs damn near popped out of his head when he saw Gizzle's infrared beam streaking inside of the car. "Yo, Dirty, pull off!" he shouted at the top of his lungs when the Trè Pound barrel appeared in plain view, its infrared beam surfing over Doo Dirty's waves, illuminating the back of his head like a glowing red halo.

"*Nigga, pull the fuck off!*" Keeno shouted even louder, struggling to get a firm squeeze on his Glock's rubber-grip handle.

"What? What is it?" Doo Dirty said, as he spun around to see what Keeno was looking at. He never got the chance. Gizzle's Trè Pound was already flaming.

Boom! Boom! Boom! Boom!

The left side of Doo Dirty's forehead collapsed, as he spun around in the front seat twisted. His final thoughts were splattered on the windshield and dash.

"Oh, shit! Oh, shit! Oh, shit!" Keeno panicked, still struggling to get a hold on his Glock .40. He palmed the handle and pushed his finger through the trigger-guard.

Boc! Boc! Boc! Boc! Boc! Boc!

He was aiming to hit Gizzle, but Doo Dirty's head was in the way. Each bullet ripped through Doo Dirty's cheeks and nose, blowing what was left of his brains out the driver's side window. A gush of blood sprang from his mouth and splashed Keeno in the face.

"Aaagghhhrrrr!" Keeno freaked out, frantically wiping the red slime from his eyes.

Boom! Boom! Boom! Boom! Boom!

Gizzle's Trè Pound roared back to life, blazing up Keeno's left thigh and groin.

Screaming in pain, Keeno dropped his .40 and wiggled down in between the dashboard and seat.

"Pussy, get'cha ass up!" Heemy snatched him out of the car through the window. "Didn't I tell you I was coming?" Heemy rambled off fast, speaking with his teeth clenched. "Didn't I tell you? Didn't I fuckin' tell you?"

"Yo, chill, Heemy, please?"

"*Chill?*" Heemy looked at him like he was crazy. "Pussy, *shut* the fuck up!"

Whop!

Heemy tagged him on the chin with a short right hook. Keeno rocked back against the car and then leaned forward, slouching into Heemy's arms.

Whop! Whop!

A vicious two-piece dropped him to the pavement face first.

"Oww!" Keeno cried out, fearing for his life. He rolled over and attempted to crawl away, but a bullet from Heemy's whistle dug into his ass crack.

Boca!

Two more shattered his shin bone through his calf muscle.

Boca! Boca!

"Aaagggggghhhhhh! *Shit!*" Keeno screamed so loudly, the devil probably heard him. He was rolling around in pain, moaning and groaning, bitching and crying. "Come on, Heemy, man, please?" He rolled over to look up at Heemy, who was towered over him. "Don't kill me, dawg, please?" he whispered in a terse, dry voice. "Heemy, please?"

"Yo, move out the way, Scrap," D-Day said to Heemy as he ran up with his chopper. He jammed the chopper lips between Keeno's, but Heemy waved him off.

"Naw, that's too easy." Heemy shook his head *no*. "Pick his ass up and throw him in the trunk. We taking him to The Swamp."

"*The Swamp?*" Keeno popped up with a new sense of urgency. "No. No. Fuck no! *Heemy, please?*"

Looking around for something to hold onto, Keeno settled on the chrome spokes in Doo Dirty's rim tire. He curled his hand around one of the spokes and held on for dear life. He'd never been to The Swamp, but had heard enough horror stories to know that if taken there, he would never be seen or heard from again.

"Hey? What the hell is going on out here?" Keeno's grandfather, Mr. Carl, called out from his doorway. He was awakened by the gunfire, but had no idea his grandson was the victim. "Wait a second." He stepped outside on his stoop. "Raheem?" The old man squinted his eyes, almost certain the man standing beside the car with a gun in his hand was Heemy. "Raheem, is that you?"

Hearing his grandfather's voice, Keeno looked back over his shoulder. "Granddaddy, run! Go in the house and call the cops!"

"*Keeno?*" The old man grabbed his heart and stumbled back into the screen door. "Raheem, what'chu doing, boy? Yalls is friends."

"Aye, yo, Pop-Pop?" Snot Box said, as he ran up to the front door. A red bandana disguised his face, and his chromed-out Dezzy was aimed at the old man's chest.

Mr. Carl dropped to his knees with his palms together, praying. "Father God, in the name of—"

Doom! Doom! Doom! Doom!

"*Noooooooooo!*" Keeno shrieked when the shots rang out, knowing that his grandfather was already dead. He rested his face against the pavement and blacked out slowly. The loss of blood from his gunshot wounds had finally taken their toll.

Heemy shook his head at Keeno, then he glanced up and down the block. The houses that were once pitch black were now lit up with their lights on. The silhouettes of the people who lived inside were standing at the windows.

"*Nosey muthafuckas,*" Heemy mumbled under his breath. He wiped the sweat from his brow with the same hand clutching his Glock, then he aimed the Glock at Keeno's left hand. It was still holding onto the rim spoke in Doo Dirty's tire.

Boca!

The dark part of Keeno's left hand exploded like a hotdog left inside of a microwave for too long.

"Pick his ass up and throw him in the trunk," Heemy said to D-Day.

"For what?" D-Day replied, nudging Keeno with the tip of his shoe. "The nigga's already dead."

"His ass ain't dead, he's just passed out. Throw his stupid ass in the trunk. We taking him to The Swamp."

As D-Day and Gizzle reached down to pick up Keeno, Snot Box pushed them out of his way, then he aimed his Desert Eagle at the back of Keeno's head.

Doom! Doom! Doom!

"Fuck you did that for?" Heemy asked Snot Box, while looking down at Keeno's blown out wig. "I told them niggas to throw his ass in the fucking trunk."

"Niggas ain't got time for none of that shit, Blawd," Snot Box replied as he wiped Keeno's blood from his pistol. "Niggas still got business to handle, and it's bad enough we hotter than a mutha-fucka. Ain't no room for none of ya personal shit."

Heemy gritted his teeth and nodded his head slowly. He'd hated to admit it, but Snot Box was right. So instead of arguing, he fired another round into Keeno, and then headed back to his truck. He didn't even care if the sirens he heard blaring in the distance pulled up before they left. He already had his mind set on holding court in the streets.

Blood of a Boss 5

Chapter Eighteen
At the CIA Building in Washington D.C.

The CIA's Assistant Director, Wilford Gleason, was seated behind his desk, leaned forward with his fingers locked together. For the past thirty years, he'd been living a secret life, showing multiple faces to the people who knew him. His late father, Michael Gleason, was once the same way. But now that Michael was dead, Wilford, the oldest of his ten children, was the only one remotely slick enough to fill his shoes. His youngest son, William, who was now the Pennsylvania Attorney General, could have easily been his second choice, but Wilford was the *one*. Aside bearing a striking resemblance to his late father, he'd been groomed by Michael since the age of nineteen to replace him as the hidden figure behind The Conglomerate. It was he who decided where and what went down, secretly pulling the strings to the world's most prolific, unequivocally matched, secret society of gangsters. Not even its members knew his true identity. To them, without ever seeing his face or hearing his voice, he was only known as *Mr. Shadow*.

The legend of Mr. Shadow spanned back to the 1940's, during the country's second world war. But it's roots could be traced back to the prohibition era of the1920's. Wilford's grandfather, Sir Melvin Gleason, situated in a small Michigan town that bordered the Mississippi River, ran a bootlegging operation that smuggled whisky from The Great Lakes all the way down to the Delta. Equipped with his English wit, his peculiar knack for doing business, and his criminal ties from Chicago to New York City, by the 1930's, not even a full decade later, Melvin was worth nearly a billion dollars. But having money wasn't enough for Melvin, he wanted more; his overgrown ego was thirsty for power. His opportunity came knocking in the spring of '42, when his old friend and one-time business partner, Mr. Charles *Lucky* Luciano, the Boss of all Bosses, reached out to him from a New York prison.

Lucky, who was then serving a fifty-year sentence for tax evasion and pandering, was desperately looking for a way out. He figured that Melvin was the best way to do it. Melvin's oldest son,

Michael, had just been appointed as the CIA's Assistant Director, and Lucky, knowing that the country's biggest fear was a sabotage on the New York waterfront, was hoping he could sway Melvin into convincing Michael to give him a deal. *"The only way the Germans can hurt us is through the docks,"* Lucky told Melvin, after convincing his old friend to pay him a visit. *"The unions control the docks, and me and my friends control the unions. It'll be nothing for us to keep the docks secured. Anything coming or going will be checked and approved by us. But in exchange, Melvin, I need you talk to Mikey. Tell him I need help,"* Lucky said with a smile. *"For old times' sake."*

The proposition was brought to Michael, and out of respect for his father, and Lucky, who if it weren't for him, his family would have starved during The Great Depression, agreed to the terms.

"But only on a few conditions," Melvin told Lucky when he returned to the prison. *"When the war's over, you've gotta go back to Italy. It'll only be for a few years, or until Michael can smooth things over for you to come back. In the meantime, while you're back in the old country, we're gonna need you to reclaim and take-over the heroin network that's currently being decimated by the Fascist. We'll assist you with whatever you need, and in return we're gonna need three things: the muscle of the mafia back here in the States, twenty percent of the joint in Las Vegas that Bugsy's been running for you and Meyer, and twenty percent of all proceeds from the heroin trade; not yet, but as soon as you get back up and running. There's also another thing, and this is most important,"* Melvin said as he got up to leave, *"Michael's the point man. He'll be guiding you from the shadows, with a life-blood commitment, by you, that his identity will never be revealed to whomever you choose to do business with. From here on out, you'll refer to him only as Mr. Shadow. Those are the terms."*

Lucky agreed, and the rest was history. Michael's identity remained anonymous for the next forty-four years, and the criminal network that Lucky pieced together, up until this very day, knew him only as *Mr. Shadow*. The only difference between then and now, was that Wilford, after being thoroughly groomed by his father, had replaced Michael as The Conglomerate's point man. It was now up to him to assure that his family remained in power. But in order to do so, he needed an inside man. He figured that because his father had Lucky, and then later down the line Big Angolo, he too would need someone on the inside to watch his back and protect his interest. The man he chose was Mumar Khalifi, the Iraqi rebellion leader who he insisted held a seat at The Conglomerate's roundtable.

After professing a blood-life oath to conceal Wilford's identity, Mumar had proven his worth many times over. Most recently, when he convinced Grip that he'd taken his side over Big Angolo's. For the past year or so he'd been playing Grip so close that he recently learned about the Title III wiretaps that were placed on Big Angolo's cell phone. The information was passed along to Wilford, and Wilford, using his CIA connections, intercepted the wiretap transcripts.

The Title III transcripts were nothing short of a goldmine. Not only was Wilford made aware of Big Angolo's secret plot to murder Grip and then hand his legacy over to Sonny, he was further made aware of Big Angolo's connection to Gangsta, which ultimately led to an additional wiretap being placed on Gangsta's cell phone. The information contained therein revealed Gangsta's connection to Joaquin and Juan, and further exposed the formulated plot between them to kill Sonny and Grip, and then take over the Roundtable with Gangsta seated as the new head chair.

Unfortunately, what Grip, Gangsta, and the remaining bosses from the Roundtable failed to realize was that Big Angolo, like Lucky Luciano before him, was only a figurehead. The Conglomerate's head chair was only a façade, a powerless position similar to the U.S. Presidency. The true power belonged to the Gleason Family, and Wilford was determined to keep it that way. But in order to do so, he needed keep things quiet. The Penn's Landing massacre, followed by the CNN segment where Detective Phoenix mentioned The Conglomerate by name, was too close to home. It was time for Wilford to take action. So, after pulling the plug on the CNN news segment, he shut down the internet long enough to remove any traces of the yacht party video, and then summoned Mumar to his office.

Still seated behind his desk, leaned forward, with his fingers locked together, Wilford was staring the brown skinned Iraqi dead in his eyes. Mumar, seated on the opposite side of his desk, stared back at him. From the look on his face, he appeared to have no fear. But on the inside, his thumping heart was yearning for Allah's mercy, praying that he wasn't held responsible for the way things had spun out of control in the past few hours. He'd been given the task of calming the beef between Grip and the bosses who opposed him. But after learning that Diablo was back in the States, and that Juan was responsible for the helicopter that shot up Nahfisah's yacht party, he knew the unwanted attention would ultimately fall back on him.

"Come on now, Mumar, relax." Wilford smiled at him, graciously enjoying the smell of fear that was oozing from Mumar's pores. "In fact," Wilford flipped the lid on his cigar box, then spun box around to face Mumar, "take one of these. It'll calm you down and take away the edge. I need you focused, Mumar. *Focused*. You seem a little tense right about now. Go on and take one." He gestured for Mumar to choose a cigar, then selected one for himself. "I know you're a hookah man, but I promise you," Wilford flashed him a smile, "these are the finest hand-rolled cigars between here and Havana. You ought'a be accustomed to Cuba by now. I mean, after all, you've been spending enough time over there with Gervin to know a good stogie when you see one. Am I right, or am I right?"

"Nahm." Mumar nodded his head *yes*, taking in a deep breath. He was twirling the cigar between his thumb and index finger, and looking at it as though it were a spiritual bomb, one that would explode in his face the second he placed it to his lips. His dedication to Allah was something that he'd taken to heart, knowing that in order to be granted success in this life and the next, his mind, body, and intentions needed to be pure.

Successful are the believers, Mumar thought to himself, reflecting back on a hadith he learned as a child. He licked his lips and slowly wiped the sweat from his furrowed brow.

"Here," Wilford said as he leaned across the desk with his flamer on high, "let me light that for you."

Reluctantly, Mumar placed the cigar between his lips, then he leaned in closer to catch the flame. A cloud of smoke appeared in front of his face, as his lungs rejected the burn. He coughed twice, then at Wilford's gesture, sucked in another pull from the stogie. Coughing even more, he followed Wilford across the room with his eyes. Wilford opened the window at the front of his office and inhaled the fresh air. Looking out the window at the D.C. skyline, he sat his cigar on the window's ledge, and then stuffed his hands inside of his pockets. A sinister smile spread across his bony face when Mumar began coughing uncontrollably.

"Water Hemlock," Wilford blurted as he turned back around to face Mumar, who was now down on his knees, still coughing and clutching his throat with both hands. "Such a beautiful plant, is that Water Hemlock. Lilly white flowers that grow in umbrella like clusters. The tiny little notches in its leaves that stop just short of the tip. Ironically, it's just as deadly as it beautiful. In fact, it just so happens to be the deadliest and toxic plant in all of North America."

"What—did you—do to me?" Mumar stammered between gasp. His brown skinned face had a yellowish tint, his tomato, red eyeballs were popping out of his face like the peepers on a lemur and on both sides of his face, from his neck to his ears, his gooey looking veins were bulging out of his skin like a colony of earth worms slithering to the surface at the slightest hint of a rainstorm. "I can't—breathe!"

"Well, that's what it does, Mumar," Wilford antagonized, stomping out the cherry on Mumar's cigar. "The thick rootstalk of a Water Hemlock contains a number of small chambers. Each chamber containing a brown liquid so poisonous that a single drop can kill an elephant in as early as fifteen minutes. But in your case, Mumar, it shouldn't take that long. The two tablespoons sprayed over the tobacco you just finished smoking, should do the trick in about five—four—three—two—one."

"Subhanna—llah!" Mumar gasped, then coughed up a thick glob of white phlegm. His limbs began to shake, and the smell of his released bowels filled the room. Wilford covered his nose and continued taunting him with the deadly symptoms caused by the plant.

"Excessive salivation and frothing from the mouth. Muscles twitching. Dilation of pupils. Ugh." Wilford shuddered from the sight of Mumar's poppy eyeballs, which by then had turned into burgundy globs with purplish slime oozing out. "Rapid pulse breathing. Tremors. Violent convulsions. Yep." He nodded his head, as Mumar's entire body began to wiggle and shake. "Grand mal seizures. Skeletal and cardiac myofiber degeneration and necrosis. Coma. And then finally—"

"*Augh*!" Mumar heaved and then froze in place with his phlegm coated mouth locked wide open.

"—death," Wilford finished his sentence. "You know I liked you, Mumar, I really did." Wilford said as he squatted down beside Mumar's head. "Just as trustworthy as grandpappy's old hound dog. But unfortunately, your services are no longer required. It's bad enough I allowed you to see my face, and even if I didn't, with all of this inner bickering amongst the Roundtable, it was only a matter of time before I cleaned house. I gotta keep 'em guessing, Mumar. Wouldn't you agree?"

"*Umm-hmm*," he imitated Mumar's reply while placing his hand under Mumar's chin and nodding his head *yes*.

"Why, sure it is, Mumar. See, now, I knew you'd agree with me. My brother, William, doesn't think so, but we're gonna prove him wrong, aren't we?" He again nodded Mumar's head *yes*.

"That Moreno kid? Sontino? He's exactly what the doctor ordered. Young. Ambitious. Fearless. Who better than to rectify things, huh, Mumar? Aww, come on now, Mumar, don't look at me that way. *Fix your face*", he raised his voice and then lowered his tone, "you're making me upset. No? Well, fuck you, then, you fucking, sand nigger. Goddamned desert monkey."

Wilford stood erect, then reached back with his right hand and removed his handkerchief from his back pocket. Wiping the phlegm and slime from his hands, he returned to his desk and plopped down in his high-back, soft leather chair.

174

"Everybody's got a plan. They all got a fucking plan," Wilford mumbled under his breath, chuckling at the thought. "That is, until I punch 'em in the mouth," he stated like a schmuck. "Alexa, call William."

"Calling William," the programmed Alexa chimed back.

The speaker on Wilford's landline began to ring.

"Yeah, Wilford. I'm here," William's voice came through the speaker a few seconds later.

"I need you to get Gervin on the phone. You tell him that Mr. Shadow has reviewed everything relevant pertaining to his next appointment as the Boss of all Bosses, and that his ultimate decision is to support him and Sontino. You also tell him that Sontino's going to be released from custody first thing in the morning, and that the both of them are expected to attend the board meeting with The Conglomerate on Monday at midnight, sharp. During that time, Mr. Shadow will announce his appointment of Sontino as the next head chair."

"And that's it?" William asked him. "What about the members of The Roundtable responsible for breaking the peace treaty?"

"Any and all responsible will unequivocally be held accountable. For now, I just need you to reel in Gervin. You already know what to tell him."

Click!

After disconnecting the call, Wilford lounged back in his chair. Looking down at Mumar, who's head and shoulders were sticking out from underneath his desk, he shook his head and scrunched his nose.

"For Christ sakes, Mumar. You fucking stink."

Chapter Nineteen
At the Private Airport in Teterboro, New Jersey

The Madam sat quietly in the back seat of her Range Rover. She was looking out the window at the Sprinter Van to her left where Annie and the girls were seated inside. After locking eyes with Annie for a brief second, she closed the curtain and returned her visage to the flat screen that was built into the headrest she sat behind. For the past five minutes, she'd been talking to Alexis on *Skype*.

According to Alexis their mission was nearly complete, as her and the two giants were back at La Casa Moreno finishing what they'd started. Shabazz and Aziz, pursuant to Grip's orders, were piled in the back of her Navigator waiting to be dropped off at Mosque #12. Rahmello and Heldga were buried out back and Olivia's decapitated remains were stinking inside of a duffle bag. The duffle bag was placed in the back with Shabazz and Aziz. The next step was dropping the bag off on the courthouse's steps. Then after that, flying down to Miami until the morning of Sonny's trial when Alexis would fly back to Philly to support her man.

Hearing this, The Madam was pleased. The last phase in solidifying her alliance with Grip was taking out Olivia to keep her from testifying against Sonny. So now that Olivia was no longer a threat, Grip's master plan to take over The Roundtable and crown Sonny as the new king was more of a reality than a vision. And because Alexis, her only daughter, was carrying Sonny's unborn child, The Madam assumed that would make her status among The Conglomerate that much higher, possibly even higher than Grip's.

"Manman, I'm sorry," Alexis apologized for disobeying Grip. "Had I known everything that was going on, I wouldn't have done it. I was only trying to be there for Sontino, knowing he would have done the same for me."

Listening to her daughter speak, The Madam could sense the weariness in her voice. There was something bubbling under the surface that Alexis was hiding from her. Exactly what, The Madam didn't know. But what she *did* know was Alexis had never been successful in hiding her true feelings from her. Even on the rare occasions she tried, The Madam could always see right through it. She could see through it now.

"Pitit-fi, eske ou anfôm? Kisa ki pa bon?"

"Wi, Manman, I'm okay," Alexis slowly replied, the sound of her voice betraying her own words.

"Eske ou kwè sa?"

"Yes, Manman, I'm sure. There's nothing wrong. If it was, I would tell you."

Still suspicious, The Madam inquired about the baby. "Eske se titit?"

The question brought tears to Alexis' eyes. She desperately tried to keep from crying, but she couldn't help it. In a matter of seconds, she was balling her eyes out and telling her mother about the secret she'd been keeping. How three months ago her and Gangsta had a one-night stand, and how the baby she was carrying could possibly belong to him instead of Sonny.

"*Pitit-fi?*" The Madam spoke with compassion. "Konbien fwa?"

"I already told you," Alexis sobbed. "It only happened once."

"Ki dat doule?"

"It was back in May, the same night we flew out to Cuba."

"You mean the same night I introduced you to him?"

"Wi," Alexis confirmed. "And if you remember, after our meeting, me and Terrance flew back to Philly while you and Grip stayed in Cuba. Well, that's when it happened. We were smoking and drinking, and then one thing led to another. I never intended for it to happen, but it did. Then a few days later, me and Sontino got together for the first time since we reconnected. So, basically, I slept with both of them in the same week."

"Does Terrance know that you're pregnant?"

"No," Alexis replied meekly.

"And what about Sontino? Have you mentioned any of this to him?"

"No, he doesn't even know that I'm pregnant. He's already going through so much, that I didn't want to add any extra stress on him. I just told him that when he comes home, we need to sit down and talk. I'm going to explain everything to him, then?"

"Like hell you are," The Madam quickly retorted. "You're not going to tell him a goddamned thing. As far as we're concerned the two of you are together, and that's his child."

"But, *Manman*," Alexis whined.

"But, Manman, nothing. That child is our only leverage. I'm serious, Alexis. Don't you say shit, not a goddamned word. Eske ou tande?"

"Wi, Manman, I understand."

"Good. Now, y'all finishing handling what y'all need to handle. We'll speak more about this when I return to Miami."

The Madam disconnected the call, and for the first time noticed the Gmail envelope that was situated in the top left corner. She clicked open the envelope and saw it was a message addressed to The Roundtable from Mr. Shadow. The email read:

To: The Members of The Conglomerate
From: Mr. Shadow Date: July 5th, 2015
RE: Emergency Meeting (See Attachment)

The Madam clicked open the attachment and saw it was a video. She pressed down on the *Play* button and began watching.

The first thing that appeared on the screen was a bloated face with curly black hair and a bushy long beard. A smashed, blackened cigar was dangling from the left side of his mouth. Traces of pink, bloody phlegm was caked up along the length of his beard.

"What the hell is this?" The Madam squinted her eyes and leaned in forward, trying to make sense of what she was seeing.

The camera's scope was so closely zoomed in, the bloated face filled out the entire screen. Its poppy, bloodshot eyes were a dark purple. The running liquid spilling from the cracks reminded The Madam of two crushed grapes.

"Is that Mumar?" she blurted out loud, as the camera's scope began to retract. "That *is* Mumar," she stated with flare, looking at the screen with big, wide eyes.

Slowly but surely the scope broadened, giving The Madam a clear view of Mumar's decapitated head. It was placed in the center of an oakwood desk. Behind the desk, seated in his high-back chair with his face blurred out, was the infamous Mr. Shadow.

The Madam could feel her heartbeat increasing. In the fifteen years she'd spent as a member of The Roundtable, this was the closest she had ever come to seeing Mr. Shadow's face. Normally, whenever he had to send them a message, he would send it through Big Angolo. But never had Mr. Shadow, ever, not even once, sent them a message firsthand. Clearly, this was a sign that things were about to change.

"Members of the Roundtable," Mr. Shadow slowly began to speak, his distorted voice disguised so well it was impossible to identify the true sound. *"I regret to inform you that your leader and head chair, Big Angolo, is no longer among the living. Some of you, I know, are already aware of this, as your actions over the past twenty-four hours have demonstrated.*

According to Mumar, here, there's been rumblings between you for over a year now. All of which pertaining to who's going to be crowned as the next head chair in the wake of Big Angolo's death.

"And mind you," he grabbed a fistful of Mumar's hair and lifted his head up for the camera to see, *"this is all coming from him. Now, how true it is?"* He shrugged his shoulders, while still holding Mumar's head. *"I'm still pretty much undecided. But what I do know is that some of you have professed your loyalty to Big Angolo, while a few others have taken sides with Grip. At the same time, at least two of you, despite professing your loyalty to either side, have been harboring your own aspirations to take over as The Conglomerate's next boss. Who you are and who's side you're own, I won't go into detail. This is something we'll discuss at a later date. For now, though, what I will do is shed some light on the bullshit that happened earlier tonight in Philadelphia."*

He tossed Mumar's head in the trashcan beside his desk and then lounged back in his chair, slowly wiping the blood from his hands with the handkerchief he pulled from his top desk drawer.

"These rumblings between you have escalated to the point they are now detrimental to our organization's existence. The likes of which being so uncouth, that earlier this evening our organization

was mentioned by name on the CNN news. All of this despite being warned that anyone in violation of the peace treaty established by Big Angolo, would feel the wrath of everyone else seated at the Table. To those of you responsible, I'm here to inform you that your actions I deem indelible. You've made your move, so now it's time that I make mines.

"*The meeting tomorrow night between Grip and those of you who support him, have been canceled. This is nonnegotiable. Every last one of you, forty-eight hours from now, will be present at the Waldorf Astoria in New York City for our annual meeting. It's a little off schedule, but it's necessary. At this meeting, I'll be addressing two issues. The first issue is my selection of who's going to replace Big Angolo as the new Boss of all Bosses. The second issue will revolve around the peace treaty. Those of you responsible for breaking it, will be dealt with accordingly. Anyone who fails to attend, for any reason whatsoever, will automatically be sanctioned to* death."

The video stopped, and The Madam shook her head. She wasn't one of the members responsible for breaking the peace treaty, but Grip was. He didn't know it, but she was well aware of the secret he had stashed away back in Jardines De Le Reina. It was a secret that could potentially not only affect him, but her as well. At that point, she needed to make a decision. Either continue supporting Grip, or throw his shifty ass to the wolves.

***

"Dominic, pull over," Grip commanded as he turned off the video he'd just finished watching of Mr. Shadow. He fired up a stogie and rolled down his window, as Dominic pulled over on the side of the road. The two vehicles trailing behind did the same. The three-vehicle convoy was less than a mile away from the private airport, and even though Grip had his band of soldiers already stationed there, he knew he needed a few minutes to get his head together before speaking to The Madam.

What Grip knew, and what The Madam didn't, was that her Range Rover, the same as Alexis' Navigator, was kitted with a tracking device that Alejandro had planted a few days earlier. The data collected from the tracking device indicated that The Madam, prior to flying down to Cuba the day before, had driven out to SCI Graterford, presumably to pay a visit to Alvin. This information, coupled with the threatening undertone of Mr. Shadow's words, was more than enough for Grip to reconsider his entire strategy.

The partnership between Grip and The Madam was predicated on the fact she had already infiltrated Big Angolo's ranks. Consequently, she was given the task of reporting back to Grip any and all developments pertaining to Big Angolo's secret plot to have him annihilated. She was also given the task of keeping tabs on Gangsta. So now that Grip had been made aware of the secret allegiance between Gangsta and Alvin, and that The Madam had driven out to the prison to visit Alvin, he couldn't help but to wonder if The Madam was playing both sides. Not once did she mention her detour to the prison, nor did she reveal the full extent of Gangsta's plan. Had it not been for the tracking device and the secret camera stashed inside of Gangsta's Denali, Grip would have never known.

"*This stanking bitch,*" Grip mumbled under his breath, thinking of all the numerous ways The Madam had to be playing him. "*This whole shit about saving Annie and the kids, was all a goddamned ploy. This bitch is try'na rock me to sleep and then fatten me up for the slaughter. We'll see about that. She must'a forgot who the fuck she's dealing with. I'm Gervin Muthafuckin' Moreno.*"

Grip sucked in a slow, deep pull from his stogie, and then blew the smoke out into the cool night air. Satisfied that his thoughts were together, he ordered Dominic to continue driving towards the airport. He looked back at the bench seat behind him, where Nahfisah was still crying. Omelly was right beside her, strapped down in his car seat sound asleep. He patted Nahfisah on the knee, and then turned back around when his cell phone began to vibrate. He took the phone from his cup holder, then he looked at the screen. The caller was William Gleason.

"This is Gervin," Grip said when he accepted the call. He always assumed that William was Mr. Shadow, but this was something he chose to keep to himself.

"Good evening, Mr. Moreno," William's voice came through the phone. "I'm calling on behalf of Mr. Shadow. I've been instructed to inform you that after reviewing all information relevant, Mr. Shadow has decided to support you as the next head chair, with Sontino next in line to be groomed as your replacement."

"Oh, yeah?" Grip cracked a smile. "Sure shit. My petition was made on behalf of Sontino, but showing him the ropes until he's ready to takeover is fine by me. The kid's a natural, he's gonna do just fine."

"And speaking of Sontino," William stated calmly, "he's scheduled to be released first thing in the morning. You and Sontino will be formally appointed forty-eight hours from now, before the entire Roundtable. Your presence is required, so don't miss it. The Waldorf Astoria, Monday, midnight sharp."

Click!

"Hot damn!" Grip smacked his palms together, then quickly quieted down when Omelly began to stir in his sleep. "We did it. We fucking did it," he spoke in a low voice, placing his hands on Dominic and Alejandro's shoulders.

"Congratulations, Señor." Alejandro looked back and smiled.

"It's been a long time coming, Senor," Dominic chimed in. "Ju and Sontino deserve it."

Smiling from ear to ear, Grip sat back in his seat and then placed a call to Sonny.

Ring! Ring! Ring!

"Yo?" Sonny's voice came through the phone. "You at the airport wit' my mom and the kids?"

"We're actually just now pulling into the parking lot," Grip replied. "I'll get your mother on the phone as soon as we arrive at the hanger. And just so you know, you're outta there first thing in the morning. So, start packing your bags."

"And that's a fact?" Sonny shot back quickly.

"That's an *actual* fact," Grip replied with a chuckle. "And there's one more thing. We did it, Sonny. We fucking did it. We're the next ones up, you and me."

"Next ones up? The next ones up for what?" Sonny was confused.

"The next head chair, the Boss of all Bosses. They're making me the new number one, with you in the wing being groomed as my number two."

"So, I see you still stuck on this Conglomerate shit." Sonny was unimpressed. "I keep telling you ain't none of that on my radar. That's *ya thing*. Me, personally, I honestly don't give a fuck. The only thing I'm worried about is going at these YBM niggas. Then after that, reestablishing my team so my young bul, Heemy, can takeover. I'm done with the game, Grip. I'm out."

Grip shook his head.

"Well, I'll tell you what. How about we wait until tomorrow when you're finally out of there and we get'chu down to Cuba. Then once we do that, the two of us can sit down and talk."

"If you say so," Sonny slowly replied, already knowing that no matter what his grandfather said, his mind was set on leaving from the game. He'd been feeling that way for years now, and after everything that he'd just experienced with his mother and the kids, he knew it was the last straw. He couldn't afford to give the game everything in his life that it hadn't already taken. It was time to walk away.

"I'm gonna leave a few of my guys behind. They'll be waiting outside of the jail to pick you up when they release you."

"Nah, I'm good," Sonny declined. "That's not necessary, I can handle it myself. I still have a few loose ends that I need to tie up. Then as soon as I'm finished, I'ma fly down to pick up my mom and the kids."

"Well, just hold on a few seconds, we're pulling into the hanger. I'm gonna get your mother on the phone."

"More or less."

Grip sighed when he pulled the phone away from his ear. He was silently obsessing over the notion that Sonny would ruin his plans. His grandson didn't know it, but their new appointments at The Roundtable were nonnegotiable.

Askari

Chapter Twenty

Despite being saved by the beautiful brown-skinned woman who identified herself as Alexis' mother, it was still hard for Annie to discern whether or not her and the girls were safe. Her gut feeling was telling her they were being protected. But even then, in the back of her mind, she couldn't escape the thought they were being held hostage.

The Sprinter Van they were seated in was parked inside of a 5,000 square foot hanger. The two private jets that were previously inside had been rolled out to the clear port, where an army of ten soldiers were lined up and down the runaway. An additional army of fifteen were scattered throughout the hanger. Each soldier was standing at attention and had an M-16 clutched in both hands.

Looking out of the window at both groups, Annie could see they represented two separate armies. In addition to their different colors of camouflage, the squad leaders, on the rare occasions they spoke, commanded orders in two different languages.

The fifteen soldiers scattered throughout the hanger, the same as the two men seated up front, spoke Creole. But the ten soldiers standing outside spoke Spanish. There was also a notable difference in their skin complexions. The Spanish speaking soldiers were a tanned, light brown, while the Creole speaking soldiers were a shiny, crisp, black; a few of them even darker than the rapper Lil' Boosie. It was all quite confusing. Why would two separate armies be working together for one common cause, a cause in which Annie was still undecided?

Annie looked down at Keyonti, who had drifted off to sleep. The soft sounds of her cute, little bear cub snores reminded Annie of Sonny, who as a small child made the same exact sounds while he slept. Thinking about Sonny, Annie's eyes began to water.

"*Come on, Annie, you gotta stay focused,*" she mumbled under her breath, knowing she needed to be strong for the sake of her babies. "*Queen strength,*" she encouraged herself, wiping the tears from her eyes with her bloodstained sleeve. "*Queen strength, Annie. Queen strength.*"

After gaining control of her emotions, she ran her fingers through Keyonti's hair and then leaned over to kiss Imani's forehead. She then cut her eyes at the two Haitians seated up front. She sized them up from one man to the other, then settled back in her seat and continued looking out the window.

On both sides of the Sprinter Van, parked about ten feet away, were two tinted-out Range Rovers. The woman who identified herself as Alexis' mother was seated in the Range Rover to the right. The windows on the Range Rover to the left were rolled down, showing that the vehicle was empty. Another vehicle, a jet-black Chevy Suburban, was parked at the rear of the hanger, quietly situated against the far-left wall. The 5% tinted windows were too dark for Annie to see inside, but that didn't stop her from trying.

Who the hell is in there? Annie thought to herself, while staring at the two-armed guards who were posted at the rear and front bumpers. Like the ten soldiers standing outside, they appeared to be of Latin descent. Their camouflage was also the same color, which indicated to Annie they were members of the second army.

What the fuck is so special about that truck? If anything, shouldn't them muthafuckas be guarding us? I'm not feeling this shit. I'm not feeling this shit at all.

Still uncertain as to whether or not her and the girls were being protected or being held hostage, Annie closed her eyes and said a quick prayer.

"Please, Lord. Please let us be okay."

No sooner than the words left her mouth, a triple black Chevy Suburban cruised into the hanger. A black Mercedes Sprinter Van cruised in behind it. Directly behind the Sprinter Van, was a second Chevy Suburban the same make and model as the first.

The three vehicles came to a stop, and a band of soldiers hopped out the Sprinter Van. Moving with precision, they quickly formed a four-man point around the first Suburban. Situated, they spun around about face.

Looking at the first Suburban, Annie was more flabbergasted than afraid. The back door cracked open slowly, and a thick cloud of cigar smoke wafted up into the air. Stepping out behind the smoke, was an older version of her late husband, Easy. Annie recognize him immediately. There were no mistakes about it. The light skinned man with the aqua-blue eyes, the chiseled face and the slicked back, salt-and-pepper hair was the same man who rescued her family from the ambush at Easy's funeral. It was Gervin "Grip" Moreno.

Moving with the grace of a boss, Grip stepped away from his SUV and casually made his way across the hanger toward the tinted-out Suburban in the back corner. He popped open the back door, and then reached inside.

"What the hell?" Annie said to herself, looking at the man who stepped down from the back seat. A gray potato sack was pulled over and tied around his head. His height, weight, and stature were all similar to Grip's. The clothes he wore made the two men appear to be identical.

"Take him outside to the plane," Grip commanded, speaking to the two soldiers who were guarding the SUV. Each man grabbed the subject by one of his arms, then carefully escorted him to the first plane.

Grip sucked in a heavy pull from his stogie, blew his cheeks out, and then parted his lips so the smoke could flow out. Looking at the first Suburban, he pointed at the Sprinter Van where his daughter-in-law and his great granddaughters were waiting.

Dominic, receiving Grip's message, climbed out from behind the steering wheel. He cracked open the back door and a crying Nahfisah climbed out. Omelly, who was wrapped in a blanket and sound asleep, was cradled in Nahfisah's arms.

"Ju come now. No worries," Dominic said as he grabbed Nahfisah by the elbow. He led her towards the Sprinter Van, where Annie was already climbing out.

"Mama Annie," Nahfisah cried as she melted into Annie's arms. "They tried to kill us. They killed Flo. He shot her right in front of me."

"Ssshhh. You be quiet now," Annie consoled as she held Nahfisah tightly. "The girls are in there, and I don't want them seeing you like this. They've been through enough already. The last thing they need is seeing you all worked up and crying. So, get it together for me. Can you do that?"

"Umm-hmm." Nahfisah nodded her head *yes*. She handed Omelly to Annie, then she wiped the tears from her eyes and stepped up inside of the Sprinter Van.

"Señorita, dis for ju." Dominic handed Grip's cell phone to Annie. "It's Sontino calling for ju to speak wit."

Annie accepted the phone, then she looked over and locked eyes with Grip. "*Thank you,*" she mouthed the words and then kissed Omelly on his forehead. "*Thank you.*"

"*Don't mention it,*" Grip replied, as he nodded his head and placed his hand over his heart.

Annie slipped back inside of the Sprinter Van, and Dominic replaced the two Haitians that were seated up front. He drove the van outside to the first plane, as the ten soldiers who were stationed on the runway came back into the hanger. The twelve-foot-high garage doors descended from the ceiling, closing with a loud *click*.

Grip flicked his cigar, then he took off walking towards The Madam's Range Rover, stopping in his tracks when her seventeen soldiers stepped in towards him. His Cuban banditos stepped in even closer. Both armies were locked, loaded and ready to blast. Grip turned his head from left to right, then he winked his eye at The Madam, who was now looking at him through her rolled down window.

"Suspenn," she ordered her men to stand down. "Alè lot bo. Avansè." She shooed them away with the flick of her diamond studded hand.

The seventeen Haitians lowered their weapons and backed away slowly. Grip gestured for his men to do the same. He then moved around the back of the Range Rover and climbed in on the back-passenger's side. Settling back in the seat, he closed the door and then looked over at The Madam. Her concerned brown eyes were hidden behind the lenses of her black, oversized Michael Kors. But even then, Grip could feel The Madam's uneasiness. Her trembling hands and steady toe tapping indicated as much.

"You've got a lot of explaining to do, Gervin. *A lot of explaining*," The Madam said as she removed her sunglasses.

"Is that right?" Grip said, as he removed another stogie from his front pants pocket. Twirling the stogie between his right thumb and index finger, he looked at the headrest where the video of Mr. Shadow was playing on repeat. He then looked up and locked eyes with The Madam.

"So, where do you want me to start?"

"You can start by telling me what happened to Joaquin and Chachi. I *know* you, Gervin. I know you held them responsible for Diablo going rogue."

"I did the thing to both of them muthafuckas," Grip replied without the slightest hint of remorse. "Chopped 'em to pieces, and then tossed they asses in the ocean for the sharks to eat. Those stupid muthafuckas should have stayed down in Brazil. At least that way, it would've been harder for me to hit 'em. But because they were stupid enough to fly up to Cuba, the only thing they did was stick their heads in the lion's mouth. Now, with me being the lion," he placed the stogie in front of his nose and inhaled deeply, "what else was I supposed to do? So, I chewed 'em up, and spit 'em the fuck out. It's the nature of the fuckin' beast."

"And that's the problem." The Madam pointed at the video of Mr. Shadow. "It's because of you, we're in violation of the peace treaty. Now, how in the hell are we supposed to get around that?"

"Easy," Grip replied, while reaching back down inside of his pocket. He pulled out the cell phone he confiscated from Joaquin, then he pulled up the text message that was sent to Jorge. "Take a look at this." He handed Joaquin's phone to The Madam. "This is how we get around it."

Looking at the message, The Madam's blood began to boil. The order that was given to Jorge, was for Jorge and two of his men to fly up to Philly to kidnap Annie and the kids. But what struck The Madam as odd, was the address given and the specified time. There was absolutely no way Joaquin could have known Annie's home address, and the specified time for Jorge to kick in the front door, was the same exact time that Grip told Delaware Fats to arrive at the house, eight o'clock sharp. So, clearly, Grip was the one responsible for sending the message.

The Madam shook her head in disgust, while giving the phone back in Grip. It sickened her stomach to know that she was rocking with a man so cold, he was willing to sacrifice his own family solely for the sake of his personal gain.

Grip smiled at her, already knowing that she read between the lines—that he was the one who sent the message, acting as though he was Joaquin.

"The way I see it, the peace treaty was violated the second them muthafuckas attempted to kidnap my family. That text message proves it. So, technically, all I did was retaliate. Them muthafuckas made a move, so I countered."

"You countered? Countered, how? You're the one who sent Jorge the message."

"Says who? *You*?"

"Gervin?"

"Don't Gervin me, I knew what the fuck I was doing. The plan was for Delaware Fats and his Wilmington crew to catch him in the act, kill his ass, and then report back to me. But, obviously, things didn't turn out quite the way I planned. You and your crew popped up and knocked him off first, which is still good. It places blood on both of our hands, making you just as guilty as me."

"You've gotta be shitting me." The Madam flashed him an incredulous look. "And what about Sontino's family, *your family*? What if Jorge would have kidnapped them? They would have been dead by now."

"Possibly." Grip shrugged his shoulders, displaying how selfish and black hearted he truly was. But on the flip side, assuming that would have happened, had I killed the men responsible, Sontino would have had no other choice but to praise me. The same applies if I rescued Annie and the girls before they were kidnapped. Either way, it was a calculated risk—one that I took, one that I stand by, and would absolutely take again if ever deemed necessary."

"And just what in the hell do you think Sontino's gonna do when he finds out? Do you really think he's gonna go for this shit?

That he's gonna bow down and conform to what you *claim* to have done for him. You're smarter than that, Gervin. You've *gotta* know better."

"Who gives a fuck what Sontino conforms to." Grip's lip curled with anger. "His ass ought'a be grateful that I set things up the way I did. It's because of *me*, and the moves that *I* made, that he's being released first thing in the morning. I *spoke* to William, Geraldine. I spoke to him just a few minutes ago, and guess what? It's endgame. *Checkmate*. They're crowning me as the next head chair. Sontino's gonna wait in the wing as my second-in-command. So, if nothing else, Sontino better be smart enough to conform to *that*. And if he isn't? Well, fuck it, it wouldn't be the first time I shed the blood of a boss."

The Madam was so angry that her eyelids began to flutter. The feeling of being outwitted and manipulated had her stomach queasy, and her palms sweaty.

"So, the Columbians?" The Madam questioned with her eyelids squinted. "The ambush at the party? That was you?"

"Actually, it wasn't. But it's still something that works to my advantage. It's another justification for smashing one of my enemies at The Roundtable. It was fucking perfect! That sonofabitch, Juan, he'll be lucky if he lives long enough to see the morning.

"So, now," Grip paused for a second and pulled out his solid gold lighter, "that brings me to you."

"That brings you to me? And what about me?"

"Look out the window, I need to show you something."

"Show me, what?"

Instead of replying, Grip shot her a look that said, "*Bitch, you better do what the fuck I told you.*"

The Madam looked at him skeptically, then she checked his hands to see if he was holding a weapon. The only thing he had was a lighter in one hand and his Cuban cigar in the other. Satisfied that he wasn't setting her up to blow her brains out from behind, The Madam turned around slowly and looked out of the window. As far as she was concerned, nothing appeared to be out of the ordinary.

Their two armies were standing at attention, with every eye in the building zoomed in on the Range Rover.

"So, what am I supposed to be looking at?" The Madam asked while still looking out the window. "What is it that you wanted to show me?"

"*This*!" Grip said, as he pressed down on the lighter.

The second his Cuban banditos saw the spark, they spun around quickly, aiming their M-16's at The Madam's soldiers. The seventeen Haitians never had a chance to react. The bullets were already flying.

Bdddddddddddddddddddddddddddddddddddddddddoc!

Thick clouds of gun smoke permeated the air, as blood, guts, and brain matter decorated the hanger and clung to The Madam's tinted-out windows. A slew of bullets crashed into the Range Rover's side, but not a single one penetrated its bulletproof exterior.

The Madam, seeing the dead bodies of her men, was so hot that her body began to tremble. But even then, her slick wit and gangsta regalia remained intact. Nostrils flaring, she licked her lips and inhaled deeply, turning back around to face Grip.

"Humph," The Madam scoffed as she looked Grip dead in his eyes. "If you were planning to make me cum, you could have knelt down and sucked my pussy. At least that way I would have squirted in your mouth, instead of my goddamned panties."

Grip's rage-filled eyes became two wide slits. He tossed his cigar in The Madam's face, then he reached out and grabbed her by the neck with both hands.

"You fucking bitch," Grip snarled at her. "I trusted you, and you fucking crossed me!"

"Ger—Gervin, wait!" The Madam stammered, as she struggled to pull Grip's hands away from her neck. She kicked her legs and twisted her body, all the while digging her fingernails into the bones of his wrist. "God—damnit. Gervin, *wait*!"

"Wait, shit, bitch, I'ma fucking kill you!" Grip snarled at her, squeezing so hard that a glob of snot sprang from her nose. Her thick, fat tongue rolled out from between her lips, and the slobber that rolled off the tip slinked down and coated the back of Grip's left hand.

"Grrrrrggghhh!" The Madam gurgled and gasped, feeling dizzy and woozy from the sudden lack of oxygen. She raked her fingernails down the front of Grip's face, and he roared like a beast.

"You should have never crossed me, Geraldine! You should have never fucking did it!"

"What—are you—talking about? Grrrrrggghhh!"

"Bitch, you cut a side deal with Gangsta and Alvin? You knew what they were up to, and you never told me. And for that," Grip gritted his teeth and squeezed even harder, "you're gonna fucking die!"

The Madam's eyes popped open, as the color began to drain from her face. Her struggles against his strength became weaker and weaker, and when the pressure from a violent snap cracked the base of her vertebrate, her lifeless body sank down to the floor of the Range.

"Stanking-ass bitch," Grip snarled through his teeth, finally releasing his hold from The Madam's neck. He sat back in the seat, then he leaned over and removed his handkerchief from his back pocket. Wiping The Madam's spit from his hand, he looked down in the seat where she previously sat, and saw that her cell phone was lying face up with the screen lit. The time digits of an outgoing were plastered on the screen. The running time indicated the call had been activated six minutes earlier. The Madam didn't know it, but she accidentally butt dialed the *call back* button when Grip first made his move towards her SUV, and she was prompted to tell her men to stand down.

"Look at this fucking shit," Grip blurted out loud when he grabbed the phone and saw the outgoing call had been placed to Alexis. Even worse when he placed the phone against his ear, he knew from the silence that everything he said about breaking the peace treaty and placing Sonny's family in danger had all been recorded by Alexis' voice mailing service.

"Sonofabitch!" He lowered his head in disappointment, realizing how bad he fucked up. "*I can still fix this,*" he mumbled under his breath. *"I can still fix it. All I gotta do is find Alexis, and then kill her before she listens to the message and gives it to Sonny. That's all I gotta do, and I'm in the clear. I can still fix this."*

Vrrrrm! Vrrrrm! Vrrrrm!

An incoming text message vibrated The Madam's cell phone, causing Grip to flinch. Curious, he disconnected the call to Alexis, and then pressed down on the Messenger bubble.

"Bruno? What the fuck?" Grip squinted his eyes when he saw the message had been sent by Bruno, another one of his former soldiers that he placed in position when he green lighted the YBM. Bruno, the same as The Reaper, was one of the YBM's top enforces. He was also the only member from the gang who received the death penalty when they were all indicted. He flipped his conviction a few years later, and was subsequently sentenced to Life Without Parole. Twenty years in, and serving his time at SCI Graterford, he was still working for Alvin as his top enforcer. He was also Alvin's bodyguard and cell mate.

The message log between Bruno and The Madam spanned over the past two weeks, and the more Grip read, the more it fucked him up to know that he'd been wrong about The Madam. Instead of crossing him, she was actually on top of her game, using Bruno to keep tabs on Gangsta and Alvin. Even her trip to the prison before she flew down to Cuba, was actually a visit between her and Bruno, and not Alvin; the text messages confirmed it. Moreover, according to Bruno's last message, the million dollars The Madam wired to his offshore account had just cleared, and he was waiting for her final order to take Alvin out.

"Patterns, my old friend. Patterns," The Madam's voice rang clear in the back of Grip's mind, as he thought about his longtime friend, and how her sick, twisted wit was just as vicious as his. He looked down at The Madam's dead body, then he looked back at the phone.

Tap! Tap! Tap!

Alejandro tapped on the window.

"Señor Moreno, ju ready move out?"

Grip looked at Alejandro, then he looked back down at The Madam. The damage was already done and there was nothing he could do to change it.

Tap! Tap! Tap!

"Señor Moreno, de pilots are waiting."

"Alright, Alejandro, just gimmie a second," Grip replied tersely. He looked down at The Madam once more, then he set his sights on the phone in his hand. He reread Bruno's last message, then he pressed his thumb on the *reply* button. The message he sent back was a simple one.

Kill him.

Askari

Chapter Twenty-One
Back at The County Jail

"Lexis' mom? And you're sure about that?" Sonny asked his mom when she told him about Alexis' mother being the one who saved her and the girls. The fact that Alexis' mother was somehow linked to Grip, was something that he couldn't wrap his head around. "That doesn't make any sense. *I* don't even know Lexi's mom. I never met her before. So, how the hell is she tied into Grip?"

"How the hell should I know?" Annie replied with an attitude, her anger increasing by the second. "All I know is she saved us. And had it not been for her, me and the girls—"

"Don't even say it," Sonny cut her off. "I can't even stand to think about that shit."

"*Don't even say it?*" Annie snapped at him. "Not the fuck at all. I'ma say what I need to say, and your black ass is gonna listen. Now, I don't know what the fuck it is you got going on, or how deep you done dug your ass into this shit, but I'll kill your ass myself before I let you destroy this family. We could've been killed, Sontino. *Dead*! Every last one of us. Me. Fat-Fat. Mani. Nahfisah. *All of us*! Talking about some goddamned don't even say it. Boy, you done bumped your fucking head."

It never dawned on Sonny that his mother would be upset, even though she had a right to be. He never even considered it, he just assumed that because her and the girls were safe, that everything was okay. But clearly, it wasn't. And now because he realized how traumatized she actually was, the last thing he wanted to do was argue with her. So, instead of replying, he just held his tongue and allowed her to vent.

"I'm sick of this shit, Sontino. I can't take it, and I won't. And the same goes for these kids. First it was Riri and the baby, then it was your dad, and then Brian and his family. How many more of us need to die? Tell me. How many more, before you realize this fucking shit isn't worth it?"

"Listen, Ma, I know y'all done been through some shit, and I'm sorry y'all had to go through that. But what's done is done, and there's nothing I can do to change it. You telling me how much I fucked up, don't change nothing. I'm just grateful that you and the girls are safe, and that Nah was able to make it off that muthafuckin' yacht. Other than that, I don't know what else to say."

"Boy, you got a lot of fucking nerve. Talking about some god-damned what's done is done, and ain't nothing you can do to change it. You ought to be ashamed of yourself, Sontino. *I'm ashamed.* I'm ashamed that you're my goddamned son."

Annie's last remark brought tears to his eyes, it sliced him so deep. He wanted to tell her that her own hands were covered in blood, and that the life her and Easy exposed him to, as a child, were the makings of the monster that he grew to become. But what good would that have done? She would have only denied it and further placed the blame on him. So, instead of saying what he felt, he switched gears hoping he could hurry up and end the call. His re-lease was only a few hours away, and he needed some time to sit back and get his head together. Especially where it pertained to Alexis.

"A'ight, so this is what's going on," Sonny said with the pain in his heart seeping through his words. "I talked to Grip, and he's flying y'all down to Cuba. It's already set up for me to be released in the morning, so as soon as I'm outta here, I'ma fly down to come get y'all."

"You can do whatever the fuck you want, but I'm telling you now the shit stops here. Either you walk away from this shit, or you walk away from us. You can't have both. I won't allow it."

Click!

Sonny pulled the phone away from his ear, then he looked up at his wall full of family pictures. Shaking his head, he reflected back on his mother's words. Everything she said reaffirming in his heart what he'd previously stated to Grip: that his time in the game was over. That it was time to walk away and not look back.

Struggling to separate his feelings from his thoughts, he sat qui-etly for a few more minutes and then got back to business. He needed to know what connections Alexis had to Grip, and for what reason she chose to keep it a secret. So, he went to his call log and pressed down on Alexis' number, exuding frustration when she sent him to voicemail.

"What the fuck is up wit' this broad? Answer ya fucking phone."

He disconnected the call, and then called right back.

Ring! Ring! Ring!

"You reached Alexis. Leave it after the beep."

Beep.

"Fuck is you sending me to voicemail for? Hit me back as soon as you get this message. I need to holla at'chu."

After disconnecting the call, Sonny laid back on the bunk and stared up at the ceiling. He was thinking about the last time he and Alexis spoke on Tango, and how strange she was acting.

***

A Few Hours Earlier

"What'chu wearing all black for? Ain't you supposed to be going to my sister's party?"

"I was planning to, but I can't. Something just came up that I need to take care of," Alexis spoke in a voice that was all business, nothing close to the sweet sound Sonny was expecting.

"Yo, where you at right now? It's dark as hell in the background."

"I'm up the block from ya peoples' house."

"My peoples' house? What'chu mean, La Casa Moreno?"

"Umm-hmm."

"But, what'chu doing up the block? Ain't no houses up there, it's just a bunch of woods."

"Listen, Sontino, I love you too much to keep playing these games with you."

"Games? What games? You're confusing me right now, Alexis. What the fuck is going on?"

"All I can say is that when you come home next week, there's a few things we need to sit down and talk about."

"Next week?" Sonny shot her a funny look, wondering how she knew the intricate details of his case. "Yo, who the fuck you been talking to? And who the fuck is that standing behind you?" He lashed out when he caught a glimpse of the big, black, dark-skinned man who was roaming about in the background.

"I'm not even try'na go there right now, Sontino. Just know that I love you, and that I'm out here riding for you."

Click!

***

Back to the Present

"What the fuck is up wit' this broad, and how the fuck is she connected Grip?" Sonny asked himself, as he hopped down from the bunk and relit the Wood he was smoking prior to Grip calling him.

Thinking about Alexis, it was all beginning to make sense. Their reconnecting after ten years of not speaking to one another was one thing, but the way she was able to finesse her way into a job at the county jail and being placed on his housing unit, was too straightforward to be a coincidence. There was also the situation with his missing warrant—how Alexis was the person who gave it to him, and how the return address on the envelope was labeled: *From A Friend.* It further concerned him how Alexis knew the intricate details of his case, and now that her mother was the one who saved his family from being kidnapped, the conclusion that Alexis had been spying on him for Grip was inescapable.

"This grimy-ass nigga," Sonny stated to himself, inhaling a thick puff of smoke. "All that family shit he was kicking was a bunch of bullshit. He still sees me as an enemy. That's the reason he was using Alexis to keep tabs on me. He was afraid I would rat him out to the feds. *And this bitch?"* He shook his head and sucked in another pull from the Wood. "These bitches ain't shit. First Daph, and now her. All this time she had me thinking she was down for a nigga, that she loved me and had my back. Only to find out she was working for Grip. She probably woulda killed me, had this nigga told her to do it. This shit is crazy."

Vrrrrrm! Vrrrrrm! Vrrrrrm!

Sonny's iPhone vibrated and scooted around on the pillow where he left it. He grabbed it from the bunk, then he set his eyes on the screen. The caller was Savino.

"Yeah, nigga, what's up?" Sonny said when he accepted the call, exhaling the smoke from his last pull.

"I was calling to check on you, to see if you heard anything new about your mother and the kids. I've been worried sick thinking about them," Savino lied through his teeth. He couldn't have cared less if Annie and the girls were safe. His real reason for calling was to check Sonny's temperature, praying Sonny softened his stance since revealing he knew about the shipments of coke, he'd been giving to Rahmello.

"Yeah, they good," Sonny replied, then he hit the Wood until the cherry crackled. "No thanks to you."

Savino flinched, judging from Sonny's voice that his anger was still intact.

"Well, ah, just so you know, a few minutes ago, I received an email from William Gleason, the Attorney General. The Commonwealth's case against you was rescinded. They're releasing you from custody first thing in the morning."

"I already know that," Sonny's voice was cold. "Again, no thanks to you."

"Well, I, umm, I just wanted you to know."

"Yeah, whatever, nigga. Get the fuck off my phone," Sonny hissed at him, then he disconnected the call. After taking another pull on the Wood, he flushed it down the toilet, then he placed a call to Heemy. It was time for Savino to get his issue.

Askari

Chapter Twenty-Two
At the YBM Headquarters

It was a quarter to four, and the intersection of 54th and Kingsessing was dark and deserted. A chilly, brisk wind swept through the block, as the cool mist from an early morning shower drizzled down slowly. Heemy could hear the raindrops pelting against his windshield. He was seated behind the steering wheel of his SS Impala. Snot Box was right beside him in the passenger's seat, and D-Day and Gizzle sat quietly in the back. Parked behind them, in four separate Escalades, were the homies who survived the ambush at Nahfisah's party. Their number totaled was thirty-one, and all eyes were fixed on the third house from the corner.

"You sho' this the house, Blawd?" Snot Box asked while stuffing bullets down into the clip of his Desert Eagle. His red bandana was tied around his face, and another flag was draped over his palm to shield his fingerprints from the bullets he was loading.

"From what I can see," Heemy replied, then he pointed out the bear-like beast that was roaming around the front yard. "According to Smitty, it's the third house from the corner with the German Shepherd behind the fence. So, yeah," he nodded his head slowly, "that's gotta be the house."

"Fa'sho," Snot Box said while stuffing another bullet down inside of his clip. He was just about to load another one when Sonny's ringtone chimed from his cell phone. "Aye, gawn and answer that fo' me, Blawd. My muh'fuckin' hands is tied."

Heemy grabbed the phone from his center console and pressed down on *accept*. He already knew from the ringtone that the caller was Sonny.

"Peace, Almighty."

"*Heemy?*" Sonny questioned the sound of his voice.

"Yeah, it's me, bro. What's poppin'?"

"Why the fuck you ain't answering ya phone? I just banged ya jack like four fuckin' times."

"I ain't even got it no more, I had to get rid of it."

"Fuck you do that for? You knew I'd eventually have to call you."

"Shit got crazier than a muthafucka out here. The boys is on my top, talking 'bout I'm wanted for all these muthafuckin' bodies. They ran up in my mom's crib, and the bitch gon' call me try'na line me up to get booked. I *had* to get rid of that jawn, bro. I had to. I ain't have no other choice. Then on top of that, they got my face on the news."

"*They got'cha face on the news?*" Sonny shot back. "And how the fuck that happen?"

"Nahfisah's party," Heemy said with a sigh. "One of them nosey muthafuckas was filming that shit, and they got me on camera bustin' at The Reaper. Somehow the cops got they hands on the video, and now it's all over the news. They even playing that shit on CNN."

"Damn." Sonny shook his head and ran his fingers through his beard. His purpose for calling was to place a hit on Savino, but now he just wanted to make sure his lil' nigga was straight. "So, why the fuck you ain't somewhere laying low? For all that, you shoulda flew down to Cuba wit' Grip and my folks."

"Nah, that's out, bro. At this point, I 'on't give a fuck. It is what it is. The only thing I'm focused on the YBM, and I ain't taking off the press. So, either the boys kill me, these bitch-ass niggas kill me, or I'm killing everything I get my hands on. Straight like dat. Muthafucka's shoulda killed me when they had me."

"More or less." Sonny sighed, already knowing that Heemy had his mind made up. "So, where y'all at right now?"

"We on these fuck-niggas' doorstep."

"Oh, yeah? And how y'all find out where they was at?"

"Smitty. When I went to go holla at him, he gave me the address."

"A'ight, well handle y'all business and be careful. Then as soon as y'all finished, hit me right back. I got sum'n I need to tell you."

"More or less."

Click!

"What the homie talking 'bout, Blawd?" D-Day asked from the back seat.

"He said Bishop the fuck up."

"So, let's get it, then," Snot Box said as he loaded his clip back in its groove.

Click! Clack!

He chambered a round, and then climbed out the car. Heemy, D-Day and Gizzle did the same. After signaling for the homies in the four Escalades to stay on point, they crossed the street and crept up the sidewalk towards the fence.

Roof! Roof! Roof! The German Shepherd went crazy the second he saw the four men creeping. He took off running, but was jerked back and slung through the air when the iron chain connected to his collar stopped short a few feet away from the fence. *Uggghhhrrrrr!* He popped back up and made another charge at the fence, only this time he stopped before the chain could jerk him. Pulling forward, he was clawing at the dirt, barking and growling and foaming at the mouth.

Roof! Roof! Roof! Uggghhhrrrrr! Roof!

Boca!

Urn!

"Damn, Blawd, what the fuck you shoot him for?" Snot Box looked at Heemy. "Them muthafuckas in the house prob'bly heard that shit."

"Fuck them niggas, and fucked that dog," Heemy snarled back. D-Day and Gizzle smirked. Snot Box just shook his head.

Looking back and forth between the front door and the windows, Heemy led the troop as they marched up the walkway towards the house. He was just about to kick in the front door, when Snot Box stepped forward and waved him off.

"Ssh," Snot Box blew on his finger, signaling for Heemy to be more discreet. He reached his hand out and twisted the door knob. Surprisingly, the door was unlocked. He looked back at Heemy and raised his eyebrows. The look that he gave him said, "*See? Now, stop moving so goddamned fast.*"

Heemy scowled at him, then he nudged him aside. He pressed his Glock against the door, and then pushed it wide open. Stepping into the vestibule, he crouched down low with his burner leading the way. The small space was cold and damp, and the smell of German Shepherd reminded him of a dirty white boy who'd been caught in the rain.

The second door in the vestibule was slightly wedged open, and a sliver of light was seeping out through the crack. Heemy pushed open the door, then he popped up ready to blast. Snot Box stormed in behind him. D-Day was next with both hands gripping his chopper. Gizzle played the anchor, swinging his twin toolies from left to right, ready to wet the first thing moving.

"Yo, Heemy, where the fuck is these niggas at, Ike?" Gizzle gritted his teeth.

Heemy looked at him, then he looked straight ahead through the dining room and into the kitchen. The lights were on, but the first floor appeared to be empty.

"I'm saying, though, Scrap, you sure this the right house?" D-Day whispered to Heemy. He was standing at the bottom of the stairs with his chopper aimed up at the second floor.

"I ain't sure, bro. I *think* it is," Heemy was forced to admit.

"Nah, this the right muh'fuckin' house," Snot Box whispered. He was holding up the empty bag of *Nut Shit* that he just grabbed from the coffee table. "Y'all niggas check upstairs." He pointed at D-Day and Gizzle. "Me and Heemy gon' search the first flo' and the basement. The first shot heard, come running. That goes for both sides."

Everybody nodded their heads, and then broke off in separate directions. D-Day and Gizzle crept up the stairs, while Heemy and Snot Box moved through the dining room. The closer they got to the kitchen, the more they heard the sounds of Meek Mill's *Tony Story 3* playing in the basement.

"It's somebody down there," Heemy said after pulling open the door and seeing that the basement lights were on. The loud aroma of bud smoke smacked him in the face.

Snot Box, thinking fast, located the light switch. He flicked off the lights, and then quickly stepped away from the door. He assumed that whoever was down there would surely come upstairs to investigate. But after waiting for a minute or so, it confused him when nothing else happened. Instead of hearing movement, or someone complaining, the only thing he heard was the music playing.

"*Fuck it,*" Heemy mouthed the words, looking at Snot Box. "*I'm going down there.*"

"*Not yet.*" Snot Box waved him off. "*Lemme see sum'n first.*" He flicked the light switch on and off with his left hand, aiming his Desert Eagle down the stairs with his right.

"*Man, fuck this shit,*" Heemy scrunched his face up, sick of playing games. He crept his way down the stairs, only to find that the basement was empty. After turning down the music, he checked the bathroom and then looked behind the mini bar in the far-left corner. The only thing he found was an empty Hennessey bottle, an ashtray full of cigarette butts, and a Blunt clip that was left on the coffee table. He picked it up and noticed the tip was still warm. Whoever was smoking must have just left it behind.

"Yo, Snot? Heemy? Y'all good down there?" D-Day shouted from the top of the stairs. He and Gizzle had just finished searching the second floor. The three bedrooms, the bathroom, and the hallway closet were all empty. But what they did find was ten bricks of dope, a trash bag full of *Nut Shit* bundles, and two duffle bags full of money.

"Yeah, we good, bro. But these pussy-ass niggas ain't here," Heemy called back, already knowing that the house was empty.

"Fuck it, at least we ain't leaving this muh'fucka wit' nothing," D-Day said as he and Gizzle descended the stairs. "These bitch-ass niggas were holding like a muh'fucka. Look." He held up a brick of dope in each hand.

"And it's eight more of them muthafuckas we left upstairs in the kitchen," Gizzle stated, who unlike D-Day, was still clutching his pistol in both hands. "We also found two duffle bags full of fetty.

That, and a trash bag full of bundles. Niggas hit the jackpot in this muthafucka, Ike. Nephs."

Snot Box looked back and forth between D-Day and Gizzle, then he brought this gaze back to Heemy. "So, what'chu wan' do, Blawd? You know it's only a matter of time befo' them niggas come back, bein' as though they left all this money and work in this muh'fucka. I say we stick around and wait fo' 'em?"

Heemy thought about it, then he shook his head *no*. He was thinking about Smitty, and wondering if the old man led him into a trap.

"Come on y'all, we out," Heemy said as he brushed past Snot Box and trotted up the stairs. "Sum'n ain't right."

"And what about the shit we found?" D-Day asked, still holding up the two bricks of dope. "I know you ain't telling us to leave it."

"Whatever y'all found, take it outside to the car," Heemy said as he stepped back into the kitchen. He looked on the table at the thrash bag, the two duffle bags, and the eight bricks of dope. He reached out to grab one of the duffle bags, and then spun around with his Glock aimed high.

Scurrrrrrr! Ba-Boom! Wham!

"Yo, what the fuck was that?" Snot Box asked when he stepped into the kitchen behind D-Day and Gizzle. He looked at Heemy, then simultaneously they both looked at the front door.

"It's a fucking set up!" Heemy shrieked, as he took off running towards the door. He was expecting to hear the gunfire from the homies they left outside. But instead, the only sound he heard was a car horn blaring.

Brrrrrrrrrrrnnnnnnnnnn!

Stepping outside, the high beams on a pearl white Lexus forced Heemy to shield his eyes with the back of his hand. The homies they left outside were crowded around the Lex ready to start blasting. It was crashed into the fence and had thin strands of smoke seeping out the grill. The driver's side door was cracked open, and the dome light was on. Inside of the car, slumped behind the steering wheel, was the last muthafucka Heemy expected to see.

"Look at this bitch-ass nigga," Heemy snarled under his breath, aiming his Glock at Bushnut through the windshield. He ordered the homies to give him some room, then he pulled open the driver's side door.

Bushnut's left arm was dangling at his side, mangled from a stray bullet that tagged him in the shoulder. His white, Versace linen suit was covered in blood, and his jig sawed face was still sliced up and torn from the punishment Heemy gave him with the bottle. It had taken everything inside of him to swim back to the pier after jumping off the yacht. And now that he had finally made it back to the YBM headquarters, he was passed out in the front seat.

"Aye, yo, Blawd? Who the fuck is that?" Snot Box asked, as he ran over with his Desert Eagle aimed at the Lexus. "This nigga one of 'em?"

"Yeah, his ass is one of 'em," Heemy replied, still looking down at Bushnut. His iced-out chain was covered in blood, but still blinging. Heemy reached down and snatched it from his neck, then he held it up for Snot Box to see. "Look at the charm. It's the same as the stamp them niggas be using on they dope bags."

"Oh, so his mark-ass is one of the bosses, then?" Snot Box's nostrils began to flare. He jammed his toolie to the left side of Bushnut's neck, in the exact same spot where Heemy stabbed him with the bottle.

"Hold up, Snot. Chill." Heemy gestured for him to lower his toolie. "If anybody knows where to find these niggas, it's him. We can't kill him, we need him."

"Well, fuck it, then." Snot Box said, moving the gun barrel from Bushnut's neck to his left leg. "I ain't gon' kill him. But I'ma definitely wake his punk-ass up."

Doom!

"Aaaaggggggggghhhhhhhhh, *shit*! Muthafucka, god—*damn*!" Bushnut shouted when a fiery burn violated his left thigh. The bullet hole was so big that a lemon would have fit.

"Nigga, get'cha mark-ass up out the car!" Snot Box growled, then he reached down and grabbed Bushnut by the back of his shirt. He was struggling to pull Bushnut from the car, but Bushnut wasn't having it. He was screaming and crying, and clawing at the air trying to find something to latch onto.

"*Nooooo! Noooooo! Somebody get this nigga off me! Aaaaggggggggghhhhhhhh!*" Bushnut screamed for his life.

"Nigga, *shut* the fuck up!" Snot Box snarled with his teeth gritted.

Doom!

The Desert Eagle roared back to life, blowing a chunk of meat out of Busnut's right leg and hip. He flew across the console and banged his face against the passenger's side window. The impact was so hard that his face and head went straight through the glass.

Crash!

"Fuck is you doin'?" Heemy snapped at Snot Box, who was still struggling to pull Bushnut from the car. His unconscious body was loose and limber, but too heavy for Snot Box to move. "Stop playing, and snatch him out the fuckin' car."

"I'm trying, Blawd. This muh'fucka heavy as shit."

"Watch out," Heemy said, as he stepped forward and handed his gun to Snot Box. Gripping Bushnut around his ankles, he pulled him from the car with ease. "Now, stick his ass in my fuckin' trunk," he stated to two of the homies who were standing around the Lexus.

The two homies went to work quick. One man grabbed Bushnut by his ankles, while the other man grabbed him by his wrist. Together, they drug him across the street, and then down the block to Heemy's Impala.

"Here," Heemy said, as handed his car keys to another one of the homies. "This the one right here." He showed him the key that opened trunk. "Lock his ass in, and I'll be over there in a minute. The rest of y'all, we moving out. So, get back in y'all trucks. And Snot, lemme see ya phone right quick. I need to call Sonny back, so I can tell him what's going on."

Snot Box pulled out his cell phone and passed it to Heemy. "And what about the money and work?"

"Who gives a fuck?" Heemy glared at him. "If y'all want it, go get it."

Snot Box gave him a strange look, then he looked back at D-Day and Gizzle. "Come on, y'all. Let's go back and get it."

"Yeah, Heemy, what's up?" Sonny's voice came through the phone. "That wasn't even fifteen minutes. Them niggas was sweet like that?"

"Nah, bro, them niggas wasn't even in there. The only thing we found was money and work. Two duffle bags, ten bricks of dope, and a trash bag full of bundles. But don't none of this shit make sense. It just doesn't feel right. All this money and work, and ain't *nobody here*?"

"And Smitty's the one who gave you the address, right?"

"Facts."

"Well, there you go right there," Sonny pointed out the obvious. "I told you not to trust this nigga, it ain't no telling what these niggas is up to. For all we know, they might'a set you up for the feds. Matter of fact, y'all niggas hurry up and get outta there."

"I'm already on it," Heemy said, then he looked over at Snot Box, D-Day and Gizzle. They were already returning from the house with the money and work. Heemy made a gesture for them to go back to his car, then he took off walking behind them.

"We did find sum'n, though. The mission wasn't a total waste."

"And what'chu mean by that?" Sonny asked him.

"This faggot-ass, Bushnut. We caught him outside slumped on his wheel, and crashed against the fence."

"Y'all didn't kill him, did y'all? We can use him to find out where the rest of them niggas be laying they heads at."

"I already know," Heemy replied, subconsciously looking at his trunk when he said it. "We taking him to The Swamp. I know The Butcher got sum'n that'll make his ass talk."

"That's a fact," Sonny replied, thinking about the pig farm in Bucks County where they tortured their enemies. "But don't kill him, just keep him on ice. I should be there in a few more hours."

"*A few more hours*?" Heemy's octave exuded confusion. "They letting you out? I thought you wasn't going to court until two weeks from now."

"I thought the same thing, but they're releasing me in the morning. Grip had it worked out for my charges to be dropped. And that brings me to another thing. Have you heard anything from Alexis? I've been try'na call her, but she keeps on sending me to voicemail."

"The last I heard from her was a couple of hours ago," Heemy said, then he stopped walking a few yards away from his car. Snot Box, D-Day and Gizzle were already inside, and he didn't want them hearing what he and Sonny was talking about. Especially Snot Box, who on the ride over, was talking shit about Sonny, calling him a nut for fucking with Grip knowing he killed Mook. He asked Heemy what he thought, but Heemy remained quiet. His loyalty was to Sonny, and that's where he drew the line. Big Homie from the west or not, Heemy didn't give a fuck. Whoever wanted it, could get it; Snot Box included. So now that he finally had the chance to speak to Sonny in private, he decided to keep it that way.

"I called her when we first pulled up in front of Nahfisah's house," Heemy continued while looking back at the four Escalades that were lined in the middle of the street. He then returned his gaze to his passenger's side window, knowing that Snot Box was watching him through the tint.

"You called her, and said what?"

"I was calling to see if she could keep an eye on Nahfisah for me, while I stepped out to handle my business."

"And what did she say?"

"She told me she was coming."

"And that's the last time you talked to her?"

"Yeah, that's the last time we spoke," Heemy confirmed. "She was supposed to had fell through like I said, but that was right before Grip rolled up. Then after that, I left the house to go see Smitty. So, if she did come through, I woulda missed her. Why, what's up wit' her? She good?"

"That's what I'm still try'na figure out," Sonny took his time replying. "It's a lot of iffy shit going on, and Alexis got her ass stuck dead-smack in the middle of it."

"Damn, bro, you know it's funny you said that," Heemy stated, thinking about he and Alexis' last conversation. "I can't say how, or who the fuck told her, but she knew about ya mom and the kids being missing. She didn't come right out and say it, but was indirectly saying that she knew about it."

"And that's a fact?"

"That's an *actual* fact."

"So, what exactly did she say?"

"She told me they were safe, and not to worry about 'em."

"And this was *before* Grip came through to pick up my sister?"

"It was right before he rolled up, and that's the reason I ain't say nothing. I figured you already knew. And you know what else," Heemy added, remembering he and Alexis' last encounter, "when we were back at La Casa Moreno, right before we left out for the party, she was hiding in the pool house. Her, and these two big-ass Haitian niggas."

"Hiding in the pool house doing what?"

"I 'on't know. But whatever it was, they were hiding it from Rahmello. All I know is that she told me to keep my eyes on Nahfisah, and to make sure that I kept her safe. I asked her what was goin' on, but she wouldn't say. She just said that when the time's right, it'll all make sense."

"Did you get the feeling she was moving on some grimy shit?"

"To keep it a hunnid, bro. Naw. The vibe I got, was that shorty was on some rydin' shit. Like she was moving out for the team."

"More or less," Sonny's voice trailed off. He was thinking about Alexis, comparing everything he knew about her, to everything that Heemy had just told him. Maybe Heemy was right. Maybe Alexis was working with him and not against him.

"A'ight, so back to business," Sonny said, once again separating his thoughts from his feelings. "Y'all niggas take Bushnut to The Swamp, but don't kill him. I still have a few questions that I need to ask him."

"Say less," Heemy replied. "So, what time you want me to come pick you up from the jail?"

"You're not," Sonny shut him down. "Ya lil' ass gon' stay at The Swamp, and lay low until I get'chu out the country. Send Snot

Box instead. Tell him, he's gotta be here around nine o'clock. That's the time they be letting niggas out."

"Yo, Sonny, I'm telling you, bro. This nigga, Snot Box, this nigga ain't right, bro."

"I already know," Sonny revealed, "he was talking shit about me fucking wit' Grip. I wouldn't have expected anything less. But that's mainly my fault, because I kept him in the dark."

"You kept him in the dark about what?"

"See, this is the thing, Heem. Grip, Lexi, Gangsta and Alvin, Rahmello, *Savino* all these muthafuckas been dibbing and dabbling, and moving out on they own plans. But what they all failed to consider is that I've been plotting and planning, and working on a scheme of my own. That's the reason I need Snot Box to come and get me. It's time I start putting my shit together."

Chapter Twenty-Three
In Camden, New Jersey

"Keys, what time is it?" The Reaper asked, as his cold dark eyes scoured the block. He and Kia were parked outside of Heemy's apartment building, in one of the most poverty-stricken neighborhoods in all of Camden. They'd been sitting there for the past half an hour, and the more they waited, the more The Reaper was beginning to feel antsy. Had he known they'd be staking out a neighborhood so ghetto, he would have driven Murda Mont's MPV, instead of Killah Kye's Pepsi-blue Crown Vic. Its tinted windows were dark enough to conceal their identity, but its chrome 24's had them sticking out like a skinny bitch at a fat camp.

The address that Smitty gave him was a dark, dilapidated, five story building that was covered in graffiti. The only signs of life were the alley cats and stray dogs that occasionally darted from one ally to another, and the early morning dope fiends who came and went; each one looking so spaced-out and zombified, he might as well been watching an episode of *The Walking Dead*.

Kia, who was sitting in the passenger's seat beside him, looked at him, and then looked back down at her iPhone. Her twin .45's was laying across her lap, and she was holding her phone with both hands. Her thumbs were texting like a muthafucka.

"It's twenty minutes to four," she told him after checking the time on her toolbar. "You might as well kick back and relax. Ain't no telling when this nigga might pop up, and that's assuming he pops up at all."

"And that's what I'm talking 'bout," The Reaper replied, his sixth sense kicking into overdrive. "The type of money the young bul be making, you really think he be laying his head in a place like this? This a muthafuckin' trap house. This nigga don't live here, ain't no goddamned way."

Kia didn't reply, she just continued texting.

"Stop playing wit'cha phone, and pay attention. This shit is serious," The Reaper said, then adjusted his shotty so the rubber-grip handle was close by his hand. The barrel was aimed at Kia, but was more so done out of a habit than it was personal. Kia noticed it, but her unflappable demeanor was too gangsta to be bothered. She was just as ruthless as he was, and the thirteen bodies under her belt proved it.

"So, what you think, Keys? You think Smitty's on some bull-shit? That he lied about the address?"

"Nah." Kia shook her head *no*, but was still texting. "That doesn't make any sense, he'd be working against his own interest. I mean, look at all the dope we been moving for him, pressing niggas and making 'em sell that shit. At the rate we going, we'll have the city on lock by the winter. Now, ain't that the reason he put us on in the first place?"

"Yeah, I hear what'chu saying, but fuck that," The Reaper replied, looking at the ran down building. "That muthafucka ain't never played fair when it came to me. Ever since me and Alvin was kids, he ain't never been nothing but a muthafuckin' liar. I never trusted him then, and I still don't trust his ass now."

Kia shot him a strange look, not exactly following what he was saying. She started to ask him what he was talking about, but he was already climbing out the car.

"Come on, Keys, we running up in this muthafucka."

"But I'm saying, though," Kia stalled, then quickly thumbed down on the *send* button. "Don't you think it'd better if we wait? At least a little while longer?"

Click! Clack!

The Reaper chambered a round, and then stuck his head through the crack in the door. "Muthafucka, I ain't asking you. I'm *telling you*. Now, come the fuck on. We running up in this muthafucka."

Kia shook her head and sighed, and then climbed out the car two guns strapped.

"Hold up, Keys, wait." The Reaper held up his left hand, sig-naling for Kia to move cautiously. He was looking up the street, where a black minivan was cruising down the block. It was a jet-black, late modeled MPV, with a set of fog lights glowing at the bottom.

Gripping his shotty with both hands, The Reaper aimed it at the minivan "You see these niggas creeping?"

"Yeah, I see 'em," Kia replied as she moved around the back of the Vic.

"You think it might be him?"

"I 'on't know." Kia shrugged her shoulders. "It's too dark to see."

The Reaper squinted his eyes, as the minivan cruised down closer. There was something about it that pegged him as familiar. Looking at the fog lights, he thought about Murda Mont, remembering the day he had them installed.

"Yo, I *knew* I recognized them dumb-ass lights! What the fuck is Mont doing here? And how the fuck he know where this nigga live?"

The answers to his questions was standing right behind him.

About ten minutes after leaving the YBM headquarters, Kia received a text message from Alvin telling her to kill The Reaper. In turn, she forwarded the message to Killah Kye and Murda Mont, and told them to drive out to Camden. They'd been texting back and forth for the last half an hour, ever since her and The Reaper pulled up in front of the building on 2nd Street. And now that Killah Kye and Murda Mont had finally arrived, it was time to get busy.

The minivan rolled to a stop, and The Reaper lowered his shotty. The last thing he ever expected was that his own crew would carry out a hit on him. But when the side door swung wide open and Killah Kye jumped out with his chopper aimed at his grill, he trembled from the notion that death was around the corner. His fate was already sealed, and there was nothing he could do to stop it.

"You bitch-made muthafuckas," The Reaper flummoxed in a low, defeated voice, closing his eyes when he felt Kia's .45's being placed against the back of his neck.

Boom! Boom!

The two hot slugs ripped through The Reaper's neck and exploded out the front of his face. The force from the blast knocked him forward, chest first into Killah Kye's chopper.

Boc!

The thunderous blast spun him like a top, and sent his blood and guts spraying through the air. His shotgun hit the pavement with a dismal *clink*, and then he dropped to his knees with his arms around Kia's waist. His face was hot, but his body was cold, and every time he sucked in a breath, a burgundy blood cloud erupted from his chest and back.

"Ugh. Ugh. Sss. Sss."

"Ssshhhh," Kia shushed him with her .45 pressed against her lips. The .45 in her other hand was slowly caressing the top of his head, massaging him so nice, that had The Reaper not known any better, he would swear Kia was consoling him.

"K—Kia, what the fuck?" The Reaper gurgled up a mouthful of blood, as he looked up into Kia's eyes. The dim, glossy look in his own had the same look of despair that he placed into the eyes of so many others.

"Sss. Sss. Ugh. Ugh."

"Don't fight it," Kia spoke to him calm. "Just let it go."

"Ugh. Ugh. Ugh."

"I've got a message for you. From Alvin."

"Ugh. Ugh. Sss. Sss."

"He said your services are no longer needed."

"Ugghhh. Ugghhh."

"So, you know what that means." She pressed her .45's against both sides of his dome. "YBM, baby."

"Uggghhhhh!"

Boom! Boom! Boom! Boom!

***

A Half an Hour Later

Bushnut's entire body was a stiff, tight, blistering pain; its agony unfathomable. Conscious now, he wished that he had a gun so he could blow his own brains out. Anything to make the misery stop was fine by him. The pain from the gunshot wounds to his legs and hip trickled up his torso, enjoining with the hot flame that torched his left arm and shoulder. The triple darkness of being locked inside of a trunk, had him feeling like a fetus trapped inside of a womb. He could smell his own feces, taste his own blood. Steadily, he could feel himself rocking with the rhythm of the car.

Ba-Bump. Ba-Bump. Ba-Bump.

Eeeeeeeeiiiiiiiii!

The loud squeals of the pig troops crowded around the slop troughs on both sides of the road, was enough to make Bushnut tremble and scream. He didn't know it, but he'd been taken to *The Swamp*, a rural death camp in Bucks County where many men before him had gone, but was never seen again.

Up ahead, perched on a small hill at the top of the road, was an old, white, three-story, colonial style house. The Butcher, dressed in his dingy blue overalls with no shirt underneath, was patiently standing out front. The Godfather, his super-sized, eight-hundred-pound hog, was laying down beside him.

"Come on up a little closer," The Butcher's high-pitched voice pierced the air, as he waved down the five vehicles. Heemy's SS Impala rolled to a stop. The four Escalades broke off into two pairs and pulled in beside him.

The Godfather stood up at attention, with his glowing red eyes keyed in on the Impala. His pink, pudgy snout was slimy and hot, and thick slobber globs coated the cracks of his mouth. Incited by his gluttonous hunger, he groaned and squealed, and then squealed some more, taking in the sweet, savory scent of Bushnut's blood.

The Butcher looked at him and smiled. It was time to feed.

Chapter Twenty-Four
In Miami, Florida

"Come on, Juan, answer ya fucking phone," Gangsta mumbled under his breath. He was standing at the entrance of the Miami International Airport, chain smoking Newport's and calling Juan for the umpteenth time since arriving at the airport. His American Airlines flight, Flight 127, from Philly to Miami, was scheduled to arrive at 3:30 am. But due to a one-hour delay back in Philly, coupled with the airline's lack of WiFi, there was no way to call Juan and tell him that he was running late.

Usually, whenever Gangsta flew down to Miami, Marcos, the old Spanish man who chauffeured Juan's Maybach, would already be parked out front waiting for him. Laying on the back seat, per Gangsta's request, would be a P89 and two extra clips. But on this trip, and mainly because he was running late, the Maybach, Marcos, and the P89 were nowhere to be found. Gangsta was sick.

"What the fuck is wrong wit' this nigga?" Gangsta mumbled some more, as the phone continued ringing. *"He knew I was coming, so why the fuck he ain't answering his phone? Un-fucking-believable."*

After disconnecting the call, Gangsta flicked the Newport he'd just finished smoking, and then fired up another one. The feeling of being assed out and stranded without a pistol was the worst shit ever; an egregious violation of the most essential rules of the game—never go to work without a tool, and that it was better to be caught with it, than be caught without it.

Out of all times, why now? Gangsta questioned himself, as he inhaled a mouthful of smoke. *In the middle of a war, and my stupid-ass ain't got as much as a muthafucking pocketknife. This shit is crazy. If it ain't one thing, it's a muthafucking 'nother.*

It was still the Fourth of July weekend, so despite being five o'clock in the morning, the airport was fairly crowded. This was something that Gangsta acknowledged, but even then, his guilty conscience had him standing with his back against the wall. His paranoid eyes were shifting from left to right, cautiously scoping everything around him that moved.

If there was one thing he learned from his time spent working for Grip, was that a hit could come from anywhere and in a manner that was least expected. So, when a group of female strippers strutted towards him and filed into the airport, he studied each one close. Their bubblicious titties and juicy phat asses were enough to make a preacher lust. But instead of lusting, Gangsta was thinking survival. His shifty eyes were moving from one woman to the next, carefully watching their hands and checking to see if they had any weapons. Because sexy or not, a woman was just deadly as a man. Murder and Malice, were the perfect examples. Both women were sexy as hell, and at Grip's command, had murdered more men than Gangsta could count.

Fuck all this being without a burner shit, Gangsta thought to himself, as he took another drag on his Newport. *For all that, I'll just fly my ass back to Philly. Fuck Juan.*

After taking his last drag, he flicked the cigarette and then turned to head back into the airport's lobby. He pulled open the door and stepped one foot inside, but then turned back around when he saw Juan's Maybach pulling up to the entrance. The silver and black, two-toned, sedan had a panoramic roof and shiny chrome rims. The driver's side window was rolled down, and Marcos was seated behind the steering wheel.

"Hola, Papa. Ju finally make it," Marcos said with a smile. "I figured ju was running late, so I swing past and pick up some food. Ju like arroz con pollo?" He held up the chicken and rice platter that was laying across his lap. "It's de best in all of Miami, lemme tell ju. Ju wan' some?"

"Nah, I'm good. Just take me to see Juan," Gangsta replied as he climbed into the back of the 'Bach. As usual, his P89 and two extra clips were waiting for him on the back seat. He snatched up the P89, ejected the magazine to make sure it was loaded, and then shoved it back in the groove. *Click! Clack!* He chambered a live round.

"So, what ju think about LeBron James?" Marcos asked as he pulled away from the entrance. He was looking at Gangsta through the rearview mirror.

"Say what?" Gangsta looked at him like he was crazy.

"LeBron James? What ju think about him? Ju know leave Miami to go back to Cleveland? He leave de weatherrrr, de beautiful womennnn, de moneyyyy. Jus' to go back to Cleveland. I think LeBron go loco. What'chu think?"

"Yo, Papi, is you fucking serious?"

"Whaaa'? Ju no like LeBron James?"

Instead of replying, Gangsta shook his head and closed the partition.

"*Well, fucka ju, too,*" Marcos mumbled under his breath, then he stuffed his face with a mouthful of chicken and rice. "*Fuckin' punto.*"

The entire ride from the airport to Juan's mansion had taken a total of fifteen minutes. The 85,000 spare foot mansion was located on Kirkstone Lane, in the Lake Butler Sound gated community. The Maybach stopped at the front gate, where Marcos had his retina scanned. After verifying his identity, the guard at the watch booth awarded his entrance. The iron gates slid back slowly.

Zzzzzzzzzzz. Click.

Cruising at a calm ten miles per hour, Gangsta sat quiet in the back seat taking in the extravagance of each mansion they drove past. Each mansion was just as opulent as the next, but none compared to the mega mansion that Juan called home. The large estate was so big that two La Casa Morenos could have easily fit inside, and still there would have been room left over.

The Maybach stopped at Juan's gate, and another retina scan awarded their entrance. They cruised up the driveway where every luxury vehicle from Rolls-Royces to Lamborghinis and Bugatti's were lined in a row; each car was a two-toned silver and black, the same as the Maybach. Marcos pulled up to the front of the house and stopped at the pavilion. Parked underneath was another Maybach and a Rolls-Royce Phantom.

Reclined back in his seat, Gangsta stared at the ceiling slowly cracking his knuckles. He was thinking about Grip, still perplexed that his uncle was two steps ahead, instead of five steps behind. There had to be a common connection, but exactly what, Gangsta didn't know. He searched his mind for every logical answer, but nothing he thought of was sufficient enough to calm his curiosity. For the life of him, he just could not figure it out.

"Maybe I might'a over placed my hand," he stated aloud, then released a long, heavy, stressed-out sigh. "Hopefully, me and Juan can put our heads together and figure something out. And if we can't, we can always revert back to Big Angolo's original plan. At least that way, I can still kill Grip and be able to save face with Sonny. Alvin won't like it, but fuck him. If The Madam handled her business, his ass should be dead by now. And if she didn't, I can still hit him whenever I want. It's not like he's going anywhere. His ass got a life sentence."

The sound of raindrops beating down on the car forced Gangsta to look out the window. The drastic change in the weather struck his soul like an omen. A few seconds ago, the light blue sky was illuminated by the rising of an early morning sun. But now, and seemingly out of nowhere, the light blue sky was a dark gray abyss. Thick rain clouds blotted out the sun, and the raindrops that poured down were bigger than jelly beans. Constant and consistent, they splashed against the window.

Thwat. Thwat. Thwat.

Gangsta placed the P89 on his hip, and then stuffed the two extra clips in his front pants pocket. Gritting his teeth, he climbed out the car and made a dash for the pavilion.

Ka-Whack! Ka-Whack! Ka-Doom!

A thunderous boom sounded from the sky, with a striking flash of lightening. The thunderous crack was so intense, that the car alarms on the Maybach and Phantom alerted simultaneously.

Wheeuuu! Wheeuuu! Wheeuuu!

Gangsta looked back at the two vehicles, then he turned back around facing the door. He pressed the intercom button to his left, and then looked up at the camera box protruding from the door frame.

"Yo, Juan, it's me. Open the door."

Wheeuuu! Wheeuuu! Wheeuuu!

"Yo, Juan?" Gangsta raised his voice after pressing the intercom button once more. "It's me, Gangsta. Let me in and send somebody to turn off these muthafuckin' car alarms. These loud-ass muthafuckas is driving me crazy."

Wheeuuu! Wheeuuu! Wheeuuu!

"Yo, Juan, man, what the fuck?" He looked up at the camera with his arms stretched wide. Shaking his head, he again pressed down on the intercom button.

Ka-Whack! Ka-Whack! Ka-Doom!

A forceful wind gust swept through the pavilion, knocking Gangsta off balance. He turned his back to the breeze and began wiping his face from the rain that swept in with it. Irritated, he kicked the bottom of the door and pounded on it with his fist turned sideways.

"*Yo, Juan?* Stop playing and let me in! I'm starting to get wet out this muthafucka!"

Ka-Whack! KaWack! Ka-Doom!

"What the fuck?" Gangsta blurted out loud, as he snapped his head to the right. In the corner of his right eye, he caught a glimpse of a woman. She was dressed in a housemaid's uniform and running so fast, it was clear to Gangsta that someone or *something* was chasing her.

"What the fuck is going on around this muthafucka?"

Moving towards the mansion's east wing, he whipped out his P89 and clutched it with both hands. His heartbeat quickened and his eyelids squinted, suspiciously looking at the door where the woman sprang from. It was thirty yards away, but still he was able to see the bloody palm prints she left behind when she pushed it open.

Ka-Whack! Ka-Whack! Ka-Doom!

A flash of lightening lit up the sky, as the rain fell harder. The dark gray sky became darker by the second, and the closer Gangsta moved towards the door, the tighter he clutched the pistol. The massive barrel was aimed at the door, which was flapping back and forth with the heavy wind that swooped in from the east and west.

"Yo, what the fuck is going on?" Gangsta shrieked, then abruptly stopped in his tracks. He was looking at Juan's Neapolitan Mastic, who he knew as "Feo". The large, gray canine came limping out the house with his neck ripped open. He looked at Gangsta, then collapsed dead on the spot.

Subconsciously, Gangsta stepped back quickly. He looked down at Feo, and then cautiously set his sights on the door. He knew from his previous visits that he was standing at the mansion's east wing dining room. His P89 was aimed at the threshold, but it was hard too dark to see inside. In addition to the lights being turned off, the gloomy gray sky was now a smoked out black, almost darker than night.

"Yo, Juan? Chi-Chi? Y'all in there?"

Ka-Whack! Ka-Whack! Ka-Doom!

A flash of lightening lit up the door and dining room, giving Gangsta a brief glimpse of the horror that lay inside. The naked dead bodies of Juan and Chi-Chi were left on the floor, bent forward with their asses in the air. Their decapitated heads were stuck between their legs, stitched into the flesh of their ass cheeks and thighs. The faces of both men were facing the door, and their dangling eyeballs hung low by the sockets.

Gangsta was spellbound. Shaken beyond words, he spun on his heels and hauled ass back to the Maybach. The engine was silent, but the motor was still running.

"Marcos, lemme in! Lemme the fuck in!" Gangsta shouted while tugging on the back-door handle. "Fucking Marcos, man, shit! Open the fucking door!"

Looking over his shoulder, Gangsta reached out and tried the handle on the driver's door. The door swung open, but Marcos was gone.

"His ass can get left, for all the fuck I care. Fuck that!" Gangsta declared, then he hopped in behind the steering wheel. He threw the transmission in *drive*, and then marked out with the door still open.

Zzzzzz.

"What the fuck is that noise?"

Zzzzzz.

"That noise? That noise? What the fuck is that noise?"

It wasn't until he stopped at the gate, that he realized the partition was being descended. He looked into the rearview mirror, hoping to see Marcos. But instead of Marcos, hunched forward and leaned so close that Gangsta could feel him breathing down his neck, was the King of Darkness.

Diablo, dressed in the housemaid's uniform, sat quiet with his nostrils flaring. His nose, mouth and chin were covered in blood from when he chomped down on Feo's neck. His skinny face was tilted to the right, and the devil horns protruding from his forehead were covered in sweat. His serpent-like tongue eased through his lips, and then his mouth opened wide. Squealing like a beast, he lunged forward slamming into Gangsta with his razor-sharp fangs.

Eeeeeeeeeeeiiiiiiiiiiii!

Chapter Twenty-Five
Somewhere Over the Atlantic Ocean

Comfortable and spacious, and soaring through the sky at a blistering 561 mph, Grip's G650 was scheduled to land in Cuba within the next two hours. The luxury mega jet was cocaine-white with solid gold trim, and had MORENO 1 embroidered on its tailfin. Its interior, beginning with a full gallery, was fitted with four cabins; and each cabin was connected by a twelve-foot pathway. The first cabin, eloquent and roomy, was a master lounge with two curving sofas. A built-in bookshelf added to its homelike feel, and a marble chess table with platinum and gold pieces occupied the corner. The second cabin was Grip's favorite. A state-of-the-art mini bar with golden barstools and tufted, silver divans decorated the space. Positioned on the wall, directly above the bar, was an 84" TAG TECSLATE television. The third cabin, fitted with a nine-man conference table, was where Grip held his meetings; and in the fourth cabin, sectioned off for privacy, was a master suite with a king-size bed. A 65" flat screen hung on the wall adjacent to the bed, and placed beneath the screen, was a black and gold cashmere sofa from The House of Versace.

Standing at the entrance of his master suite, Grip was looking down at his king-size bed; his visage moving from one face to the other. Annie and Nahfisah were knocked out on the ends of the bed, while Keyonti and Imani were stretched out in between. Omelly was placed in the center.

Slowly and meticulous, and one at a time, Grip began studying the faces of his granddaughter and great-grandchildren. Aside from earlier, where he first encountered Omelly and then briefly saw Nahfisah back at the airport, this was his first time actually seeing the faces of his offspring. In each one, he clearly saw the remnants of his own. The feeling inside of his chest was something that he never expected. The conflicted mixture of guilt, grief, abandonment, love, care and concern, was enough to bring tears to his eyes. It reminded him how cold and cruel he'd become in a world so vicious.

What the fuck is wrong with me? He questioned his previous actions, regretting the fact that he deliberately placed his family in danger. *This is my lineage, my legacy. And I was willing to throw it all away? For what? Money? Power? For everything that I already have, which will one day all belong to them? And then, Sontino? Rahmello?* He shook his head slowly and began wiping the tears from his eyes. *I've gotta make this shit right. Whatever it takes. I've gotta step up and be the man to my family that my father never was. There's no other way.*

"Paw-Paw?" the soft sound of a feminine voice snapped Grip from his thoughts. He looked down and saw Keyonti standing at the edge of the bed. He rubbed his eyes, shook away the cobwebs, and then leaned in closer to better see his granddaughter's face. He couldn't believe his eyes. Keyonti, with her smooth, chocolate complexion, her curly black hair and aqua-blue eyes, was a dead ringer for his late mother, Gabriella Moreno.

Keyonti squinted her eyes, then slowly tilted her head to the side. She knew that her Paw-Paw Easy had gone up to heaven to be with Jesus, but the man standing before her looked just like him. The only difference was that instead of Easy's hazel-brown eyes, the eyes of the man staring back were the same color as hers. She tilted her head back straight and then reached her arms out, demanding Grip to pick her up from the bed.

"Up-up."

Reluctantly, Grip reached down and grabbed the little girl by the waist. Scooping Keyonti up into his arms, he inhaled the scent of her hair and slowly pressed his nose into her soft, chocolate cheek. The little girl giggled, and Grip did the same. The tears in his eyes came down like a flood.

"Uhn-uhn." Keyonti shook her head *no*. "No, no cry. No, no cry."

"Okay," Grip whispered with a smile on his face. He used his free hand to wipe his tears away, then he kissed Keyonti's forehead. He would never imagine that holding his great-granddaughter would feel so good.

"Did you know my Paw-Paw Easy?" Keyonti asked him with an innocent face. "You and my Paw-Paw look alike. My daddy, too."

Grip closed his eyes and inhaled deeply. Nodding his head, he reopened his eyes and said, "Of course I knew your Paw-Paw Easy. He was my son."

"*You're my Paw-Paw's daddy?*" Keyonti was amazed; her blues eyes locked on Grip's. She rubbed his face and examined it close. "And what about my daddy? Do you know my daddy, too?"

"Umm-hmm." Grip nodded his head. "Your daddy's my grandson. So that means you're my great...my great-granddaughter," Grip choked on his words. He tried to fight the feeling, but could not stop his tears from falling.

"Didn't I say no, no cry?" Keyonti chastised, speaking as though she were someone's mother. Using both hands, she reached up and wiped his tears away.

Grip smiled, completely intoxicated with the instant love he felt for her.

"I'ma call you my Big Paw." Keyonti nodded her head. "Okay?"

"Yes, ma'am." Grip nodded his head, accepting the name she gave him.

"And from now on, I'm Fat-Fat." She smiled at him, then pointed down at the bed, where Imani and Omelly were still knocked out sound asleep. Looking back and leaning in to Grip, she whispered in his ear, "That means I'm your favorite."

"Yes, *ma'am.*" Grip chuckled and squeezed her tight, amused by her Moreno wit. The little girl was a true queen in the making, someone who would one day bolster his empire to astronomical heights. All of this he knew, from just one conversation.

"Fat-Fat tired now." Keyonti pointed back down at the bed. "I wan' go back to sleep-sleep."

"Yes, Love, whatever you want," Grip replied, then he carefully sat her back down on the bed. "If you need...*Big Paw,*" he stated with a smile, loving his new moniker, "I'll be right out here." He pointed towards the third cabin, where Alejandro and Dominic were seated at his conference table. "Okay?"

"Umm-hmm," Keyonti replied with a yawn. She buried herself back under the covers, and nestled in close to Annie.

Alejandro and Dominic went quiet the second they saw Grip stepping back into the cabin. They looked at one another, and then looked back at Grip.

"What is it?" Grip questioned, as he plopped down in his high-back chair. He could tell from the look on their faces that a new development was discovered. "Is it Alexis? Rudolpho and Philippe, they found her?"

"No, Señor, not yet." Alejandro shook his head. "Without de tracking device, dere's no way Alexis be found. Our only chance is a few more hours."

"*A few more hours*?" Grip looked at him a strange. "And what the hell is that supposed to mean? What's so special about a few more hours?"

"Sontino, Señor."

"Sontino?" Grip's eyelids squinted.

"Si, Señor." Alejandro confirmed with a nod. "If ju remember, Señor, from wha' ju say on de recording? Ju say Sontino be released first thing in de morning. Chances are, Alexis be dere to pick him up. If she do, Rudolpho and Philippe know to move in. Until then, only we can do is wait."

Grip leaned back in his chair and cracked his knuckles. His situation was a lose-lose. Prior to a few minutes ago, his mind was already set on killing Alexis. But now, after his unexpected change of heart, he realized that doing so would only make things worse. Being as though Alexis was pregnant with Sonny's child, to kill her would be like killing Riri all over again. And for that, Grip knew without a doubt that Sonny would never forgive him. But still there was the potential threat that if Sonny heard the message, and assuming he already hadn't, their relationship would go back to what it once was, and had always been.

"So, wha' ju want we do?" Alejandro asked him.

234

Grip remained silent, carefully weighing his options. About forty minutes earlier, he reached out to Felix Dubois, a billionaire tech tycoon, who was also one of the members from The Roundtable who supported his movement. After explaining to Felix exactly what happened, he requested that Alexis' cell phone be wiped clean, free from all messages, texts, outgoing and incoming calls. Felix confirmed that clearing Alexis' cell phone records wouldn't be a problem. But he also mentioned one caveat: that if Alexis had already forwarded the message to another device that he didn't know about, there was no way to track it down. So, even then, there was still a possibility that Alexis heard the message and had sent it to Sonny, or had it stashed away waiting for the right time to pull Grip's card.

"Señor? Ju no gimmie me no answer."

"Get Rudolpho and Phillipe on the phone," Grip spoke slowly, already regretting his decision. "You tell them muthafuckas I said to kill her. But under no circumstances, *none*, is Alexis' body ever to be found. I want her so gone, that on Judgment Day, not even God can find her. You got that?"

"Si, Señor," Alejandro replied, then he grabbed his phone and placed a call to Rudolpho.

"Dominic," Grip looked at the young Cuban, "go down and grab me a drink from the bar. A double shot of Louie Thirteen, on the rocks."

"Si, Señor." Dominic nodded his head, then he got right to it.

Vrrrrrm! Vrrrrrm! Vrrrrrm!

The cell phone that Grip confiscated from Joaquin began vibrating on the tabletop. Grip grabbed it and looked at the screen. It was the message he'd been waiting for. After learning that Gangsta was flying down to Miami to link up with Juan, Grip, acting as though he were Joaquin, sent a text message to Diablo. He gave Diablo the order to fly down to Miami to take care of Gangsta and Juan, and then told him that a private jet was waiting for him at the airport in Northeast Philly. So, now that Diablo had taken care of business, he was replying to Grip's last message informing him the job was done.

Grip pressed down on the Messenger bubble and began reading.

"Here ju go, Señor," Dominic said when he returned with Grip's drink. He handed over the double shot of Louie, and then sat down in the armchair to Grip's left. "Wha's dat?" He pointed at cell phone, seeing the way Grip was looking at it. "Dat's him, de one dey call Diablo? He really go and do what'ju say?"

"Take a look for yourself," Grip said, as he handed Dominic the cell phone.

Dominic looked at the screen, then he looked back at Grip. A broad smile spread across his face, as he shook his head in disbelief. "*Señor?*"

"I know, right?" Grip smiled back, then he took a sip of his drink. "I've been planning this shit for the last ten months. The Devil works for me now."

Chapter Twenty-Six
Back at SCI Graterford

The possibility that Gangsta would cross him was always something that weighed heavy in the back of Alvin's mind. But it wasn't until AJ was transferred to the county jail, rather than the state prison like he and Gangsta negotiated, that Alvin first knew Gangsta was on some bullshit. The plan was for AJ to be transferred to SCI Graterford, where he and Alvin could be reunited after twenty-five years of being apart. But instead, he was transferred to the county jail and placed on the same exact housing unit as Sonny. The more Alvin thought about it, the more he realized it was all done intentionally; that Gangsta, knowing AJ would seek revenge for what happened to Daphney, would do his best to murder Sonny.

Even worse, and what Gangsta didn't know, was that his and The Madam's sloppy attempt to turn Bruno against Alvin, was something that Alvin knew about all along. Bruno told him about it the second he returned from his visit with The Madam. According to The Madam, it was never Gangsta's intention to make Alvin his second-in-command. Instead, he was motivated by the YBM's manpower, knowing he could use them to distribute the cocaine he'd eventually start receiving from Juan. The only reason Alvin didn't react, or reveal what he knew, was the million dollars they offered to pay Bruno for the hit. He set it up so that the offshore account the money was sent to, was actually an account belonging to his long-time attorney, Mario Savino.

"Yo, Bruno, lemme see ya phone," Alvin said as he rolled over and sat up on the bottom bunk. "My muthafuckin' battery just died."

Bruno handed Alvin his cell phone, then he handed him the second cup of coffee that he just finished pouring for him.

"I can't *wait* to see the look on these nigga's faces," Bruno said as he climbed back on the top bunk. "Especially, this nigga, Sonny. His ass so smart, that he's stupid. Too busy worrying about all the wrong shit."

"You can say that again," Alvin stated with a chuckle. He dialed Savino's number, then he placed the phone against his ear.

Ring! Ring! Ring!

"Bruno?" Savino's voice came through the phone.

"Nah, this ain't Bruno, it's Alvin. Did that paper land?"

"Yup, the confirmation came through about an hour ago," Savino confirmed. "But you still have to wait another twenty-four hours before it clears. Then after that, it's all yours."

"That's a muthafuckin' bet," Alvin replied, already thinking about his next move. "And Savino, man, thanks again, man, fa'real. After all these years, you were the only muthafucka who stuck by my side and never gave up on me. I really appreciate it, fam. Straight up."

"Don't mention it," Savino replied. "It was an honor representing you."

"No doubt." Alvin cracked a smile, then he disconnected the call.

Laying back on his bunk, Alvin pulled out the legal mail he received from Savino two days earlier. It was a court order from the Pennsylvania Supreme Court. He flipped it open and began reading:

Detective Adam Smith, whose credibility we deem irretrievably depraved, provided false testimony and fabricated evidence that led to the 1990 conviction of Alvin Rines. WHEREFORE, and in the interest of justice, We the Court find that the 1990 conviction of Alvin Rines for murder, racketeering, and drug trafficking was unconstitutional. This Court hereby rules that Alvin Rines' conviction and sentence be immediately VACATED.

After reading the court's decision for the fiftieth time since receiving it, Alvin shook his head and cracked up laughing. It was a long twenty-five-year battle, but Savino had somehow managed to pull it off. Not only for Alvin, but for his twenty-three codefendants as well. The cherry on top was The United States Supreme Court's decision in *Miller v. Alabama*, which further made a way for AJ to be released from custody. It was a new day and time, and the city of Philadelphia would surely be flipped upside down.

"Hey, yo, Bruno?"

"Yeah, A, what's up?"

"The city thought my first run was legendary, just wait until they see the *new* me. I'ma show these muthafuckas how a *real* boss move."

To Be Continued...
Coming Soon
Blood of a Boss 6

About the Author

My pen name is *ASKARI*, but I'm known throughout the city of Philadelphia and surrounding counties as S-Class. Prior to writing books, I was one of the hottest up and coming rappers in the city. This was in the early 2000's, prior to social media. But I still had a strong buzz, blazing mixtapes and rocking clubs from Jersey to New York City. In October 2001, my homie, Peedi Crakk, was signed to Roc-a-fella Records, and being the real nigga he is, he took our entire crew along for the ride. Our sole mission was to lock down the rap game and get our families out the hood. Unfortunately, in February 2003, just as my career was beginning to take off, I was arrested and charged with a murder that I absolutely did not commit. There was no physical evidence linking me to this crime: NO GUN, NO FINGERPRINTS, NO DNA, NO VIDEO SURVEILLANCE, NOTHING!!! The entire case hinged on the identification testimony of one alleged eyewitness, who initially described the shooter as *A DARK-SKINNED BLACK MAN WITH A SUNNI MUSLIM BEARD*. However, as you can see from my pictures, I have a light brown complexion, and at the time of this crime, I was eighteen years old with a baby face. I had no beard whatsoever.

At my trial, the district attorney's case relied exclusively on the testimony of this one eyewitness; the same witness who knew me prior to this incident, but described the shooter as a completely different person. This witness was a convicted felon, currently serving time for an unrelated matter. He did, however, state for the record that he was promised leniency in exchange for his testimony against me. This witness testified that at the time of this incident, he was standing on the corner selling crack cocaine and that he was under the influence of alcohol and drugs. He further testified that he only had a partial view of the shooter's face, as the shooter was wearing a hoody sweatshirt, with the hood up over his head. He also indicated that the crime scene was not well lit. During cross examination, he revealed that after this incident, he went around the neighborhood asking people "What happened?", and that another individual *TOLD* him that I was the shooter. This witness' identification testimony was so suspect and unreliable, that even the trial judge acknowledged there was the possibility of a misidentification.

In addition to shortcomings of this witness' identification testimony, the recording of his 911 call was mysteriously missing from the evidence file. Not only that, but the investigating detectives, for unknown reasons, failed to make an appearance at trial. As a result, they were never questioned about the integrity of their investigation. Even worst, according to police reports, there was at least one eye-witness to this crime who the detectives never interviewed. I made numerous attempts to have my trial counsel locate and interview this witness, but my attorney failed to do so. THIS WITNESS MAY HAVE VERY WELL BEEN THE ONLY OPPORTUNITY I HAD TO PROVE MY INNOCENCE. BUT UP UNTIL THIS DAY, HE HAS NEVER BEEN PROPERLY IDENTIFIED, LOCATED AND INTERVIEWED!!!

Sadly, despite all of the witness' shortcomings and a notable lack of physical evidence, the jury convicted me of first-degree murder. My trial lasted TWO DAYS!!! SMFH!!!!

Man, when I tell you I was crushed.... I couldn't believe it. Moreover, I couldn't understand. How could something like this happen? How the fuck could I be convicted of something that I didn't do? Excuse my language, but I'm angry as hell!! Please, try to understand.

Yet and still, in the midst of the bullshit, I knew that I had to remain humble, positive and prayerful. I knew that I had to remain diligent in my fight to prove my innocence, while at the same time conducting myself as a man, standing firm on the principles that my mother and father instilled in me as a child. I have not wavered, and I never will. I shall and must continue to fight for my freedom; that's just my nature.

I was only twenty years old when I was kidnapped by the system. I was a father of three beautiful children. I was working two jobs and busting my ass in the studio every day, primed to be the next Jay Z. I was also working with the youth in my community as an assistant coach on our little league football team. But I guess none of that mattered. I once seen a civil rights documentary where an ignorant Klansman stated: "When we get ourselves all riled up to hang us a nigger, any nigger will do." It's about to be 2018, and for nearly fifteen years, I've been in prison for a crime that I didn't commit. Maybe to them, I'm just another nigger. SMFH!!!!

You know, it's funny when I sit back and think about my life. I thought that I'd be triple platinum now, captivating audiences with my creativity and word play. I guess I still am, but instead of a microphone, I'm using a pen. Still focused on using my creativity to open the doors that confine me. Whether they be the doors that kept a young brotha locked in the hood, or the doors that currently have a brotha locked behind bars. Either way, I will be free.

To my real family and friends, fans and supporters, I love y'all from the bottom of my heart. Words could never express my gratitude. And to the big homie, CA$H, thank you bro. When I was down and out, sitting in a cell, looking for a way out, I came across *TRUST NO MAN*. In your dedications and acknowledgements, you gave me a new outlook, a new source of motivation. It was then that I picked up a pen, and I'm determined to never put it down.

Always,

Rayshon "ASKARI" Farmer

Submission Guideline

Submit the first three chapters of your completed manuscript to ldpsubmissions@gmail.com, subject line: Your book's title. The manuscript must be in a .doc file and sent as an attachment. Document should be in Times New Roman, double spaced and in size 12 font. Also, provide your synopsis and full contact information. If sending multiple submissions, they must each be in a separate email.

Have a story but no way to send it electronically? You can still submit to LDP/Ca$h Presents. Send in the first three chapters, written or typed, of your completed manuscript to:

LDP: Submissions Dept
Po Box 944
Stockbridge, Ga 30281

DO NOT send original manuscript. Must be a duplicate.

Provide your synopsis and a cover letter containing your full contact information.

Thanks for considering LDP and Ca$h Presents.

Coming Soon from Lock Down Publications/Ca$h Presents

BOW DOWN TO MY GANGSTA

By **Ca$h**

TORN BETWEEN TWO

By **Coffee**

THE STREETS STAINED MY SOUL **II**

By **Marcellus Allen**

BLOOD OF A BOSS **VI**

SHADOWS OF THE GAME II

TRAP BASTARD II

By **Askari**

LOYAL TO THE GAME **IV**

By **T.J. & Jelissa**

IF LOVING YOU IS WRONG… **III**

By **Jelissa**

TRUE SAVAGE **VIII**

MIDNIGHT CARTEL IV

DOPE BOY MAGIC IV

CITY OF KINGZ III

By **Chris Green**

BLAST FOR ME **III**

A SAVAGE DOPEBOY III

CUTTHROAT MAFIA III

DUFFLE BAG CARTEL VI

HEARTLESS GOON VI

By **Ghost**

A HUSTLER'S DECEIT III

KILL ZONE **II**

BAE BELONGS TO ME III

A DOPE BOY'S QUEEN III

By **Aryanna**

COKE KINGS V

KING OF THE TRAP III

By **T.J. Edwards**

GORILLAZ IN THE BAY V

3X KRAZY III

De'Kari

THE STREETS ARE CALLING II

Duquie Wilson

KINGPIN KILLAZ IV

STREET KINGS III

PAID IN BLOOD III

CARTEL KILLAZ IV

DOPE GODS III

Hood Rich

SINS OF A HUSTLA II

ASAD

KINGZ OF THE GAME VI

Playa Ray

SLAUGHTER GANG IV

RUTHLESS HEART IV

By Willie Slaughter

FUK SHYT II

By Blakk Diamond

TRAP QUEEN

RICH $AVAGE II

By Troublesome

YAYO V

GHOST MOB II

Stilloan Robinson

CREAM III

By Yolanda Moore

SON OF A DOPE FIEND III

HEAVEN GOT A GHETTO II

By Renta

FOREVER GANGSTA II

GLOCKS ON SATIN SHEETS III

By Adrian Dulan

LOYALTY AIN'T PROMISED III

By Keith Williams

THE PRICE YOU PAY FOR LOVE III

By Destiny Skai

I'M NOTHING WITHOUT HIS LOVE II

SINS OF A THUG II

TO THE THUG I LOVED BEFORE II

By Monet Dragun

LIFE OF A SAVAGE IV

MURDA SEASON IV

GANGLAND CARTEL IV

CHI'RAQ GANGSTAS IV

KILLERS ON ELM STREET IV

JACK BOYZ N DA BRONX II

A DOPEBOY'S DREAM II

By **Romell Tukes**

QUIET MONEY IV

EXTENDED CLIP III

THUG LIFE IV

By **Trai'Quan**

THE STREETS MADE ME III

By **Larry D. Wright**

IF YOU CROSS ME ONCE II

ANGEL III

By **Anthony Fields**

FRIEND OR FOE III

By **Mimi**

SAVAGE STORMS III

By **Meesha**

BLOOD ON THE MONEY III

By J-Blunt

THE STREETS WILL NEVER CLOSE II

By K'ajji

NIGHTMARES OF A HUSTLA III

By King Dream

IN THE ARM OF HIS BOSS

By Jamila

HARD AND RUTHLESS III

MOB TOWN 251 II

By Von Diesel

LEVELS TO THIS SHYT II

By Ah'Million

MOB TIES III

By SayNoMore

BODYMORE MURDERLAND III

By Delmont Player

THE LAST OF THE OGS III

Tranay Adams

FOR THE LOVE OF A BOSS II

By C. D. Blue

Available Now

RESTRAINING ORDER **I & II**
By **CA$H & Coffee**
LOVE KNOWS NO BOUNDARIES **I II & III**
By **Coffee**
RAISED AS A GOON I, II, III & IV
BRED BY THE SLUMS I, II, III
BLAST FOR ME I & II
ROTTEN TO THE CORE I II III
A BRONX TALE I, II, III
DUFFLE BAG CARTEL I II III IV V
HEARTLESS GOON I II III IV V
A SAVAGE DOPEBOY I II
DRUG LORDS I II III
CUTTHROAT MAFIA I II
By **Ghost**
LAY IT DOWN **I & II**
LAST OF A DYING BREED I II
BLOOD STAINS OF A SHOTTA I & II III
By **Jamaica**
LOYAL TO THE GAME I II III
LIFE OF SIN I, II III
By **TJ & Jelissa**
BLOODY COMMAS I & II
SKI MASK CARTEL I II & III

KING OF NEW YORK I II, III IV V

RISE TO POWER I II III

COKE KINGS I II III IV

BORN HEARTLESS I II III IV

KING OF THE TRAP I II

By **T.J. Edwards**

IF LOVING HIM IS WRONG…I & II

LOVE ME EVEN WHEN IT HURTS I II III

By **Jelissa**

WHEN THE STREETS CLAP BACK I & II III

THE HEART OF A SAVAGE I II III

By **Jibril Williams**

A DISTINGUISHED THUG STOLE MY HEART I II & III

LOVE SHOULDN'T HURT I II III IV

RENEGADE BOYS I II III IV

PAID IN KARMA I II III

SAVAGE STORMS I II

By **Meesha**

A GANGSTER'S CODE I &, II III

A GANGSTER'S SYN I II III

THE SAVAGE LIFE I II III

CHAINED TO THE STREETS I II III

BLOOD ON THE MONEY I II

By J-Blunt

PUSH IT TO THE LIMIT

By **Bre' Hayes**

BLOOD OF A BOSS **I, II, III, IV**, V

SHADOWS OF THE GAME

TRAP BASTARD

By **Askari**

THE STREETS BLEED MURDER **I, II & III**

THE HEART OF A GANGSTA I II& III

By **Jerry Jackson**

CUM FOR ME I II III IV V VI VII

An **LDP Erotica Collaboration**

BRIDE OF A HUSTLA **I II & II**

THE FETTI GIRLS **I, II& III**

CORRUPTED BY A GANGSTA I, II III, IV

BLINDED BY HIS LOVE

THE PRICE YOU PAY FOR LOVE I II

DOPE GIRL MAGIC I II III

By **Destiny Skai**

WHEN A GOOD GIRL GOES BAD

By **Adrienne**

THE COST OF LOYALTY I II III

By Kweli

A GANGSTER'S REVENGE **I II III & IV**

THE BOSS MAN'S DAUGHTERS I II III IV V

A SAVAGE LOVE **I & II**

BAE BELONGS TO ME I II

A HUSTLER'S DECEIT I, II, III

WHAT BAD BITCHES DO I, II, III

SOUL OF A MONSTER I II III

KILL ZONE

A DOPE BOY'S QUEEN I II

By **Aryanna**

A KINGPIN'S AMBITON

A KINGPIN'S AMBITION **II**

I MURDER FOR THE DOUGH

By **Ambitious**

TRUE SAVAGE I II III IV V VI VII
DOPE BOY MAGIC I, II, III
MIDNIGHT CARTEL I II III
CITY OF KINGZ I II
By **Chris Green**
A DOPEBOY'S PRAYER
By **Eddie "Wolf" Lee**
THE KING CARTEL **I, II & III**
By **Frank Gresham**
THESE NIGGAS AIN'T LOYAL **I, II & III**
By **Nikki Tee**
GANGSTA SHYT **I II &III**
By **CATO**
THE ULTIMATE BETRAYAL
By **Phoenix**
BOSS'N UP **I , II & III**
By **Royal Nicole**
I LOVE YOU TO DEATH
By Destiny J
I RIDE FOR MY HITTA
I STILL RIDE FOR MY HITTA
By **Misty Holt**
LOVE & CHASIN' PAPER
By **Qay Crockett**
TO DIE IN VAIN
SINS OF A HUSTLA
By **ASAD**
BROOKLYN HUSTLAZ
By **Boogsy Morina**
BROOKLYN ON LOCK I & II

By **Sonovia**

GANGSTA CITY

By **Teddy Duke**

A DRUG KING AND HIS DIAMOND I & II III

A DOPEMAN'S RICHES

HER MAN, MINE'S TOO I, II

CASH MONEY HO'S

THE WIFEY I USED TO BE I II

By Nicole Goosby

TRAPHOUSE KING **I II & III**

KINGPIN KILLAZ I II III

STREET KINGS I II

PAID IN BLOOD **I II**

CARTEL KILLAZ I II III

DOPE GODS I II

By **Hood Rich**

LIPSTICK KILLAH **I, II, III**

CRIME OF PASSION I II & III

FRIEND OR FOE I II

By **Mimi**

STEADY MOBBN' **I, II, III**

THE STREETS STAINED MY SOUL

By **Marcellus Allen**

WHO SHOT YA **I, II, III**

SON OF A DOPE FIEND I II

HEAVEN GOT A GHETTO

Renta

GORILLAZ IN THE BAY **I II III IV**

TEARS OF A GANGSTA I II

3X KRAZY I II

DE'KARI

TRIGGADALE I II III

Elijah R. Freeman

GOD BLESS THE TRAPPERS I, II, III

THESE SCANDALOUS STREETS I, II, III

FEAR MY GANGSTA I, II, III IV, V

THESE STREETS DON'T LOVE NOBODY I, II

BURY ME A G I, II, III, IV, V

A GANGSTA'S EMPIRE I, II, III, IV

THE DOPEMAN'S BODYGAURD I II

THE REALEST KILLAZ I II III

THE LAST OF THE OGS I II

Tranay Adams

THE STREETS ARE CALLING

Duquie Wilson

MARRIED TO A BOSS... I II III

By Destiny Skai & Chris Green

KINGZ OF THE GAME I II III IV V

Playa Ray

SLAUGHTER GANG I II III

RUTHLESS HEART I II III

By Willie Slaughter

FUK SHYT

By Blakk Diamond

DON'T F#CK WITH MY HEART I II

By Linnea

ADDICTED TO THE DRAMA I II III

IN THE ARM OF HIS BOSS II

By Jamila

YAYO I II III IV

A SHOOTER'S AMBITION I II

By S. Allen

TRAP GOD I II III

RICH $AVAGE

By Troublesome

FOREVER GANGSTA

GLOCKS ON SATIN SHEETS I II

By Adrian Dulan

TOE TAGZ I II III

LEVELS TO THIS SHYT

By Ah'Million

KINGPIN DREAMS I II III

By Paper Boi Rari

CONFESSIONS OF A GANGSTA I II III

By Nicholas Lock

I'M NOTHING WITHOUT HIS LOVE

SINS OF A THUG

TO THE THUG I LOVED BEFORE

By Monet Dragun

CAUGHT UP IN THE LIFE I II III

By Robert Baptiste

NEW TO THE GAME I II III

MONEY, MURDER & MEMORIES I II III

By **Malik D. Rice**

LIFE OF A SAVAGE I II III

A GANGSTA'S QUR'AN I II III

MURDA SEASON I II III

GANGLAND CARTEL I II III

CHI'RAQ GANGSTAS I II III

KILLERS ON ELM STREET I II III

JACK BOYZ N DA BRONX

A DOPEBOY'S DREAM

By **Romell Tukes**

LOYALTY AIN'T PROMISED I II

By Keith Williams

QUIET MONEY I II III

THUG LIFE I II III

EXTENDED CLIP I II

By **Trai'Quan**

THE STREETS MADE ME I II

By **Larry D. Wright**

THE ULTIMATE SACRIFICE I, II, III, IV, V, VI

KHADIFI

IF YOU CROSS ME ONCE

ANGEL I II

By **Anthony Fields**

THE LIFE OF A HOOD STAR

By Ca$h & Rashia Wilson

THE STREETS WILL NEVER CLOSE

By K'ajji

CREAM I II

By Yolanda Moore

NIGHTMARES OF A HUSTLA I II

By King Dream

CONCRETE KILLA I II

By Kingpen

HARD AND RUTHLESS I II

MOB TOWN 251

By Von Diesel

Askari

GHOST MOB II
Stilloan Robinson
MOB TIES I II
By SayNoMore
BODYMORE MURDERLAND I II
By Delmont Player
FOR THE LOVE OF A BOSS
By C. D. Blue

<u>BOOKS BY LDP'S CEO, CA$H</u>

<u>TRUST IN NO MAN</u>

<u>TRUST IN NO MAN 2</u>

<u>TRUST IN NO MAN 3</u>

<u>BONDED BY BLOOD</u>

<u>SHORTY GOT A THUG</u>

<u>THUGS CRY</u>

<u>THUGS CRY 2</u>

<u>THUGS CRY 3</u>

<u>TRUST NO BITCH</u>

<u>TRUST NO BITCH 2</u>

<u>TRUST NO BITCH 3</u>

<u>TIL MY CASKET DROPS</u>

<u>RESTRAINING ORDER</u>

<u>RESTRAINING ORDER 2</u>

<u>IN LOVE WITH A CONVICT</u>

<u>LIFE OF A HOOD STAR</u>

STRAWBERRY-LIT MAGAZINE INTERVIEW

Q. How long have you been writing?

A. I've been writing music since I was six years old, so writing was always inside of me. In fact, my mother was a writer. As far as writing novels, I've been doing that for about nine years now.

Q. What inspires you to write?

A. The main inspiration behind my pen are without a doubt my life struggles and experiences. I've been through and seen a lot when it comes to the game, so writing about the game is something that comes easy to me. Not to mention, I have a peculiar way with using words to paint pictures. I'm also a big fan of street lit, so after reading countless books I decided to pen my own. It wasn't, however, until the first time I read *Trust No Man* by the big homie, CA$H, that I took writing seriously. To know that bro was locked down for all that time and was still using his God given talents to entertain, gave me the motivation to do the same. Ironically, after five years of shopping around for a publishing deal, CA$H was the one who signed me. So, shout outs to the big homie, CA$H and Lock Down Publications. (Smile)

Q. Are your characters based off people you know?

A. I would say loosely inspired, but greatly exaggerated. My stories are strictly entertainment, nothing more.

Q. When preparing to write what are some things you need to get in the mood to write?

A. The first thing I need is a nice, hot shot of green tea with honey. Then after that, I listen to R&B and zone out.

Q. Tell me a little bit about your latest release or series.

A. My latest release is Blood of a Boss 5, the fifth installment of my first street lit series, which is a total of six books. It's a story about a family of Gangstas, spanned over four generations. It's raw, hardcore, vivid and witty; everything you'd expect from the street lit genre. The readers love it, and I'm anxious to see how they respond to it. Shout outs to the readers, by the way.

Q. Where did the concept come from this release?

A. I'm from Philadelphia, and in Philadelphia there's basically four generations of notoriously known Gangstas: The Italian Mafia in the 50's and 60's; The Black Mafia in the 60's and 70's; The Junior Black Mafia in the 80's and 90's; and in the 2000's to present, a generation of wild young buls willing to do whatever for the bag. So, I thought it'd be dope to tie all four generations into one family.

Q. What do you hope the readers get from this story?

A. Well, I definitely want to keep them on the edge of their seats and biting their nails, anxiously anticipating what's going to happen next. That's the main reason I take so long between releases. I always write with my readers in mind, knowing they expect nothing but heat when it comes to this serious. But most important, I want to show my readers the other side of the game; how everything isn't as flashy as it seems, and how consequences follow every action.

Q. If you could write in another genre what would it be?

A. As far as I know, it's a genre that currently does not exist, and that's Sci-Fi/Street Lit. I've got some heat in the bag that I'm working on, far different than what's considered the norm. Hopefully, the readers will catch on.

Q. Describe yourself in three words.

A. Focused. Determined. KING.

Q. What is next for you?

A. Definitely, screenwriting. But first, I want to establish myself as one of the best in street lit. I haven't hit the main stream yet,
but I will. I believe that I'm a strong enough writer to do it. So, all
the big dawgs in the game, I'm on y'all heels! (Smile)

Q. Tell us something about your next release.

A. My next release, *Shadows of The Game*, will be available
soon after BOSS 5 is released. It's an urban drama about a young
mother struggling to raise her teenaged sons in a Trump America,
where young black men appear to be perpetual targets. It's actually
the flip side and a spinoff to my Blood of a Boss Series, telling the
story of a family who was victimized by one of the characters in
Boss. So, basically, it's based on the harsh side of the game that it's
rarely spoken about. I honestly feel it's my best work.

Q. What sets you apart from other writers in your genre?

A. In the Street Lit/Urban Lit genre, we're all pretty much talking about the same thing: money, drugs, sex, and gunplay. So, to
separate myself from the pack, I focus on two things: the uniqueness
of my storyline; and conveying my storyline so vivid, that my readers feel as though they're watching a movie instead of reading a
book.

*Q. What would you tell an inspiring author who is looking to
get into the publishing industry?*

A. If you're a Street Lit/Urban Lit author, the industry is overly
saturated with titles. So, in order to stand out from the rest, you need
to focus on your storyline. Be vivid and concise with your wordplay,

and never rush to release a project. Your writing career can only go as far as the readers take you. So, take your time and give the readers everything they want and deserve.

Q. How can readers connect with you?

A. They can contact me on social media:
Facebook: Rayshon Askari Farmer

Made in the USA
Las Vegas, NV
23 January 2024

84797475R00144